THE LOST BOOK OF
ADANA MOREAU

THE LOST BOOK OF

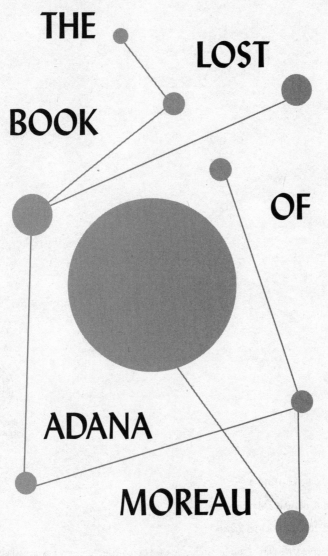

ADANA MOREAU

A NOVEL

MICHAEL ZAPATA

HANOVER
SQUARE
PRESS

HANOVER
SQUARE
PRESS™

ISBN-13: 978-1-335-01012-4

The Lost Book of Adana Moreau

Hanover Square Press
22 Adelaide St. West, 40th Floor
Toronto, Ontario M5H 4E3, Canada
HanoverSqPress.com
BookClubbish.com

Printed in U.S.A.

For Mom, Dad and Vic.

And in memory of Matt Davis.

THE LOST BOOK OF
ADANA MOREAU

Truly do we live on Earth?

—Nezahualcoyotl

THE DOMINICANA

May 1916–August 1930

His father was a pirate. He had black skin and was a pirate. Regardless of his occupation, or maybe because of it, he was charming and warmhearted and loved listening to most anybody who had a story to tell. His mother was a servant to an old Spanish sugar plantation family just outside of San Pedro de Macorís. It was said she had Taíno blood in her veins and never lied. She had long, coffee-colored hair and all she had known her entire life was the plantation house where she worked with her mother, the seas of the Antilles, and her parents.

On May 16th, 1916, the American Marines landed on the island and her mother and father were killed in the ensuing guerrilla war waged by the peasant gavilleros against the Marines, who, according to her father, were nothing more than tígueritos hired by greedy American businessmen who wanted to force them off their land to expand the sugar plantations. The night before her parents' deaths, she had been half-asleep watching an ashy-faced owl perched outside her bedroom window when she heard her parents in the kitchen. She got out of bed. It was nearly midnight.

"We should leave now," her mother said.

Her father put his finger to his lips and her mother nodded.

"In the morning," her father whispered.

Her mother and father stood in the kitchen and held each other and she noticed there was blood on her father's pants. She understood then that her father and mother were gavilleros. When her mother spotted her over her father's shoulders, she smiled and went to her. Her mother stroked her long, coffee-colored hair, just as she had done when she was a child, and told her that the world was the same as it ever was and not to worry.

First thing in the morning, the American Marines came to their home. They dragged her parents outside, bound their hands, and made them kneel in the sand. She heard the shots while hiding under their little village house where there were small pools of water and dirt and sand and dirty-ashen seashells. Once in a century, her father had told her, the sea flooded the land and for a time neither existed.

Two days later her family's employers decided to leave for New York City or back to Madrid, she couldn't remember, but the important thing is they fled to a city that wealthy people have been fleeing to for centuries. The last thing they told her before speeding off in a taxi was that the Antilles were brutal and she was one of the last of a brutal race. She thought of her mother, who had worked for the Spanish family for nearly thirty years. She was sixteen. She didn't want to go home, so she lived alone in the plantation house for two months, wandering from room to room, eating what was left in the kitchen, cleaning as she had done before, and sleeping for days at a time on a bed that had once belonged to a queen from the House of Bourbon.

One afternoon, she packed her clothes and left the plantation house. She headed west, toward Santo Domingo, sometimes walking for long stretches at a time along the coast which was dotted with estates and villages without names (or rather names she had never known) and sometimes riding in the back of a cart driven by a sugar worker who understood without saying so that she was the daughter of murdered gavilleros. For five weeks she wandered the streets of Santo Domingo, which were like the streets of a labyrinth, and ate fish and bread scraps at the market. At night, she slept on park benches and dreamed of future civilizations and an endless seabed full of strange luminescent creatures.

At the end of five weeks, she met an American in the market who said he was trading with the gavilleros and the American Marines. She didn't know why, but she told him the story of how the American Marines had killed her parents. He listened without saying a word. When she was done, he said that he was really a pirate. He said that he gave the gavilleros a deep discount and sold shoddy equipment to the American Marines at high prices. He was making money hand over fist. He apologized for talking so much and then he said she was beautiful. He said he had never seen a more beautiful woman in the Caribbean than her. She told him that his Spanish was good, if a little outdated. He said that he also spoke French and some Arabic. The pirate studied her face for a moment and then said he could get her on a ship that would take her to New Orleans. She shook her head.

"Why not?" asked the pirate.

"Americans are greedy tígueritos," she said, "they're shit."

"And me?"

"I don't know yet. Maybe you're shit. Maybe you're not shit."

Still, she thought about her prospects on that occupied island and decided to leave Santo Domingo. On the ship voyage she met a boy who looked out of place. He had deep, sky-black eyes. When she asked the boy where he was from, he said he was from nowhere.

"So, you're an orphan," she said.

"An orphan," he said and smiled politely.

"Like me," she said.

Like everybody, she thought. Orphans are all the world really has left.

For four days, she lived on the deck of the ship and slept near the orphan boy. She listened as he talked about war and mechanical soldiers and an eternal library that he would one day discover and never leave. He's mad, thought the servant girl. He spoke Spanish well enough, but sometimes he sang in a language that she didn't understand. The songs were like a melismatic trance. One morning, in the middle of a song, he stopped singing and told her that the ship was entering the eye of the Gulf of Mexico.

"How do you know where the eye is?" she asked the boy, teasing him.

"Just look," he said and shrugged.

The sea was deep blue and alien and as vast as the sky. She imagined that in the distant future the end of the world would have its origins there and for some unknown reason this put her at ease. When the ship arrived in New Orleans, the pirate was waiting for her. A few days later, he asked for her hand in marriage and she said yes.

On April 7th, 1920, Maxwell Moreau was born in a one-room apartment near the Barracks Street Wharf. His mother labored for seventeen hours and during painful bursts of activity she squeezed her eyes shut and tried to focus on the smells of coffee and bananas and boiled crawfish and the blows and whistles of faraway ocean liners. This was something, she thought, that all mothers giving birth in New Orleans probably did. When Maxwell Moreau finally came out, the pirate knew that his son would not be a pirate like him, spending his life on the surface of the sea, a loud and violent sea that swelled with creatures and myths and drove men to early deaths or, worse, to an asylum.

He swore to it and told his wife that their son had ochre eyes, which were the pigment of earth.

The baby Maxwell Moreau cried and cried and his mother held him to her breast and whispered son et lumière, which was something her husband had taught her to say in French and which meant *sound and light* and was everything the earth wasn't.

The Dominicana and the pirate soon bought a home on Melpomene Avenue. Occasionally, the pirate worked for a wealthy Creole smuggler, often for long periods of time at sea or by river and then by marsh in order to help him hide jugs of Cuban rum in the trunks of cypress trees or guard him as he tried to strike deals with Isleños, laughing or rather pretending to laugh, which was a type of threat, at least according to the pirate who listened to most anybody with a story to tell, especially an inscrutable Isleño. He might as well have pistols for ears and a shotgun for a tongue, he might as well start a gang war, the pirate once told his wife, but he still went and worked for the wealthy Creole smuggler and she still saw him off and waved as he boarded a motorboat. Sometimes, when the wealthy Creole smuggler turned his back to the pirate, he saluted him in mockery of the United States Navy. Then, more often than not, the Dominicana stood and chatted with the wealthy Creole smuggler's wife in the lilting heat and saunter of the Louisiana sun and watched the trill of fishing boats and egrets drift over the Mississippi River as if they were comets lost in the creation of things.

At three, Maxwell Moreau began to wander. He liked sound and light and he followed it everywhere like how the ancient Hebrews followed celestial clues and iconographic fever dreams in the desert. One day a hornet entered the house on Melpomene Avenue and stung Maxwell. He didn't cry. In fact, when the hornet flew out the back door and into a garden of sunflowers, Maxwell followed it. The hornet flew into another yard and then another before finally landing on a tree. A dog with a half-black muzzle was chained up to the tree and when it saw Maxwell it began to bark. Maxwell thought that the dog was even more interesting than the hornet. He walked over to the dog, but stopped just short of the length of the chain. The dog barked and barked and Maxwell smiled and smiled. He teased the dog and because Maxwell was canny like Sisyphus he eventually figured out how to untie the dog without the dog biting him. The dog disappeared for some time and Maxwell waited. Just before dusk, the dog returned and lay down near the tree. Then Maxwell lay down near the dog with his body pressed against the earth, a pulsating earth with heartbeats, which were the dog's heartbeats, and tremors, which were the tremors of the City, and murmurs, which were subterranean rivers slipping into the lower Mississippi. He then slept in complete peace, and this is how his mother found him.

Ages ago, she thought as she picked up her sleeping son and held him close, as close as she ever had, the world must have been covered with abandoned or lost children lying on the earth. She then imagined in horror that a prehistoric flying creature must have fed on these children. Even though she knew that those kinds of creatures must be extinct, she still imagined that one had been circling vulture-like for her child and that she had arrived just in time. She had no idea where this absurd fear came from and when she returned home with her child she immediately told her husband. He said that her fears were reasonable. He said that there must have been a time when immense and terrible flying creatures fed on children. He said that there might even be a few of the monsters left somewhere in the world, maybe in India or South America.

As Maxwell's tendency to wander increased, his parents grew more and more worried and they decided to frighten him. They went to the library and since only the pirate could read he found a book called *Dinosaurs and Flying Reptiles of the Jurassic and Creta-*

ceous Eras. Maxwell sat on his mother's lap while his father read out loud to him and showed him illustrations of Pteranodons and Pterodactyls and Pterosaurs. In hushed tones they told their son that when he wandered, monstrous creatures with sword-like beaks and black wings took to the sky and searched for him. If they found him, they would devour him. When they told Maxwell this, his eyes lit up. He squirmed and laughed and his parents realized that they had made a terrible mistake.

Yet one thing did seem to work. Maxwell's mother noticed that when Maxwell had a book directly in front of him he was less prone to wandering. She took him back to the library. At the library, she met a librarian named Afrah or Afraa or Annan, depending on who was speaking to her. For example, visitors to the library or city officials called her Annan, but family members and friends—of whom she had many—called her Afraa. Her husband was the only person who called her Afrah, which was really the same as Afraa, but her husband pronounced the "ah" with a lilt that could only be described as the lilt of someone who was deeply in love. She was half Persian and half Haitian and she made it a point to tell the Dominicana that she lived in the Marigny, which in the 19th century was full of Haitian refugees and which was now full of mixed families, musicians, and writers.

Afraa spoke of Haiti in the same way other people spoke of violent love affairs. More than a few times she said that St. Peter would never let her through the gates of heaven on account that she would be incredibly bored there. Heaven would be like a very boring Port-au-Prince, she would say, one without the madness of survival, one without the sea, one without women like her mama whose curves swelled with the seasons. The Dominicana and Afraa quickly became close friends. She called Maxwell a little island mestizo and she called his mother the kindest Dominicana she had ever met, which was the truth.

At first, Afraa gave the Dominicana spoken English lessons at the library each Wednesday and Friday afternoon. Later, in addition to the library lessons, Afraa would visit the Dominicana each Monday night at her home on Melpomene Avenue. They would eat red beans and rice and then Afraa would read out loud for the Dominicana and her son. Translated into Spanish, she read Persian poetry, Assyrian myths, Greek myths, and African myths. She read the poetry of Sor Juana Inés de la Cruz and the fables of José Núñez de Cáceres, the Dominican revolutionary. She read Latin American pastorals, modernismo poetry, and indigenismo novels, which, the librarian said, were all simulacrums of *Don Quixote*. That book, she explained, was the one from which all others were endlessly replicated. So, of course, she also joyfully read *Don Quixote* for the Dominicana and her son. Translated into English, she read a slim Russian novel titled *We* by Yevgeny Zamyatin. She read British plays and American short stories. She read the horrifying and elegant works of Edgar Allan Poe. She also read *Adventures of Huckleberry Finn* and *Moby Dick*, which, the librarian suggested, would help the Dominicana make sense out of the American character. The American character, the librarian theorized, was obsessed with movement and tyranny, like a madman, and different from the European character, which was obsessed with systems and order, like a lieutenant, and also very different from the Latin American character, which was obsessed with the abyss of time, Aztec labyrinths, and the Minotaur who wandered both. The Madman, the Lieutenant, and the Minotaur, the librarian said, constituted the entire history of the New World. In time, by listening to each word and following along with Afraa's smiling eyes, the Dominicana learned how to read.

For his fifth birthday, Afraa bought Maxwell a gift. It was a copy of *The Book of the Thousand Nights and a Night*. His favorite story in the book was called "Tale of the Ensorcelled Prince," which is about a ruler whose wife casts a spell that changes him into half stone, half flesh. One night, while his mother was tucking him in, Maxwell imagined that his flesh was turning to stone. He smiled and told his mother.

"What is that like, mi amor?" she asked, thinking of her parents and imagining that like her son she too was turning to half stone, half flesh, unable to see them or call out to them or reach them through the passage of time, which moves forward, always forward (or rather that was the impression it gave her), and masks existence.

Maxwell closed his eyes and imagined that his veins were cracks in stone and that his skin was hard and gray, but he fell asleep before he could answer.

Around this time, Maxwell learned how to write. Afraa taught him the following words: *Maxwell, men, women, talk, stone, day, dog, sky, earth*. It had taken him the most time to learn how to write the word *earth*, but once he did he wrote it ten times on a sheet of lined paper that he then slipped into his copy of *The Book of the Thousand Nights and a Night*. He then tucked the book under his arm and walked out into the yard and through the garden of sunflowers. Once he reached the yard with the dog, he patted the dog's head and continued out into a street he had never seen before, a street with a brass and drum band dressed as skeletons and feathered birds of prey, a tremendous street that made tremendous noises, and it was there that he showed a skeleton the word he had written ten times, *earth*, a word that contained everything he knew and which he imagined was the shape of a human face, and the skeleton shrugged his bony shoulders, laughed, and marched on and Maxwell followed.

Just after Maxwell's seventh birthday the pirate had a simple idea. Since they had been unable to completely cure Maxwell's wandering disease, the pirate decided that he would go on long walks with his son. The walks worked, more or less, and Maxwell's mother, who had started reading the letters of Rousseau, mentioned to her husband that maybe the world would be better if it adapted to the whims of children rather than the other way around. If streets, she said, followed the patterns and logic of children then there would never be such a thing as getting lost, there would be a certain madness, yes, but it would be a lovely madness, one capable of multiple dimensions.

At first, the pirate and his son walked up and down Melpomene Avenue. When Maxwell became bored of Melpomene Avenue, the pirate and his son walked the streets of the French Quarter, which were full of bars, delis, cafés, clubhouses, and brothels. One morning, as they walked, the pirate explained to his son that many of the poor people who lived in the French Quarter were from an island in the Mediterranean Sea called Sicily, a volcanic island inhabited for thousands and thousands of years, and that they had replicated some of that island's feverish, elegant, and innumerable histories on the very streets they walked. Sometimes, Maxwell imagined that the French Quarter was a deep-sea jungle, and he held his breath and watched people on the streets as they moved like schools of fish, octopi, and sharks. Other times, the pirate took his son to cemeteries, which were good places to wander or get lost in because they resembled mazes without solutions. On days that were especially hot and humid, the trees and tombs offered shade. One late afternoon, while lost in one of these cemeteries, Maxwell asked his father where *his* father was buried.

"The sea," replied the pirate.

"Oh," said Maxwell, "so, he was a pirate like you?"

"Yes, my father was a pirate. Like me."

"Was he a good pirate?"

"Yes. He was very profitable."

"And his father?"

"Also the sea."

"And his father?"

"Somewhere outside the city, in an unmarked plot or a public grave."

Maxwell looked at a tomb and wondered what the man inside must have looked like and whether he had been rich or poor, tall or short, smart or dumb.

The pirate then explained to his son:

"Piracy gave us freedom, mijo. My great-grandfather, who was the first pirate in our family, was born a slave and *his* father was born a slave and *his* father was born a slave and *his* father was a born a slave in an unknown African village near the sea and that village will haunt our family until the last days on Earth."

The pirate and his son found a bench under a cypress tree. Through the late-afternoon haze, the pirate pointed to a barely visible star in the sky. He then explained to Maxwell that the light of the star was dead and had been emitted millions of years ago, maybe even billions of years ago, before even the Earth existed.

"We are surrounded by dead light, mijo, by the past," he said, "but a very useful past. My great-grandfather followed that same starlight to freedom. If the instruments on my boat ever failed me, I could still use that dead light to make my way back home. That is the first lesson learned by every pirate."

Maxwell thought about faraway villages, a hole in the solar system where the Earth should've been, and dead light. He couldn't understand if all light was dead or just light from the stars. Still, it was pleasant to think about. The pirate and his son were silent for a long time. When a soft wind passed through the cemetery, they both sighed the same way—deeply and with their eyelids half-closed.

One day while working, the pirate took his son to Delacroix Island, which, the pirate told his son, was not really an island at all, but was *the end of the world*, since it was only reachable through marsh and bayous and since the people who lived there were the type of people who would inhabit the world at the end of days. The Isleños, as the pirate called them, were fishermen, trappers, and bootleggers, but they had a proper grasp of history because they were the bastard children of the French and the forsaken children of the Spanish, and some of them, abandoned bastards that they were, spoke four or five languages and made more than even the governor.

Later, when the pirate was finished in town, he told his son that he wanted him to meet someone.

"Who?" asked Maxwell.

"A very important Isleño," the pirate said.

"Okay," Maxwell replied and watched as a young girl sang a familiar song in a strange accent and hopped over a drainage ditch.

"An old pirate. One of the last. Maybe the very last," the pirate said and watched his son closely.

"One of the last," Maxwell repeated and nodded, somewhat distracted and perplexed by the young girl.

"Do you understand?" the pirate asked his son.

The old pirate's name was Cesar, although all the Isleños called him the Last Pirate of the New World. He lived in a small shack near a large marsh in Plaquemines Parish. By the time the pirate and his son arrived, the sun was already setting behind the marsh, so the old pirate told them that they would have to spend the night. Then the old pirate gave Maxwell alligator jerky and passed a bottle of whiskey to his father, which he sipped slowly. The pirate and the old pirate enjoyed each other's company immensely. As they drank, they talked about boats and boxing and the Jai Alai Club in Arabi, where the old pirate went to listen to jazz bands and to watch women sing, beautiful, clever women who reminded him of his ex-wife Cecile and who in ancient Zimbabwe or Ghana would've destroyed kings and the men who thought they were kings. They also talked about Prohibition, a boon to Plaquemines Parish, and the modernization of the South, which would eventually lead to a day of reckoning. But first they'd have to bring the Isleños a post office and some electricity.

"We can't have a day of reckoning without some damn electricity," the old pirate said and exploded into a fit of laughter.

The pirate laughed. He then looked out a window into the dark marsh and sipped from the bottle of whiskey.

"And what about the boy?" the old pirate asked. "What about his modernization?"

"Mijo, what do you want to be when you grow up?" the pirate asked his son.

"A pirate," Maxwell answered.

The old pirate got up from his chair and lit a few candles. He then explained to Maxwell that he was the Last Pirate of the New World and that he was the direct descendant of a long line of African pirates who had worked in the Atlantic Ocean and that his great-great-grandfather had come to the New World first not as a slave but as a freeman in 1809 in order to work under Jean and Pierre Lafitte in the Bay of Barataria and had died some years later in the Cartagena rebellion in Colombia.

He then told the boy that when he retired or died or when he disappeared (because death, he explained, is a great disappearing act, the ultimate Houdini trick), whichever came first, Maxwell's father would become the Last Pirate of the New World. This was something he had thought long and hard about because his own son had been killed in the Great War by German mustard gas during the Meuse-Argonne offensive in the middle of a sea-green forest. He had even gone to the forest after the war to find signs of his son, but, of course, there hadn't been any signs of his son, there hadn't been any signs of his kindness or his terror or even his last thoughts. It had been a long, pointless journey.

Then the old pirate announced that after Maxwell's father

retired or died, piracy in the New World was all over. He had post offices and electricity to look forward to. It was the end of an era and that was that.

Later that night, when the old pirate and the pirate were drunk, they spoke of the true nature of the sea, which meant that they first spoke of the sea's consciousness, its will, its intention (a vengeful intention and subterfuge like that of an Assyrian god), but during the Sino-Japanese War the old pirate had horrifically discovered that the deep maw of the sea, or Susanoo, as the Japanese sailors had called it, had no consciousness at all.

"For thousands of years," the old pirate said, "we've been praying to a brainless watery nothing."

At some point in the night, Maxwell woke up and he couldn't fall back asleep. He was too tired and too excited. He got up from the bedding that the old pirate had laid for him on the floor of the shack and crept outside into the night. On the front porch he sat on a stool and thought about the old pirate's dead son and listened to the bellow of insects coming from the marsh. After some time had passed, an isolated amount of time, as if time itself were an island or a planet the color of deep jade, Maxwell left the porch and found a path which led to the banks of the marsh. Once there, he thought about being a pirate, and stood like a sleepwalker and watched the moon, which was white and monstrous. He watched the moon for hours until it descended inexplicably into the marsh.

In the morning, they ate bread and cheese and explored the tributaries of the marsh on a flatboat. The old pirate pointed out ancient cypress trees, herons, and mud crevices where alligators had laid their eggs. He told the pirate and his son that due to the Great Mississippi Flood the city and its bankers were going to dynamite the Caernarvon levee and flood the parish. Thousands of people, including the old pirate, were going to have to find new homes and new lives. The bankers were scared of the flooding that was happening all along the Mississippi River and the business they would lose if they didn't flood the parish.

"They're trying to wash us away," the old pirate said. "We'll be refugees in our own land, but they don't give a shit. They're swine with fat pink bellies."

"Bellies that never burst open," the pirate said.

"It's all for nothing. The Mississippi'll flood upriver. They're little men who want to be millionaires, sometimes gods. They believe their greed creates the world when in fact it destroys it."

For a few minutes both men were silent, and then Maxwell, who had been lost in his own thoughts—thoughts of other worlds and dinosaurs, in particular, the Iguanodon, which, he imagined, was gentle and had the same sort of snout as a horse—spotted an alligator. He yelled and the men watched as the alligator slipped by the flatboat, its eyes shining.

On Thursday, April 28th, 1927, the old pirate came to live with the pirate and his family on Melpomene Avenue. On Friday, April 29th, the city flooded his parish. The old pirate brought a few things—a small wooden chest, a suit, a few books—and he adjusted quickly to the small home. He took Maxwell on walks through the city, which generally lasted hours. Maxwell got the impression that the old pirate was a madman and he imagined that his words were a map to a dying, insane planet.

"The Pope is diseased," said the old mad pirate to Maxwell on one of their walks. "Pope John XXIII, who was a pope from 1410 to 1415, and who was also a pirate, was particularly diseased. He had a disease where he thought he was Pope. All popes, as it turns out, have the same disease. Poets are also diseased. Most of them have syphilis, which is a sex disease that drives men to dementia. During the Sino-Japanese War, I met a famous Japanese poet who had syphilis. It was said that he hadn't left his house in twenty years, which begs the question, how had he gotten syphilis in the first place? Not leaving your home for years and years is a different type of disease, I think. This proves that poets generally suffer from multiple diseases. How did I meet him? I was responsible for smuggling a case of his poetry books into China. The Chinese loved his poetry because it sympathized with them, or that's what they thought.

"Then there's a disease where you can't feel pain. There's no name for it as far as I know, but it's still a disease. Once, I met an Indian boy in Bombay who suffered from it. He stood in the center of beggar circles and cut himself to pieces with a small, sacrificial Ram Dao sword. All the while smiling like someone who had just seen a god. He wasn't blessed by a god, though. He died jumping off a roof for an English journalist when he was just sixteen. Turns out he was mortal, which is another disease. If you think about it, everything is a disease. Youth is a type of disease-in-waiting. Old age is a clear bottle brimming with chalky, liquid disease. Money is a disease. Conviction is a disease. So are cities. Then there are diseases that are like chain reactions. Those diseases are the worst because they inflict hundreds of men, sometimes thousands, sometimes millions. All white men have a disease like this. It's called Manifest Destiny and it's why they try so hard to drown us. Then there's an Eastern disease that's similar to Manifest Destiny. It's called Amuk. The people who have this disease suffer a murderous rage, but then afterward they suffer from amnesia. It's horrible! There was a village, I remember, off the coast of Borneo, or maybe in the Philippines. Or maybe it was the Island of Java. Anyway, one day all the men in this village went mad and tore down their homes and started killing each other. By the next morning, the town had been destroyed and hundreds of men had been murdered, but none of the survivors remembered anything. They presumed a great beast had come and laid waste to everything in sight. Can you believe it? I wouldn't have, until I met a man from that village who had killed his brother. Such sadness in his eyes. Sadness. That's another disease. One of the worst. But it's not the worst. The worst is a disease called Koro, which is a disease where men believe their genitals are retracting into their bodies. Like turtle heads. This is the worst disease of all because the future of mankind resides in its ability to use its genitals. Imagine that! The future! When one day, if you think about it, all diseases will be cured or a great unknown disease will over-run mankind and condemn us all to hell."

One added benefit to the old mad pirate moving in was that the Dominicana had more free time. During the mornings, she kept Maxwell home from school, which, she told him on more than one occasion when he pleaded to go, would only poison his mind. Instead, at the kitchen table, she went over Spanish, English, history, literature, philosophy, sciences, and math with him. He particularly excelled at math. Once, when the Dominicana asked her son why he thought this was the case, he just shrugged, smiled, and told her that he could solve math problems either on paper or with his eyes closed, it didn't matter which, and sometimes even in his dreams.

During the late afternoons and some evenings, while the old mad pirate and Maxwell wandered the city together, she went to the library and continued her studies with Afraa. By this point all Afraa had to do was suggest a novel or two and send the Dominicana off into a quiet corner of the library to digest it. She spent long, humid evenings reading until the old mad pirate and Maxwell came to walk her home, or, on some occasions, bring her dinner which they had bought in the city markets. When her husband wasn't working, he came with Maxwell. On these nights, the pirate and his son would hide behind bookshelves in a variety of hide-and-seek and watch her read. The pirate would whisper to his son that he had a very beautiful and brilliant mother and Maxwell would nod. Then the pirate and his son would cough loudly, making their presence known, and the Dominicana would put her book down, playing her part as the seeker, the heroine.

Afterward, while walking home, the pirate and her son would ask her what she had been reading and she would describe the novels she had read in great detail. Then the Dominicana and her family would make up stories about Babylon or immortal warriors or space travel, after which they would walk in silence through the gray and rose–colored streets of New Orleans and think about the *possibility* of their stories, as if thinking about them made them real, which was a true reflection of literature and happiness.

In particular, the Dominicana enjoyed the horror and science fiction novels of North America and England: H. P. Lovecraft, Ambrose Bierce, H. G. Wells, and Mary Shelley (whose *Frankenstein*, she thought, had marked the dawn of a new and terrifying era), in addition to the lesser-known writers she found in literary magazines and pamphlets dedicated entirely to the genres. While she couldn't be certain why she enjoyed these writers, she thought it might have something to do with the sorts of people who came from empires—people who suffered from a sense of unreality. But through unreality, the Dominicana thought, they understood at least one important thing: that people could be other people, cities could be other cities, and worlds could be other worlds.

One night, as Maxwell's mother was helping Afraa reshelve books, she found a cutout *Times-Picayune* article about the British explorer Percy Fawcett, who, in 1925, had set out for the Amazon in search of the Lost City of Z, only to disappear. She remembered a similar story her mother had often told her about a Spanish conquistador who set out into the Amazon in search of a city of gold and eternal life, never to return. The story used to horrify her, but she had also been enchanted by it. The discovery of the *Times-Picayune* article, which coincided with her childhood memory, gave the Dominicana an idea for a science fiction novel about a heroine from the Dominican Republic. Later that night, she told her husband about her idea and he suggested, insisted even, that she write it down before she changed her mind. Shortly after, Afraa let her borrow one of the library's typewriters and she set to work on a novel entitled *Lost City*. The plot was as follows: one night in the near future, a young girl of sixteen living in Santo Domingo decides to sneak out of her house and go for a swim. While swimming, she notices a great flash of light in the northern horizon. At first, she thinks the flash of light is beautiful. Then she feels bad for thinking this because she knows the flash of light must also be terrible. Her fears are confirmed. The next day her parents die and soon others follow. By the end of the second day, hundreds are dead. By the end of the week, thousands and thousands are dead.

Santo Domingo falls into chaos. Overcome with grief, she leaves. She walks for three days, avoiding people at all costs. Some are stricken with a horrifying disease and they try to kill her. She imagines that they are zombies, after the lovesick, indentured servants of Vodou priestesses in Haiti. Eventually, she stumbles across a group of survivors getting on a ship named the *Bulukiya*. The ship is named after a seafaring adventurer in *The Book of the Thousand Nights and a Night*. She takes this as a good sign. The group of survivors let her on the ship on the condition that she work and sleep on deck. One night, in the middle of the sea, the captain transforms into a zombie and the young girl from Santo Domingo kills him. Afterward, the group of survivors elects her as the de facto captain.

For a few years, the survivors live like pirates in the Caribbean Sea. At night, sleeping under the fiery stars, the Dominicana dreams of sea monsters and mechanical soldiers and an endless library, but during the day she thinks only of the survival of the people on her ship. One day, regardless of her efforts, two large black ships attack the *Bulukiya* and the survivors are taken to Cartagena to be sold as slaves. The city resembles a ruined paradise on the edges of the earth.

In captivity, she meets an old, dying mestizo from Peru. He tells her stories about his travels before he was taken as a slave. He says that South America is a Netherworld. He says Bogotá is full of zombies. He says Quito is in ashes. He says Buenos Aires is quiet and cold and empty.

He does however tell her about a city in the Amazon where people are gathering and where humanity might have a chance. The Lost City, he says, the golden city, the eternal city. The mestizo says he discovered proof of it as a young man while traveling the world. He then shows the Dominicana a journal he found in an old library in Madrid which was written by an unknown woman in the 17th century. Some of its pages are missing and it's full of incongruous details and deranged sketches: gold fountains that emit lava, jungle spiders the size of horses, men and women with heads in the middle of their chests, and skies inhabited by cities and prehistoric beasts. The journal also has a detailed map to the Lost City. Then the mestizo tells her that he's dying and he gives her the journal. Some humid nights later, a fever devours the mestizo and he dies in his sleep. When her captors come to take the body, the Dominicana kills them and escapes.

During the day, she wanders the countryside, living off fruit and wild rice, avoiding zombies and survivors both. At night, she sleeps in abandoned village huts and dreams about her dead parents. Eventually, she reaches the edges of the jungle. The jungle, she knows, is an abyss from which she will never return.

At the start of Part 2, the Dominicana, emaciated and nearly shattered, finds the entrance to the Lost City. A man with gray eyes, who finds her lying near the entrance in a pool of blood and rainwater, nurses her back to health. Shortly after, they fall in love and build a small house together. The city, built amongst ancient ruins and hidden deep in the jungle, is not a golden, eternal city. Wanderers, raiders, and savage bands of zombies show up regularly, making life terrible for the survivors. In addition, the survivors have a hard time deciding on a political system on which to run their new society. They debate the disintegrated political systems and empires of the Old World. Occasionally, these debates lead to arguments, which then lead to acts of murder and rebellion. Sometimes, the Dominicana imagines that the survivors are zombies. She imagines that they are zombies infected with a type of amnesia. Regardless, life inside the city walls is more stable than life outside of them.

A growing number of survivors even start to believe that the Lost City holds occult or metaphysical properties that could be the key to their new civilization. One night, after making love, the man with gray eyes reveals to the Dominicana that the Lost City is a *false* Lost City. He says that as a young man his grandfather had found proof of the *real* Lost City. Your grandfather? she asks him. Yes, he says, you once met him. My grandfather disappeared years ago, he says, but I knew the moment I saw the journal in your hands that you had somehow met him and that he trusted you implicitly. Yes, she says, I met him in captivity in what remains of Cartagena. Then she says, I'm sorry, amor, he's gone. The man with gray eyes nods sadly and says that the real Lost City exists somewhere in a parallel Earth. He says he has more proof. She asks him if anybody else knows about the real Lost City. He says no one else knows, but that a few people in the city suspect he knows something.

In the middle of the night, the Dominicana and the man with gray eyes trek through the jungle in search of the Lost City. The jungle swarms with insects and the eerie songs of nocturnal birds. The Dominicana thinks that even if mankind passes into oblivion, the Earth will still contain the frenzy of life. After some time, they come upon the remains of an ancient pyramid structure, mostly hidden by overgrowth. Inside of a small, roofless room, they find two skeletons and a 17th century telescope.

The Dominicana looks through the telescope and sees an innumerable amount of stars. She imagines that the stars are the lights of Santo Domingo and she weeps.

The man with gray eyes tells her that there's more. He reveals a stone portal in the shape of a perfect hemisphere. The portal shimmers, like the surface of a silver pool. Or a distant memory. In the distance, they hear screams. A small flash of light follows. The flash of light is not beautiful. In fact, the Dominicana's skin and eyes burn and she has trouble seeing. Then she hears gnashing teeth. It's the most terrifying sound she has ever heard. The man with gray eyes tells her to enter the portal. She refuses to go anywhere without him. A zombie enters the small room, violently lurches, and then runs toward the man with gray eyes. The Dominicana recognizes the zombie as one of the survivors from the false Lost City. The man with gray eyes begs for her to go, then turns toward the zombie just as it reaches him. She enters the stone portal.

In the final Part, the Dominicana finds herself riding a train alone. The train passes through jungles and cities. Some cities seem unfinished and have spires that pierce the sky. Others are made entirely of glass or rock. Still others look like immense geometry problems or shadows that stretch into the horizon. Half of the cities throng with people and half of them are empty. The train finally stops. She steps off a wooden platform into a jungle. She understands then that she's in a parallel Earth. She waits and waits for another train, but none come. She then searches the jungle for signs of other people, but there are none. At some point, she realizes she's pregnant and she discovers a clearing in the jungle with the ruins of a city and another stone portal. When she tries to walk through the portal, nothing happens. Six months later this is where she gives birth to a boy with gray eyes.

One day, when her son is nearly nine years old, the Dominicana spots a girl bathing in a river. The girl has long legs and shining black hair. When the girl sees the boy, she runs away.

The next morning, the Dominicana notices that her son is melancholy. To no avail, they spend the next few days searching for the girl. One day, while searching, the Dominicana spots an immense creature with a sword-like beak and black wings circling above the jungle canopy. She remembers the mestizo's journal. Who was the unknown woman who wrote the journal? she thinks. How did she find her way out of this endless jungle? she wonders. But she doesn't have time to figure it out. She realizes, horrifically, that the immense creature is hunting her son.

Just before dusk, the Dominicana and her son hide in the trunk of a massive kapok tree. Night falls. Her son is terrified and can't sleep, so she spends the long night fashioning a spear from a fallen branch and telling him about the seas of the Antilles and her life on another Earth in Santo Domingo. At some point, the boy asks her about his father and she tells him, again and again, that he saved her life and that he had gray eyes, just like him. She then sings to the boy. How was the Earth created? she sings. Is this truly the only one? Where does one universe end and another begin? The boy finally falls asleep.

At dawn, when the creature attacks, the Dominicana does not lower her gaze or even close her eyes in the anticipation of death, which is nearly certain. Instead, she stands in front of her son with the spear because, really, there is no other choice.

The Dominicana kept *Lost City* in a drawer for three months, until, one late summer day, she gave it to her husband while he was packing for a smuggling trip to Cuba. The pirate read *Lost City* from beginning to end, sometimes by flashlight, out in the middle of the sea at night or in a noisy hotel room in Havana, and not only did it give him the wondrous impression that the world was an infinite cycle of worlds, he greatly admired it. When he returned to New Orleans, he told his wife that she had written a masterpiece and he took her out to dinner to celebrate.

Some days later, the Dominicana gave the manuscript to

Afraa, who, by chance, had recently met a young publisher at a party by the name of David Ellison. He had been involved with the short-lived literary magazine the *Double Dealer*, once hailed as "the Renaissance of the Vieux Carré," but he now ran the small publishing house Amulet Books. Without telling her friend, Afraa gave the manuscript to the young publisher. After one exhilarating and sleepless night of reading, he decided to publish it in the spring of 1929. *Lost City* did well, especially for the small publishing house, which was accustomed to barely breaking even, and sold its one thousand copies by September. The fantasy, horror, and science fiction pulp magazine *Weird Tales* embraced the novel and published an excerpt. *Lost City* was even considered for a prestigious award for new writers given out by Loyola University.

A few months after the release, a sharp cultural critic for the *Times-Picayune* wrote that the novel predated and enhanced William Buehler Seabrook's concept of the zombie and, in fact, upended the Western world's fascination with Haitian Vodou, reanimation, and multiple dimensions. In other words, the critic concluded, the novel *Lost City* was visionary and there was nothing in contemporary literature like it.

Other and more numerous critics called the novel maundering or grotesque or dangerously socialist, each stating in their own careful yet counterfeit way that (much like with the New Orleans Voodoo queen Marie Catherine Laveau) the suspect reason was that it came from the frail and disturbed imagination of a woman from the Caribbean.

In mid-November 1929, an old journalist from New York City who had roots in New Orleans came to interview the Dominicana. A colleague of the journalist, whom he had worked with at *The Messenger* from 1924 to 1928, mailed him the novel and suggested that in addition to a review, he should find and interview the author in person. The journalist read the novel on the long train ride from New York City to New Orleans, yet he couldn't quite make much sense out of it, or anything really, including the white and yellow landscape outside his train window, the recent events of the Wall Street Panic, or even his own life, which, he thought, had been marked by random and often meaningless events.

During the interview, the Dominicana and the journalist sat at her kitchen table and drank coffee. To start, he asked her how old she had been when she arrived to the United States. She replied she had been sixteen. He asked her what led to her immigration. At first the Dominicana didn't say anything. She sipped her coffee slowly, letting the steam fill her nostrils like a scented breeze. She then calmly explained what it was like when the American Marines came to her country in black steel ships and murdered her parents.

She told him what it was like to be an orphan in San Pedro de Macorís and then Santo Domingo, which was a cursed thing, like the lives of Pelias and Neleus, the twin sons of Poseidon and Tyro who were left on a mountaintop to die by their mother, who herself had been an orphan. And the more the Dominican writer talked, the more she realized that it didn't matter if the journalist was there or not. Really, the interview was more of a confession through which she could finally reveal something about her past—the warren of her memory, which contained immense fields of sugarcane, an island zephyr, the seas of the Antilles.

"And is this really what your novel is about?" the journalist asked.

"Oh," the Dominicana said, "I don't know. That's for others to decide."

The Dominicana and the journalist sipped their coffee in silence.

"And what do you think of this Panic?" he asked.

Before she could answer, her husband and her son came into the kitchen with a small bucket full of red beans, a basket of oysters, and French bread. The Dominicana excused herself and grabbed the basket of oysters from her husband, and kissed Maxwell on the forehead. The boy, a tall and wiry child, ran into the other room.

"My son," said the Dominicana.

"An African cricket," said the journalist, more to himself than to the Dominicana. He then glanced out the kitchen window, where the pale sun was setting, and he knew that he wouldn't write the review and that his days were numbered.

Around this time, the men and women of Melpomene Avenue began to gather on street corners to discuss the Wall Street Panic. For a short time, there was general confusion as to what would happen to their neighborhood. The confusion began when the old mad pirate started the rumor that the city would assert ownership of the neighborhood and destroy it, much like what it had done to his parish. The old mad pirate bellowed that his shack was underwater and that the city had consumed it, like a great and ravenous octopus, and that it would now consume Melpomene Avenue.

Although many people living on Melpomene Avenue believed correctly that the city was indeed an octopus grabbing everything that was rightfully theirs, the rumor was ultimately unfounded. Before long, the pirate asked his dear friend to stop spreading rumors. The pirate walked door to door and consoled his neighbors, sometimes offering advice or even small favors. In this way, the people of Melpomene Avenue soon realized that they had other things to worry about.

Regardless of the Panic, David Ellison decided that he would forge on and publish the Dominicana's second novel. In fact, he gave her a healthy advance and she started work right away on the sequel to *Lost City*, entitled *A Model Earth*, in which the city of New Orleans is a spaceship and in which there are innumerable Earths in parallel universes.

In the summer of 1930, when she was nearly done with *A Model Earth*, the Dominicana fell sick. Her advance was nearly all used up and her husband was having trouble finding work, so they didn't immediately go to a doctor. It was only when she started to have nosebleeds and when a fever kept her from writing that the pirate took her to a Welsh doctor who owed him a favor. The doctor, a capable but exhausted man nearing the age of retirement, examined the Dominicana and then told the pirate and his son that they would have to be careful with whom they came in contact.

"Is it serious?" the pirate asked the Welsh doctor.

"It's hard to be certain," the doctor replied. "I haven't seen an outbreak of typhoid since the war, but this is my third case in two weeks."

"It's serious, then," the pirate concluded.

The pirate spent every waking hour taking care of his wife. He cleaned their home on Melpomene Avenue from top to bottom. Although her appetite was waning, he cooked for her and went to the market at least once daily to barter for the best vegetables, fish, and meats. He changed her sheets three times a day and made sure that she was never alone. He couldn't stand the thought of her being alone. If he couldn't be with her, he made sure Afraa or the old mad pirate or Maxwell was by her side. At night, he lay next to her, listening to her hoarse breathing. In the mornings, before the sun rose, he got up, kissed her on her sweaty forehead, and cooked breakfast.

After a week, the Dominicana's health took a turn for the worse. She could no longer tell the difference between the stark reality of her sickness and her nightmares. She called for her dead parents in Spanish. She damned the American Marines to hell where they would be forced to march off cliffs like lemmings for all eternity. She told her husband that she wanted more than anything to swim and drown in the seas of the Antilles.

She wept and laughed in turn. During moments of lucidity, she apologized to her husband and her son and she told them not to worry and that she loved them terribly, so terribly, in fact, she felt that at any moment her heart would burst open in radiance.

The Welsh doctor stopped by every few days. One late afternoon, as he was inspecting a series of rose-colored spots near her abdomen, the Dominicana grabbed his hand. She asked if he could tell her a story, any story really, just something to help her forget the pain. At first, the doctor didn't know what story to tell, but then he thought about his childhood in Wales. The Dominicana closed her eyes and the Welsh doctor began:

"My father was a miner from Wales, South Wales Valleys, to be accurate, and we lived in a village not too far from the coal mine where my father worked. We were a Catholic mining family. Life was systematic and grim, but not without its own vigor or rare joy, a birth, for example, or a strike. Regardless of the laws on the books, it was quite common for women and children to work the mines alongside the men. The owners didn't care. Or, at most, they paid off the government commissioners.

"One night, around my tenth birthday, my father came to my room and told me that the next morning I would be going to the mines with him. Of course, it didn't come as a surprise. This was something the boys in the village expected. A rite of passage. At that time, I thought of myself as a resilient and rugged boy. Or rather, I wanted badly to be resilient and rugged since I saw my father that way. I suppose all boys fashion themselves after a perception of their father.

"The next morning my father took me to the coal mines. I had been near them, but never in them. They were obscure, sunless, yet still full of movement and labor. Damn hard labor. Once we were deep in the coal mines, my father gave me an unexpected job. Instead of handling equipment or checking the mines for ventilation, like most of the other boys my age, my father put me in charge of a gray mining pony. The job of a mining pony, he explained, was to pull mining carts. It was a strenuous and almost endless job. He told me to take the pony to the surface and watch over him for two weeks. This was the yearly allotted time that a mining pony was allowed to have a break from the mines. My father instructed me on how to put sacks on the pony's head in order to keep it from becoming upset from the light once we reached the surface. The pony, of course, was accustomed to the dark. Once on the surface, he instructed me to take the sacks off slowly, so the pony could get accustomed to the light. It was a process that reminded me of ascending into madness.

"For two weeks, every morning, I walked the pony around a field and watched as it grazed on the grass and squinted at the sky, trying to remember, I thought, the idea of natural light. At the end of those two weeks, my father instructed me to bring the pony back into the coal mines. He met me in the field and he told me that the pony would become crazed when she saw the sacks. Careful, he told me, she knows. I thought then that to the pony the mines must have been a type of hell, a dark chrysalis from which she would never be able to leave. I was right. When we put the first sack over the pony's head, she went mad. She brayed and kicked, and I remember thinking, if she could have wept she would have wept. I also remember that my heart ached for the pony in a very physical way. It felt as real as any other type of colossal pain I had ever experienced or have ever experienced since. I must have looked terrible or like I didn't want to finish the job because my father scolded me. He grabbed my shoulders and looked me in my eyes and told me that I shouldn't give the pony a second goddamn thought. At that point, I must have started crying because my father shook me. He shook me and told me that the pony had a very important, almost sacred, duty and that was to keep boys like me from working the mines for as long as possible."

One August morning, Maxwell walked to the river and snuck on a ferry headed to the Algiers rail yards. Once there, he explored the carcasses of engines and cabin cars. It smelled like metal and wet rubber, a dense, humid smell very different from his home on Melpomene Avenue, which smelled of bread, sweat clinging to paper, his father's dirty clothes, which was the thick smell of alligator skin and the marsh outside the city. Near some tracks, he found a pile of rubber strips. Using rotted wood and a matchbook the old mad pirate had given him, he started a large fire and threw the rubber strips into it.

Later, when he was bored, he sat on a crate and watched trains arrive and depart. The trains moved slowly. He imagined that they were prehistoric black lizards and he wondered what it would be like to ride one or what it would be like to gaze into their black throats. After some time, Maxwell noticed men and boys running through the rail yards. He craned his neck and watched as they jumped into an empty boxcar. Moments later, two bullmen blew on whistles and gave chase to the train, but by then the train was already receding into the deep and indistinguishable blue of the horizon. Maxwell sat back down on the crate and waited for the next train, but partly due to his hunger and partly due to the yawning humidity, he soon fell into a deep sleep without dreams.

When Maxwell woke up, it was night and the stars were out and a crescent moon hung over the French Quarter across the river. He sat on the crate and read the sky, but all he could read up there was despair. In the crescent moon, he read despair and in the light of the stars, which Maxwell knew was the only thing that remained of many of them, he read despair. Sometime later, he felt a hand on his shoulder.

"Yo, kid, I've been watching you," said the bullman. He then took out a flashlight and shone it on Maxwell.

Maxwell averted his eyes from the light, which he imagined was a yellow tentacle reaching into his thoughts.

"You meaning to run off, right?"

Maxwell was silent.

"Listen, kid, everybody runs off when they need to run off. But tonight's not your night. Go home."

Maxwell kicked at a clump of charred rubber and then took off running, but he didn't head toward the ferries, which would take him across the river and back home. He didn't want to go home. His mother would be there and he knew that she was dying.

It wasn't long before the Dominicana told David Ellison that she had destroyed the manuscript for *A Model Earth*.

"I made a small fire," she explained, as he was sitting by her bedside.

He said that it was okay, yet he knew in his heart that it wasn't okay. He felt mournful at the thought of the destroyed manuscript, which had been remarkable, and by the fact that no one else would ever read it. Briefly, he thought of his mother, or rather, the mother of his childhood, his permanent mother, an island herself, a quiet and perplexing woman adrift in an ocean of wheat, and how she had once told him in a steady and rising Yiddish voice that literature was a memory of a memory of a memory.

Then, just to say something, he told the Dominicana about a recurring dream he had after reading *Lost City* for the first time. In the dream, Charles Darwin is an extraterrestrial sent to Earth with the task of collecting specimens for an interplanetary zoo on a distant planet, a planet millions of light-years away, which resembles a native Earth with native trees and native rivers and native beasts.

"An Earth away from Earth," the Dominicana said.

"Yes, exactly like that," the publisher said.

"But then which Earth is the real one?" she asked, smiling.

The publisher and the Dominicana sat for some time in silence, enjoying a late-afternoon breeze, and soon she began to drift in and out of sleep. The publisher stood up, but he was reluctant to leave. One of the greatest writers of this young century is dying, he thought, and there's nothing I can do about it.

Later that night, in bed, in the dark, the publisher recalled the Dominicana's question and he was suddenly unsure if he was living on Earth or an unknown planet that was a replica of Earth. Sleep deserted him. How could I mistake Earth for a replica of Earth? he asked himself. And then: What would the purpose of a zoo like that be? And then, horrifically: Am I a free man on Earth or a captive in Charles Darwin's zoo? Three months later, David Ellison's publishing house collapsed and he left in ruins for Los Angeles.

Maxwell sat with his mother and they both waited. He asked her if she needed anything and she shook her head. She then spoke to him softly and said that she had tried not to wish for more time, but in the end, she did. She wanted more time. She wanted each moment to last years. She wanted her very last second to contain an eternity, in which it was always dawn or always dusk. She then held Maxwell close and said she wouldn't talk about time anymore. Instead, she told the story of how one morning when she was a girl the seas of the Antilles had brought her a pirate. She then described the Dominican Republic and the islands of the seas of the Antilles, which had been a stage setting for the Americas. But beyond that, she explained, beyond history or the mistakes of men, beyond time, which was a great and clever thief, beyond all of that, at the edge of the universe or maybe at the start and end of the universe, there was a soft murmur, a constant breath of beauty, a truth.

The End came exactly as she knew it would. But her only child, her seed, her amor, her baby, her restless Maxwell, her ensorcelled prince, her son et lumière, her true island, would go on. Into some vague and faraway year, when the world would be different and the people in it only slightly so. On and on and on.

VOX HUMANA

December 2004–August 2005

A hospice nurse called Saul to say his grandfather was having trouble breathing and she asked him to come to the house. It took him twenty minutes to walk through the fresh snow from his apartment to his grandfather's greystone on Humboldt Boulevard. Since he was young he'd possessed a strange kind of prescience regarding his grandfather's death. He anticipated sitting on the same bed with his grandfather's tiny and ruined body. He envisioned his grandfather's hands and feet and elbows and closed eyes (the nurse would close them or he would), momentously at peace, otherworldly, and the earsplitting silence between them, which resolved itself only after ten minutes or maybe twenty, he couldn't tell, but in the end, resolved itself fully when he coughed into his palm, pointlessly it seemed, and said, thank you for everything, after which he imagined his grandfather saying, it was nothing, Saul. Then he remained silent because everything that was about to happen had already happened before. His grief was already traveling backward in time from Chicago to Tel Aviv. He was already meeting himself coming the other way, like a shitty space-time opera, he thought, and then he left and the kind nurse entered the room.

Am I an orphan again? he asked himself later that day. Then he started washing his grandfather's dirty dishes, glancing out the window at the snowy dunes on the rooftops and the clouds as they raced over the city like a cavalry of gray horses, and added, fuck, I'm too old to be an orphan.

The following week, on the Friday after the funeral, he returned to work. He worked at an old small hotel by the lake which had recently been renovated and which catered to wealthy European, Chinese, and American businesses, young couples, and the occasional nouveau riche transient. The hotel was called The Atlas. The building had a brick façade, a lobby with leather couches and a fireplace, a luxury conference room, a bar, a European-style elevator, and fifty rooms (each crowned with an original ink-on-paper drawing of a god or goddess of travel; so, for example, Room 2 was Chung-Kuei, Room 7 was Min, Room 33 was Hasamelis, Room 42 was Hermes, Room 19 was Ekchuah, and so on, tactfully, but also, thought Saul, with an exhausting affectation of mythology).

On the rooftop of the hotel, there was a neglected and twisted garden worn by the irregular seasons. When business was slow or when he was on break, he went to the rooftop garden to read. For the most part, he read science fiction novels. Saul had a flexible schedule at The Atlas. There were three shifts. When he worked too early or too late he felt like a sleepwalker or a zombie. The 3:00 p.m. to 11:00 p.m. shift suited him well. His main responsibilities included reservations, check-ins, check-outs, preparations for business meetings and conferences, and responding to guest requests, which were sometimes reasonable and sometimes ridiculous or melodramatic.

He liked his boss, Romário. Once, Romário, who was half Romanian, half Cuban and who spoke of Romania like it was a bizarre crime novel and spoke of Cuba like it was an irrevocable dream, had asked Saul what it was like to be descended from Litvak Jews. He told Romário that it must be like being descended from any other group of people. Other times, it felt like his skin was the cage of his ancient fate and there was absolutely no way out of his skin. This was his fifth year working at The Atlas. He had a salary that would've been laughable to most guests of the hotel.

At seven, during his break, Saul put on his black wool coat and went to the rooftop, which was covered in a thin layer of snow. He sat on a steel bench, drank hot coffee, and read a Russian science fiction novel by Stanisław Lem called *Solaris*, which was, in short, about a thinking ocean on a distant planet. This was the fourth or maybe fifth time he had read it. At eight, he returned to the front desk. The Atlas was hosting a conference for futures traders called OpenConCon, so this kept him busy for the rest of the night.

At eleven, he put on his black wool coat and clocked out. Then he went to a twenty-four-hour FedEx to drop off a package his grandfather had asked him to send just days before his death, a medium-sized white and brown box that weighed, according to the FedEx employee, just over nine pounds, and was addressed to a Maxwell Moreau in the Department of Physics at the Universidad de Chile in Santiago, Chile. Saul smiled awkwardly and shrugged when the FedEx employee said, oohhh! Chile, since he knew neither the contents of the package nor its recipient. Then he waited for the #72 bus and some fifteen minutes later transferred to the Blue Line.

He got off at California and walked to a small Mexican restaurant near his home. He sat at a booth and ate enchiladas and read more from *Solaris*. He read more about the strange and night-marish thinking ocean and wondered if his grandfather had ever read it, but he had no idea and this made him a little miserable. He should know these things, he thought. He should remember his grandfather accurately. He should remember as much as possible about the man who had raised him, even though remembering anything always brought consequences of its own and forgetting could be a type of a gift. For a long while he watched people pass by the front window of the small Mexican restaurant. They were wrapped up like nomads, and he detected an air of melancholy and resistance about them, the American mirror of melancholy and resistance, he thought, and then he read some more until the restaurant closed.

On Sunday afternoon, he went to his grandfather's house on Humboldt Boulevard, following a guilty need to pack up and get rid of everything as quickly as possible. His grandfather had bought the house with his modest savings as a high school teacher and historian. Saul had come to live with him at the age of five, just three months after his parents were killed on March 11th, 1978, during the hijacking of a bus on Israel's Coastal Highway, a tragic event which journalists only later started calling the Coastal Road Massacre. In fact, one of the first English words he had learned, from hearing it so often in hushed tones, was *massacre*, a word, he now understood, that drew its very last breath from unreality.

According to his grandfather, his mother had met his father, an Israeli student, in a café on Devon Avenue. One year later, in 1971, they married and moved to Tel Aviv. All Saul had left of them were five photographs, which he kept wrapped in scraps of black Egyptian linen in a small wooden school box. He never looked at the photographs and he never showed them to others. He had very few memories of his parents or Israel, a nation that from time to time he imagined as a pyretic planet in another star system.

Still, occasional memories of his childhood before their deaths slipped through. Sometimes when he closed his eyes on the #72 bus or sat by himself in a late-night diner, he conjured up images of the solar-yellow Negev Desert or an iridescent skyscraper in Tel Aviv at night or a humming market in Jerusalem. But it was always in vain because his parents were nowhere to be seen in those images; they weren't even shadows or ghosts. They had died when he was still far too young to influence or direct his memories. Like in some strange Philip K. Dick novel, time had stopped existing but something like the passage of time had still left its violent mark on him. He had an unreal father and an unreal mother, lost to an unreal war.

His first true memory, incandescent and brutal, was three months after their deaths. He was on a plane sitting by a window, but the shades were drawn and the plane was dark. He was terrified of flying, of traveling alone through an empty sky. Then the man sitting next to him lifted the shades and pointed out the window and said, look, that's the Atlantic Ocean, and he looked and the sky and the ocean were the bluest things he had ever seen. They were, in fact, mirror images of each other. As long as he kept staring at the Atlantic Ocean, he told himself, he wouldn't start crying. Then the man smiled in a way that was both tender and mischievous and said, I was born there, at which point Saul understood that the man was his maternal grandfather.

Later, in silence and exhaustion, they sat in the back seat of a taxi that smelled of disinfectant and coconut and dirt, a thick smell which almost put Saul to sleep, but he couldn't sleep, he was either too tired or too excited, the taxi hurrying through the steel and cement labyrinth of the city, and then they were there, late in the evening, standing in silence and exhaustion on a stern and quiet boulevard with tall trees and streetlights that gave out a dingy, cone-shaped alien light, a dog barking from a nearby alley, his grandfather leading him toward a tall iron gate in front of a large brick house, a careful hand on his trembling bony right shoulder, a little after midnight on June 15th, 1978.

His grandfather's two-story greystone had three bedrooms, two bathrooms, a large living room connected to a box-like dining room through a short hallway, a kitchen with square windows, a large office in a converted second-story space with a desk, a black typewriter (later, a black computer), a cheap Turkish rug, numerous historical artifacts, and windows that faced east toward a flat ocean of rooftops. The front of the office had bookshelves crammed with books of a historical nature—books that had meant as much to his grandfather as people, but he never minded lending them out, either. During occasional insomniac nights as a teenager, Saul would browse through those books and he still remembered some of the names of their authors: Garcilaso de la Vega, Fernand Braudel, John Henrik Clarke, Studs Terkel, William T. Vollmann, Dorothy Porter Wesley, John Hope Franklin, Charlotte J. Erickson, Eduardo Galeano, and Howard Zinn. In addition to this collection, his grandfather had boxes of cassette tapes full of thousands of hours of interviews he had conducted through the years and ten history books with his name, Benjamin Drower, on the cover, an Americanized name that, at the age of twelve, in 1933, he had started using instead of his birth name, Benjaminas Druer. In any case, these books were seamless, unstoppable monologues and a few had even accumulated a devoted, if somewhat underground, readership. In no particular order, they were about the Atlantic Ocean from 1491 to 1945 in two volumes, the October Russian Revolution, Archimedes, a short history of neoliberalism and Milton Friedman (an economist from the University of Chicago, who, as of note, his grandfather reviled), the collected dreams and nightmares of WWII soldiers and nurses in two volumes, Ben Reitman (an anarchist and physician to the poor, who, as of note, he adored), an oral history of Chicago from 1929 to 1945, and the Maxwell Street Market.

Although seemingly erratic in subject and nature, it could be said that these ten books constituted one single enterprise and belief, which was that history and truth had nothing to do with each other. The back of the office was dusty and cavernous and had bookshelves crammed with books of a more speculative and unreal nature. These were the books that Saul had devoured during his childhood, books written (to name a few) by H. G. Wells, E. E. "Doc" Smith, Isaac Asimov, Jorge Luis Borges, Arthur C. Clarke, Stanisław Lem, Robert Heinlein, Octavia E. Butler, Ray Bradbury, Philip K. Dick, Pauline Hopkins, Theodore Sturgeon, Ursula K. Le Guin, Frank Herbert, and Samuel R. Delany. To Saul, the authors of these books were pariahs among pariahs. Sometimes, as a kid, while his grandfather worked at the other end of that large office, he would lovingly arrange these books according to the decade they were written or according to science fiction subgenres, sometimes following Asimov's strict guidelines and other times making up his own, for example, by mixing cyberpunk with space operas in an attempt to find an accord between the interior and the exterior or by giving slipstream its own bookshelf in order to think about which books could exist in the same reality, if any. The back of the office also had a large oval window that overlooked a backyard and a garage. In the summer, ivy grew on the garage and sometimes his grandfather would talk about how to grow ivy with neighbors or strangers passing through the back alley. It seemed fairly likely to Saul that his grandfather had spent the vast majority of his life happily talking to strangers. If he had to pinpoint any reasons why, he would say that his grandfather loved listening to most anybody who had a story to tell and that almost everybody loves a person who listens. He had a black gas grill and new plastic lawn chairs he had bought the summer before his death. In the winter, the backyard was often covered in a thin layer of vaguely glimmering snow. The tall iron gate surrounded the house and its lock sometimes froze over in the winter and when it did Saul had trouble getting inside, but it wasn't frozen that Sunday afternoon.

He picked up a book written by his grandfather titled *The Mathematician and the War*. The book was about Archimedes, and while sitting on the cheap Turkish rug and thumbing through its pages, Saul keenly remembered the first time his grandfather had mentioned the Greek mathematician to him. He'd been eight or nine, walking with his grandfather at Montrose Beach, when for some reason or another he picked up a stick, squatted, and started drawing geometric diagrams in the sand. There was a white sun and a white fog over the lake that day, so the city and what it contained—its green and steel colors, its penury and opulence, its skyscrapers of frantic people, in short, its complete geometry—was invisible. At some point, his grandfather, who rarely spoke to Saul like he was a child, told him that in Syracuse in 212 BCE Archimedes had been drawing geometric diagrams in the sand just before a Roman soldier under the invading forces of General Marcus Claudius Marcellus had killed him. Then he burst out laughing, a type of prolonged loving rumble, picked up a stick, squatted near Saul, and started to draw circles in the sand for Saul. According to some, he explained, Archimedes' last words were: *do not disturb my circles*. And yet here they are, he said to Saul, in the sand and fog, more than two thousand years later, undisturbed.

Since the life of Archimedes was relatively unknown, *The Mathematician and the War* was really about Archimedes' inventions— the Archimedes' screw, the immense catapults, the horrific giant crane-like claw called "the ship shaker" which could lift a ship out of the water, possibly sinking it—and the Second Punic War. But what had surprised Saul the most about *The Mathematician and the War* was not the relatively unknown life of Archimedes or even his absurd, luminous inventions, but rather his grandfather's final, sympathetic portrayal of the nameless Roman soldier who had killed Archimedes, a sorrowful and vengeful Roman soldier who in all likelihood had lost compatriots and friends to the catapults and Titan-like claws dreamed up by that squatting mathematician and who, his grandfather had written in the epilogue, "in a sad kind of way had resisted history, but, in the end, still found himself entrapped by it."

The next day, during a lull in work or during a type of daydream, Saul drew the Archimedes' circles on a pad of paper with The Atlas logo.

What the hell are these? asked Romário, later, after discovering the pad of paper with Archimedes' circles on the front desk, then, while examining them more closely, shook his head to convey to Saul that he suddenly understood everything at once, adding, I once knew a guy who walked and walked in circles like this around Plaza Vieja in Havana, yelling at the top of his lungs, "Señores, listen to me, madness is contagious," but, of course, nobody listened, they were already mad.

A few weeks later, indistinguishable weeks filled with the same endless ash-colored snow clouds, Saul was in his kitchen reading *The End of Eternity* by Isaac Asimov when he heard the doorbell ring. At first, he just sat there, transfixed by the cough-like echo of the doorbell, thinking it might be a Jehovah's Witness or some kid selling magazine subscriptions, but after it rang again and again, he put the book down and went to the door.

Through the open doorway Saul saw his friend Javier Silva or a man who might be Javier Silva standing on the porch. He was thin and had tousled, black curly hair and a two-months-old beard, sprinkled with gray at the chin, which somehow only underscored his otherwise youthful, itinerant appearance. He wore a dark green winter coat, gray trousers, a black T-shirt, and in his right hand he held a small black and gray backpack. When he saw Saul, he hugged him.

Saul, pana, it's been a while, cómo andas?

Javier explained that he had boarded a last-minute flight from Mexico City to Chicago the previous evening and would be home for a few days, at which point Saul realized that it really was Javier Silva and not a man who might be Javier Silva, a doppelgänger, for example, who had come all this way to replace him.

Saul hadn't seen Javier in the flesh since he moved to Quito, Ecuador, some ten years earlier. Occasionally, they'd write short emails in which each took great pains to inform the other that not much had changed in his life, even if a lot had changed in Javier's life and only a little in Saul's. Or every few months Javier would call from places like Lago Agrio or Arequipa or Buenos Aires since his work as a freelance foreign correspondent kept him on a manic schedule. During those years, Saul often felt a vicarious and melancholy thrill when he thought of Javier's assignments, each marked by a small inky dot on an imaginary map in his mind. Every place Javier went, thought Saul, he left something of himself, however small or intangible, and those small dots coalesced, particle-like, into letters, then words, then pages in a newspaper or magazine that Saul then read as if reading the work of a stranger.

Sometimes, over their infrequent calls, Javier told Saul that talking to him about his work was a type of catharsis. Once, during a particularly difficult period in 2000 in Ecuador when one of Javier's fixers from the Oriente had been jailed, Javier admitted to Saul that maybe he had made a mistake in choosing "this shit box of a dying career," that, at first, he had just wanted to travel through Latin America to see massive celebrations and natural disasters and political upheavals, but that had been naïve. He learned, soon enough, that the experience of those things had no essential value beyond itself.

During another call, after one of his stories about student protests in Chile had been dropped by an editor, he told Saul that sometimes he didn't see the point of journalism, that "people have an extraordinary talent for convincing themselves that what happens only happens to other people or that what doesn't exist, in fact, does exist." Still, it was apparent to Saul and to others that Javier was very good at what he did. In 2001, Javier was awarded a Maria Moors Cabot Prize special citation for investigative stories on Texaco oil spills in the Ecuadorian Amazon and the class-action lawsuit filed in a US federal court by a group of indigenous citizens in the Oriente. In 2002, he received an honorable mention for the Hillman Prize for coverage of the Argentine Great Depression. And yet, at other times, especially during those long silences between emails or calls, Saul only felt the rift of their friendship grow larger and larger.

Once, during an assignment covering shadow markets in Mexico City's Tepito neighborhood, a type of immense bazaar nicknamed Barrio Bravo, Javier met a woman named Marina Fuentes, a medical student who gave free medical treatment to street kids and workers. Afterward, Javier had gone around the city with his heart and foot in his mouth, like an "idiotic monk on a pilgrimage to Babel," until he had gathered the gall to propose. Two years after that, Javier emailed him a blurry photograph of a squirming, newborn baby girl. The subject of the email was "my beautiful daughter, Maya." Eventually, the rift of their friendship, a rift of time and space, took on the architecture and contours of an impassable wormhole.

Still, Saul sometimes told himself after those conversations on the phone, everybody who leaves eventually returns, in some form or another. Like a relentless episode of *Doctor Who*, on one side of that wormhole was Saul and Javier's shared adolescence and on the other was Javier Silva on his porch with a two-month beard and a travel backpack. Seconds or years had passed.

The first time Saul and Javier saw each other was during the first week of 7th grade in an alley near their school, which Saul routinely took to get home. They were standing in a clumsy semicircle with four or five other kids who were all sharing a joint. While they smoked, Javier, who was wiry, with boundless energy, talked nonstop about his great-uncle, Medardo Ángel Silva, a famous poet in Ecuador from a literary group called La Generación Decapitada, who had "written a bunch of weird shit about cemeteries and hunters and puppets" and who had killed himself just before his twenty-first birthday by accident or because of a girl or because of madness, nobody really knew. There was even a rumor that there might be a lost notebook or two of his poetry floating around somewhere in Guayaquil, poetry that drove its readers mad, like in a horror film.

At some point, Saul interrupted him. What does La Gen-erac-ión de-capit-ada mean?

La Generación Decapitada? said Javier with a smirk. It means the Decapitated Generation, pana. Then everyone standing in the clumsy semicircle laughed, except Saul.

The next time they saw each other was a few days later in gym class, when, during a stifling game of baseball, Javier came up to him, apologized for being such a dick, and then started telling him about his summer trip to Quito, a city of volcanoes, and how his cousins got him drunk every night and drove him around in an old jeep. For some reason, Saul told Javier that he had been born in Israel, and Javier said, that's cool, pana, even though it was clear he didn't even know anything about Israel.

After that they became indivisible friends. In short, they were newly minted Americans who saw in each other an inviolable and welcomed otherness. In 8th grade, Javier came to live with Saul and his grandfather for a few months after his parents divorced and his dad moved back to Quito for a short period of time. Later, as teenagers, they spent long hours together wandering through train yards or abandoned buildings, the deep cold fossilizing their steps in the snow. In the summers, often after work, they went to basement punk rock shows in Pilsen or rooftop parties with sandy-haired Ukrainian girls or they met up in old air-conditioned diners to eat fat pancakes or even fatter burritos or they walked block after block in the unshakable heat while Saul told Javier about the plots of the science fiction novels he was reading, novels Saul knew Javier would never read, so that, by the end of those long walks, Saul's telling of the novel *was* the novel.

Saul also remembered how, after they had both been caught ditching school for a week straight, his grandfather, who was otherwise furious, had endearingly called Javier a luftmensch, a Yiddish phrase that loosely meant *someone who exists in a cloud of possibility* and he remembered the icy-cold feeling of repulsion that had seized him one night at a rooftop party in the South Loop when Javier told him that hek had "accidentally" fucked the girl Saul loved, or rather, the girl whom he had conceivably loved from a distance, and the six months of impenetrable silence between them that followed.

But, overall, when he thought of Javier, he thought of what his grandfather had first recognized in him, the notion of (luftmensch) possibility. Javier had pined for possibility in the cracks and basements and alleys and rooftops and, yes, clouds of that invisible city, and it was this notion more than anything else that had helped Saul, an interstellar exile from Israel, form a connection between his solitary life and the world.

Still, at some point, possibility in Chicago wasn't quite enough for Javier. At twenty-one, the same age his great-uncle, the poet Medardo Ángel Silva, committed suicide, Javier, the only real friend Saul had ever had, abruptly packed up and left for Quito.

The last time Saul saw Javier was in October of 1994. They were in the Golden Nugget Pancake House on Western Avenue at 3:00 or 4:00 a.m., stoned and eating fat pancakes, bacon, and scrambled eggs. Javier was thin then too and cleanly shaven. He wore a cheap black rain jacket with the hood up and next to him on the diner booth he had a large green and black backpack which he had packed for his flight to Quito in the morning. There was a bizarre mid-fall storm, and through the diner windows the city looked like something out of a Samuel Delany novel, which is to say a dark rainy streak, an amalgamation, a feral puzzle. When they were done eating, they ordered coffee and Saul listened as Javier told him, apropos of nothing, how he had recently run into one of his father's coworkers on Wabash Avenue, a jewelry caster like his father, a recent Salvadoran immigrant who had escaped the civil war in San Salvador in 1989. The Salvadoran was happy that he had run into Javier because his father had once mentioned that his son might be interested in some of his sketches. So, of course, he asked, what sketches? To which the Salvadoran replied that he had sketches, blueprints really, of Salvadoran prisons and then he told Javier that he had spent time in five different prisons, each one like a hornet's nest inside of a hellhole, from 1984 to 1989. I didn't do anything, he said, I helped a few farmers is all, nada más, nada más, if nothing can ever really be nothing.

Then, to Javier's surprise, the jeweler took out his wallet and started handing over the sketches, five sheets of yellowed notebook paper, each tightly folded into another like bills from a long-forgotten country. At first, Javier just shook his head and said, señor, I can't take these, but the Salvadoran either pretended not to hear him or didn't care. Por favor tómelos, tómelos, he said and so Javier had no choice but to take the sketches, even though he knew he couldn't look at them standing on the street, at least not in front of the Salvadoran, which would be like staring directly at someone's scars.

Javier looked at the prison sketches later that night when he was alone. The sketches were done in dark shaded pencil and showed gates, clay floors, dusty courtyards, guard stations, and bunk rooms with cots stacked three deep where some men—he had drawn the men as stick figures, but otherwise the sketches were quite detailed and capable—squatted near coal fires and others sat under urine soaked tents of newspapers, hundreds and hundreds of men in each prison, and, lastly, open doorways that led to concrete rooms full of wooden boxes stacked against walls, each box with small barred openings the size of a book through which the men trapped inside for months or even years could look out.

What the hell am I supposed to do with these sketches? asked Javier. They'd left the diner and were walking, but Saul didn't have an answer and they both fell silent until they reached the Western Blue Line, where they hugged and said, peace, and see you soon, and where Saul thought he should tell Javier something, anything, to make him understand that he should stay, but he didn't say anything else and then just stood there for a few seconds on the sidewalk after Javier had entered the station, watching the pale headlights of cars on Western Avenue as they came and went, one after the other.

That was the last time they saw each other, Saul remembered it well, and those were the memories that came to him as they left his front porch and walked side by side that night to a dive bar down the street. A TV over the bar played a soccer game, Mexico vs. Colombia, an International Friendly according to the owner. They ordered beers and sat at a small wooden table near the back. The bar was nearly empty. For a brief time, they sipped their beers and talked about the weather in Chicago, a little unsure how to proceed, like strangers meeting for the first time in a foreign country. Maybe they had nothing else to say or maybe the opposite was true, maybe there was too much to say and they had no idea where to begin.

After talking about the weather, they talked about Mexico City, about Marina and Maya, who was already bilingual, about the Iraq War, about the American need for war, and about the fanatical landscapes of the Internet. And as they talked and laughed too it occurred to Saul that talking to Javier after all these years still gave him a sense of peaceful familiarity, as if everything they said to each other was somehow a continuation of things already said, even if, thought Saul later that night, there was still something he'd been avoiding telling Javier.

How long do people know they're dying before they begin to tell others? Or if they don't tell anybody at all, like his grandfather, how long before others discover irrefutable proof that their loved one is dying? In July, Saul found an open manila envelope full of MRI images of his grandfather's brain. Five grueling months later he died.

Saul sighed and told Javier that he was doing a little better, that he'd taken some time off work after the funeral, that he was rereading a few good science fiction novels, that he was trying to figure out what to do with his grandfather's things, but that, in the end, the stages of grief were bullshit kitsch Americana, like a black and white porcelain clown weeping behind its palms and placed next to an urn on a mantel, really just bullshit, and it all just came down to the simple fact that he missed his grandfather, a fact he suspected would always be true.

I'm sorry, pana, I didn't know, said Javier. Then he leaned forward, resting his palms on the wood table and glancing behind Saul at the single bathroom door covered in faded stickers of punk and reggaetón bands, adding some seconds later, I left a few messages, but I had no idea.

Some hours later, after they'd left the bar, Javier a little drunk, and grinning the entire time, told Saul that he wasn't just visiting Chicago but moving home. At first, he'd wanted to surprise him, but, well, fuck it, *surprise*, in November he'd accepted a good job at the *Chicago Tribune*, something steady for once, something he could sink his teeth into without it slithering away from him which was what freelance work did, it squirmed and slithered and then, if it couldn't get away, it tried to bite you and tear your flesh away piece by piece, in twenty years everybody will have freelance jobs and everybody will be broke and miserable and half-dead. Anyway, he had a job and he'd be back in a few months with Marina and Maya. He wanted Saul to meet them as soon as possible. He'd cook up some tamales in banana leaves and roasted chicken in red mole sauce, two recipes he learned from Marina's mother, Juana, who was Zapoteca and who cooked like a madwoman.

As Javier got in a taxi, he rolled down the window and leaned half his body outside and said, look, pana, it's snowing, I haven't seen snow in years. He rubbed his eyes and the burning white snow turned mustard yellow beneath the streetlights and without a word of goodbye he pulled his torso back through the open window and the taxi sped west down the street, against the wind.

A few weeks later, Saul was packing boxes in his grandfather's kitchen when he heard a thud on the front porch. Once outside, he saw a FedEx truck turning down the street and he found his grandfather's package on the bottom step, somewhat dented but still intact and still addressed to a Maxwell Moreau at the Universidad de Chile in Santiago, Chile. The package had been returned to sender.

He took it inside and called FedEx. After nearly twenty minutes of rambling conversations with two representatives, he discovered that an executive assistant to a dean at the university had initially accepted the package on behalf of Maxwell Moreau, but then, some weeks later, had sent the package back with a notice stating that Maxwell Moreau no longer taught at the university nor lived in Santiago. Did the executive assistant to the dean give any new addresses for Maxwell Moreau? Saul asked the second representative. I don't have anything like that here, sir, she said, at which point Saul envisioned a tiresome pilgrimage to Santiago, thanked her, and hung up.

Completely puzzled and sadly embarrassed that he hadn't been able to fulfill his grandfather's last request, he went to his grandfather's desk and opened the package with a pocketknife. Inside of the box was a large manuscript titled *A Model Earth*.

Saul read and reread the name of the author on the title page of the manuscript: Adana Moreau (a writer he'd never heard of before). At first, he thought it was a history book, maybe written by one of his grandfather's colleagues, but then he read the second page, which, otherwise blank, stated that the manuscript was a "sequel to the novel *Lost City*." The third page had a dedication to Maxwell Moreau, who, Saul suspected, must somehow be related to Adana Moreau. The fourth page was the start of the first chapter. The manuscript was composed of nine-hundred and twenty-four letter-sized pages.

I don't understand, said Saul out loud to himself.

After searching the office bookshelves, Saul finally found a copy of *Lost City* splayed open on his grandfather's nightstand, its pages ruffled like a dead bird. At first, he was a little shocked that he had never seen the science fiction novel in the house before, but as he picked up the book he remembered that he rarely went into his grandfather's bedroom and that the last time he had done so was to say goodbye to him after his death. The book, which was also written by Adana Moreau and which Saul then understood his grandfather had been reading some weeks or months before his death, was a first edition, published in 1929 by a short-lived (or so Saul suspected) publishing house in New Orleans called Amulet Books. On the faded cover was an illustration of a terrifying prehistoric flying creature, maybe a Pteranodon or a Quetzalcoatlus, and a stone portal in the shape of a perfect hemisphere somewhat obscured by jungle vines. The cover, so thought Saul, was a type of nod to Sir Arthur Conan Doyle's *The Lost World*, but the similarities ended there.

He thumbed through the yellowed pages, searching for some other clues as to the book's origin or nature—but, of course, it was in vain. The only thing to do was to read it straightaway, which he then did for hours while sitting on the cheap Turkish rug in his grandfather's office, just like he had done during his childhood, occasionally taking breaks to eat a snack or piss, occasionally stopping to reread a word, a sentence, a passage, all while the light outside his grandfather's office window shifted Chagall-like from black to gray to amber, while the night vanished, while the dawn broke and brought with it the damp, sympathetic breeze of a not-yet-bitter spring, truly unable to stop reading until he reached the end because it only took him the first page to know that he had stumbled upon the presence of something extraordinary.

Okay, but what the hell is it about? asked Romário the next day, dropping his voice low as a couple dressed from head to toe in white approached the front desk. They protested to Romário about the hotel's water, or something about the speed with which the water came out of the adjustable shower nozzle, and also the taste of the water, a taste like fish or algae, an unforgettable, terrible taste, according to the sulking woman who apparently couldn't shower without drinking the water.

Saul couldn't exactly tell Romário what the novel *Lost City* was about, yet he had sensed *something* the moment he had started reading it. He had sensed something in its lingering, peculiar beauty, in the Dominicana's terrible grace, in the madness of cataclysm, in the pale, feverish eyes of the zombies, in the eternal grief of Santo Domingo, in the dazzling blues of the seas of the Antilles, in the lost paradise of Cartagena, the sweet fragrance of fruit and wild rice, the stark violent greens of the jungle, the man with gray eyes, the political gossip and historical amnesia of the residents of the false Lost City, the kapok tree, the Dominicana's love-struck son, the prehistoric flying creature, and the stone portal leading to other Earths, in short, yes, he had sensed something in its parts but also something beyond its whole, like a distant horizon flickering with blue and white bolts of lightning. And then, some minutes later, he could finally see what others had possibly not seen for a long time, or maybe what his grandfather had also seen in the book all along: that every word, every sentence, every passage, every chapter, concluding in the whole vast thing, spoke of *exile*. He turned to Romário, who had been holding his silence during those minutes and was now watching the pouting couple dressed from head to toe in white leave the hotel, and said, I think it's about exile. Then Romário rubbed his eyes and rolled his neck until it cracked and said, did I ever tell you that I spent my thirteenth birthday in a goddamn boat packed with Cubans and two Romanians, I could spend all night talking about exile.

Searching online, Saul found some information on Adana Moreau. According to a sparse Wikipedia article, she was born in 1900 in the Dominican Republic, just outside of San Pedro de Macorís. At some point (the article was unclear when) her parents were killed and she sought refuge in the United States. In 1929, as Saul already knew, she published a science fiction novel titled *Lost City*. In 1930, she died of unknown causes. The name Adana Moreau also appeared in a travel magazine about the Dominican Republic, but after ten agonizing minutes of reading what he could in Spanish, Saul realized in dismay that the person in the travel magazine was a musician, a rising star, then aged twenty-seven. Adana Moreau was mentioned in a Los Angeles–based CGI artist's blog devoted entirely to the fantasy, science fiction, and horror pulp magazine *Weird Tales*. In a blog post dated June 17th, 2001, Saul read that an excerpt of *Lost City* appeared in the June 1929, Vol. 13, No. 1 issue of *Weird Tales*.

The CGI artist, in brief, explained that he had read and used references in the excerpt for a still-unfinished zombie film he and his friends were working on. There was no other information in the post, biographical or literary, about Adana Moreau.

After a few more hours of unproductive searching, Saul found an obscure encyclopedia titled *The Underground History of Latin American Science Fiction* by Arthur Vazquez, self-published in 1984, but available since 2003 as an ebook. Following an entry for Sebastián Morales, a writer from Bogotá who claimed in 1963 that his book of interplanetary travel with talkative, octopus-like extraterrestrials was, in fact, a memoir, Saul discovered a two-paragraph entry for Adana Moreau. For the most part, the entry made the (non-encyclopedic) argument that the Dominican writer should be placed squarely among the pantheon of early 20th century science fiction masters, even if she only had one novel to her name and especially because the "North American, fuck-the-rest-of-you, winners of history" had long ago decided to exile her to the far fringes of science fiction history. The entry also ended with the following: "She was succeeded by her son, Maxwell Moreau, a theoretical physicist of note who specializes in parallel universes." Saul couldn't find any other references online to Adana Moreau or any mention at all of *A Model Earth*.

The next day, Saul went to Washington Square Park, a vaguely Victorian-looking park across the street from the Newberry Library, where his grandfather had sometimes taken him as a child when researching for a new book. He sat on a bench and watched an elderly woman walking in concentric circles around and around the park fountain, like Romário's madman from Havana.

How was it even possible for his grandfather to have been in possession of an unpublished sequel to a nearly forgotten seventy-six-year-old science fiction novel? As far as Saul could remember, his grandfather had never mentioned either novel, Adana Moreau, or Maxwell Moreau to him. And what else had his grandfather forgotten to tell him or willfully concealed? Under what circumstances, for example, had his grandfather been born in the Atlantic Ocean on October 21st, 1920? He had only told Saul the fact of his birth on that flight from Tel Aviv to Chicago, but nothing more in all those following years, not even why his own parents had decided to immigrate from Vitebsk to the United States following WWI. Why didn't I ask him more when he was alive? thought Saul. And to whom then do the words and memories of a dying man even belong?

The hospice nurse had told him that this sort of thing might happen. She saw it all the time. Near the end, old memories resurfaced like "bioluminescent organisms on the crests of ocean waves," that's exactly what she had said, "bioluminescent organisms," as if she were a marine biologist instead of a nurse. The dying, she continued, often imagine themselves immersed in the remains of their lives and those memories—those bioluminescent organisms if you like—were more real to them than anything else. This can be very painful for those loved ones who still live in the present and who know so little of that past, she said and then gave Saul an empathetic smile.

Over the next few days, very warm days all over the Midwest, Saul read the manuscript for *A Model Earth* and, despite the mystery surrounding the text, he was left with the same feeling of wonder and exile he had when reading *Lost City*. The plot of *A Model Earth* was as follows: The man with gray eyes does not die. Instead, armed with a pistol from the Great War, he kills the zombie and follows the Dominicana through the shimmering portal. Once on the other side, he finds himself in the middle of a bustling tropical city called New Orleans. During the day, he searches in vain for the Dominicana. At night, sleeping on a park bench in the Plaza de Armas, the man with gray eyes dreams of interstellar travel and the face—as painted by Gauguin—of the Dominicana. Sometimes, he wakes from his dreams with a terrible sense of heartbreak, madness. The stars, he notices, are different from the ones he can see on his Earth.

One night, half-starving, he meets a jazz musician who tells the man with gray eyes he moonlights as a smuggler. I can use a man like you, the jazz musician tells him. A man like me? he asks. A man without an Earth, says the jazz musician.

Traveling through hidden stone portals on the outskirts of the city, the jazz musician and the man with gray eyes transport illicit arms, food, and technology in and out of countless other Earths. A few of the Earths are variations of his own before its ruin, but most are wildly different. One Earth is almost entirely covered in vast, warm seas, with people etching out a living among a dwindling number of archipelagos. On another, the ice age never ended. The men and women on this Earth ride wooly mammoths and build enormous machines resembling arachnids. On yet another, the Aztec Empire has persisted through the centuries and was the first civilization to develop and drop a nuclear bomb in 1897. On more than a few Earths, there are cities in the sky. The jazz musician explains to him that the *cityships*, as they are called, are filled with refugees from Earths that are no longer habitable or no longer exist. Even the city of New Orleans on this Earth is a cityship that landed long ago. Goddamn entire multiverse is full of refugees like you, he says and then he starts to laugh. It takes the man with gray eyes a moment to understand that he is laughing at the cityships, not at him. There are no traces of the Dominicana on any of the Earths to which they transport goods, nor on any of the refugee cityships the man with gray eyes searches by himself during lonely nights that show no signs of ever ending.

In the next Part, the jazz musician and the man with gray eyes receive a job to hand deliver a letter to resistance fighters. The job pays well, but they're warned it's dangerous, since there are many people on many Earths who don't want the letter to get out. Despite these warnings, they take the job. After much hardship, they finally reach the resistance fighters in a small mountainous city and deliver the letter to a soldier, a young boy really, who tells them he used to be a wheat farmer. When the soldier reads the letter, he weeps. His face, in the light of the moon, bears an uncanny resemblance to that of Simón Bolívar. Later that night, they set up camp with the resistance fighters in the cavernous lobby of a former bank in a large steel and brick building. They talk about dead languages, 20th century music, the possibility of extraterrestrials, and the unfathomable void left by a war with an empire that desired only to multiply itself across endless other Earths, including their own.

The resistance fighters also have a strange theory: they believe that an ancient civilization from an unknown Earth, maybe even the First Earth, somehow created the stone portals, but then disappeared. In the morning, the city is attacked by bomber planes. The man with gray eyes seeks cover in the bank vault. He covers his ears to the thundering noise of the bombers, gazes into the darkness of the bank vault, a darkness like a black canvas, and thinks of all the lives he never lived with the Dominicana. He thinks of all the other Earths where they had still met, fallen in love, and were never separated. Earths luminescent with pandemonium, beauty. In the morning, he discovers that most of the resistance fighters were instantly incinerated during the attack. The jazz musician is also dead. While searching for survivors, the man with gray eyes sees the haunting image of his shadow burned permanently onto the face of a concrete wall. He leaves the smoldering city in search of a stone portal. He follows an empty road west for some time, crosses a river, then treks through a valley, until he reaches a town on the edge of a sea-green forest.

In the town's plaza, a crowd stands around a large pile of burning books. A woman in her fifties or sixties holds a very large black leather-bound book with gold and red decorations on the cover. The book is extraordinary. In the light of the fire, he can make out the title, *The Book of the Thousand Nights and a Night*, a book, the man with gray eyes remembers with some melancholy, that the Dominicana loved with all her heart. The woman smiles at him, says that the book is degenerate, and throws it into the fire. The man with gray eyes understands then that the crowd is burning literature from parallel universes. In the center of the plaza, beyond the flames, he sees two men and a young girl in chains near a razed stone portal.

After stealing provisions and a horse, the man with gray eyes leaves the town. Then he crosses the sea-green forest—filled, he horrifically discovers, with the fresh mass graves of people from other Earths—grassy plains, and a snowy mountain range in a kind of dizzying ascent. The stars in the sky are aflame, spectral. Some days later, he reaches an abandoned fishing village by the sea. In the distance, he spots a large ship anchored near a rock cliff. He takes a small fishing boat out to the ship, which, he notices with some surprise, resembles one of those Spanish galleons from his Earth which set out for the New World during the 17th century in search of cities of bloodstained gold and eternal life. Once aboard the ship, he discovers that it's abandoned, like the village. Who brought this ship here? Where did they come from? Where did they go? It doesn't matter, he later thinks while exploring the holds of the ship, everything that could possibly have happened has already happened on this Earth or another. There is no such thing as history anymore. In one of the holds, he finds a working stone portal.

In the final Part, some years later while searching for the Dominicana in the streets of the cityship of Lagos, the man with gray eyes comes upon an old South American beggar shouting in a crowded street. The beggar shouts in Spanish and only the man with gray eyes can understand him. The beggar says: I discovered the true Lost City, only I know of its existence and its eternal mysteries. Then the man with gray eyes asks for proof. The beggar looks at him, takes out an old journal, and flips to a few pages near the end. The man with gray eyes recognizes the journal immediately as the 17th century one his grandfather found in Madrid as a young man. Except he's never seen the pages the beggar shows him. On those pages, there is a drawing of a great labyrinth and maps of stone portals leading to an Earth with a city simply called Z. Abuelito, the man with gray eyes says, it's me, Vivaldo, your grandson. Impossible, replies the beggar, my grandson died in the Amazon twenty years ago. With tears in his eyes, Vivaldo rips the pages from the journal and violently pushes the beggar to the street. Without looking back, he runs.

Some months later, the man with gray eyes finds himself on an Earth almost completely covered by jungles. Fatigued and delirious, he stumbles past Cyclopean ruins—massive bridges and overgrown roads, endless beehive tombs, and towering stone and metal structures inscribed with indecipherable lettering—speaking of daunting feats of engineering and a culture long since vanished. He vaguely recalls the thundering noise of bombers, darkness, a trip through a stone portal. Is this the First Earth the resistance fighters talked about? He has no way to know. In fact, he doesn't even care by then.

While exploring the ruins, the man with gray eyes finds a small village. In the village, a young girl with long legs and shining black hair tells him in Spanish that she has seen the woman he's looking for. At first, he doesn't believe the girl, but then realizes he doesn't have a choice. For three days, they trek through the jungle. The noises of the restless, vast jungle are absolute. In the distance, rising above the canopy, enormous black shadows seem to superimpose themselves on the violet and black sky. It's more ruins, the girl explains, the capital of whoever was here before us. Eventually, they reach the edges of the city and a clearing in the jungle, at the center of which is a stone portal in the shape of a perfect hemisphere.

He sees the Dominicana. She's standing over the corpse of

a prehistoric creature with a sword-like beak and black wings. Nearby, a boy is busy building a fire. Despite everything, the man with gray eyes thinks, she's alive, she's still alive, and I'm finally here. At first, the Dominicana doesn't see him. Her face is turned down toward the creature. As she peels away its reptilian skin with a long knife, she sings a song to herself and to the boy. How was the Earth created? she sings. Is this truly the only one? Where does one universe end and another begin? Then, suddenly, the Dominicana turns and sees the man with gray eyes. She smiles, slowly at first, and then all at once. Her eyes are dark green, almost black, and they seem to absorb all the light in the sky.

For the first time in my life, I have to do something rather than nothing, said Saul to himself. I have to find Maxwell Moreau.

Saul could find no contact information for Maxwell Moreau except for the now outdated mailing address at the Universidad de Chile and only itinerant information in terms of his personal biography. From two sparse interviews reposted in physics blogs, one from 1979, the other from 1992, Saul learned that Maxwell Moreau had been born and raised in New Orleans and that, after the war, during which he served in the infamous Red Ball Express supply unit in France, he returned home and worked odd jobs throughout the South and West Coast. At some point, in 1948, while working on a farm, he attended a lecture on particle physics at the University of California, Berkeley, given by the famous Japanese theoretical physicist Hideki Yukawa and, afterward, they struck up a friendship. In 1949, with a recommendation from Hideki Yukawa, who had just then won the Nobel Prize in Physics, Maxwell Moreau was accepted to UC Berkeley where he received a BS in Physics in 1952 and then a PhD in Physics in 1957.

Saul was able to find a good deal of information online about Maxwell Moreau's career after receiving his PhD, a career which spanned nearly fifty years, three continents (he left the United States, happily, it was noted in one article, in 1981), over 150 papers, and one controversial book on cosmology, *The Hidden Multitude*, published in 1978. According to a *New Scientist* article from a May 1989 issue titled "Long Live the Death of Physics," Maxwell Moreau's book introduced an inflationary model of the universe suggesting that the early universe exploded faster than the speed of light from a size smaller than a proton and then entered an inflationary phase that would last forever. Maxwell Moreau's theory of eternal inflation, alongside the work of younger theoretical physicists like Alan Guth, the article continued, led to the "jaw-dropping" implication that our universe may be only one "island universe" in an eternally inflating and self-replicating multiverse. Other equally "jaw-dropping" scientific and philosophical implications found in Maxwell Moreau's work were summarized in the same article as follows:

I. Important aspects of inflationary models of the universe and the multiverse could be borne out empirically. New insights in quantum mechanics and inflation, new studies of the CMB (Cosmic Background Radiation, the afterglow of the Big Bang) and even more advanced computing capabilities, particle accelerators, and telescope technologies may one day create the possibility of testing for alternate realities or parallel universes. In other words, observing or even interacting with other universes will no longer be pure science fiction.

II. Substantial evidence for the multiverse would precipitate the end of physics since most universes would have wildly varying properties from our own.

III. Substantial evidence for the multiverse or the quantum universe would also precipitate the end of history since all possible histories would happen infinitely or have already happened infinitely. Thus, there are universes with Earths somewhat different from ours and universes with Earths extraordinarily different from ours. In these cases, history unfolds with all possible variations. There are also universes with Earths identical to our own, perfect replicas with all the same cities, wars, mountain ranges, and seas. In these cases, history repeats itself endlessly.

After the publication of *The Hidden Multitude* and its corresponding papers, the *New Scientist* article continued, there was some praise from theoretical physicists working "in the fringes" who called the work "revolutionary" and "an elegant way forward," but, for the most part, Maxwell Moreau's theories faced harsh criticism and scornful reception by others who were either trying to settle old scores or who—it was impossible not to note—truly believed that the first prominent mixed-race theoretical physicist of his generation was a madman, a crackpot. A review of *The Hidden Multitude*, written after a small fifteen-year-anniversary reissue of the book, also appeared in the May 1993 issue of *Scientific American*. The review, written by one of Maxwell Moreau's former students, an editor at the journal *Nature*, was an impassioned defense of his work and stated in no uncertain terms that Maxwell Moreau was the heir to Hugh Everett III, who was also ridiculed by the physics establishment and, later, even Niels Bohr, for his idea that quantum effects cause the universe to constantly split into every possible alternative timeline. "Like Everett's work," the review continued, "Maxwell Moreau's theories may yet be vindicated.

"*The Hidden Multitude* has been passed down through word of mouth for a generation and has even developed into a cult-like object for young students of theoretical physics who regard reading it as a rebellious rite of passage and who often seek him out (against the advice of their professors) at the Universidad Complutense de Madrid, where he has been teaching, on and off again, since 1981 or at one of his infrequent, but noteworthy, lectures in places like Tokyo, Brussels, Copenhagen, Paris, and Istanbul."

Saul spent the rest of the day and well into the night scouring abstracts and articles by Maxwell Moreau, and even read through an abbreviated chapter from *The Hidden Multitude*, but, in the end, he really couldn't understand any of it.

In the far reaches of the infinite cosmos there are endless identical and near-identical copies of you, said Saul to Romário. Also, every decision you make in this world creates new universes. But Romário just tapped a pen against the front desk and stared at Saul like he had a strange brain fever. Saul shrugged and admitted that although he understood that Maxwell's theories were urgent and groundbreaking in the realm of physics, he understood little of them. He was just feeling his way in the dark. He couldn't comprehend *bubble universes* or the *many-worlds interpretation* or *endless doppelgängers*, let alone Maxwell Moreau's encouragement to his readers that some of these theories could be tested one day, but if he were forced to say something approximate, he would say that the theoretical physicist's theories were a type of revolution against reality or a type of endless multiplication of it, but that too was an uninformed and ridiculous thing to say. The physics behind parallel universes would probably always lie just beyond him.

At which point, Romário turned his attention to a well-dressed, thinly bearded man who was standing in the center of the lobby and yelling wide-eyed into a cell phone about an "insurrection" at work and, if he wasn't careful, the eventual "triumph of the unwashed hordes," and said, check out the asshole in this universe.

The following night Saul woke with a start and thought he was back in Tel Aviv, even though he was certain he hadn't dreamed of the city. He got up and took a cold shower, then went to his bedroom closet, where he took out the small wooden school box that had once contained postcards and Bensia pencils but now contained five photographs wrapped in scraps of black Egyptian linen. There was something incredibly beautiful and incredibly horrific about parallel universes, thought Saul as he sat on the edge of his bed. Incredibly beautiful, he thought, because the only real difference between one universe and another was merely a question of language, a question of *what if?* so much so that, over these past few weeks, he sometimes found himself asking with enigmatic curiosity and anticipation: What if I had never opened my grandfather's package? What if his brain cancer had been treatable or what if he had never had it to begin with? What if Javier had never left Chicago or I had joined him in one of those distant, foreign cities? What if my parents had never boarded bus 901, traveling from Tel Aviv to Haifa, on March 11th, 1978? Of course, he had asked himself that latter question a great number of times and he had already lived a great number of lives with them in his mind, but now, if he were to take Maxwell Moreau's theories about parallel universes at face value, he could believe for an instant that his parents were inevitably and *endlessly* alive on other Earths. And yet, horrifically, the opposite was also apparent to Saul. His parents had also died a great number of deaths on other Earths. They had fallen in love in Chicago, boarded bus 901 together in Tel Aviv, and then died shortly thereafter, again and again, each death on each Earth replicating itself with only slight variations, carrying the echoes and silhouettes of still yet other deaths. His parents were ghosts of repetition, ghosts of the multiverse, trapped in a ghastly and suffocating image continually running on a loop: led away by the barrel of a Kalashnikov rifle from bus 901 traveling to Haifa onto bus 311 traveling to Tel Aviv, howled at by members of Fatah through the stench of smoke, flesh, filth, shot in the neck (his father) and the back and stomach (his mother), then burned while dying or already dead and sprawled on a liquefying plastic bus seat.

His grandfather had never lied regarding his parents' deaths, but he had always tried to protect him. He had watered down the facts or even, from time to time, concealed them from Saul, saying things like, "You'll understand later" or "Not now" or "Your parents' deaths, Saul, were something that nobody can ever truly understand." The latter was probably true for his grandfather, because he had lost his only child, his daughter. On one occasion, as a teenager, when Saul had angrily pressed him on the matter, all his grandfather would tell him was that their deaths afterward had been turned into a spectacle by the nationalists and occupiers who always benefited from war, so there was no point in them turning it into a spectacle again.

Implicit in his grandfather's statement and the fact that he had years earlier changed Saul's surname from Mizrahi (his dead father's) to Drower (his own Americanized surname) was that his grandfather, the historian, had wanted to forget the events of their deaths.

So, Saul had very few memories of his parents before their deaths and he had no memory of the day they were killed, only what memories he could knit together from various old news reports or imagine in the middle of endless nights. And, as he sat on the edge of his bed, clutching the small wooden school box along its dull green and black edges and staring ahead into the pulsating ditch-gray and rose–colored dawn outside his bedroom window, he imagined it once again—the Kalashnikov rifle, smoke, flesh, filth, a burning bus on a coastal road—their deaths only multiplied by Maxwell Moreau's incomprehensible theories.

In mid-June, Javier and his family moved into a two-story, single-family brownstone near Palmer Square Park. Afterward, Saul and Javier's friendship continued in the same fashion, unshakable if occasionally tense, but also now shaped by the forces of an oscillating wormhole straining to connect their youth and adulthood.

Some days later, on a warm Friday with low white clouds, as they watched Maya play freeze-tag in a playground with two other little girls, all speaking a type of invented Spanglish (mancha estatua, corre over there, death de frío), Saul told Javier all about the manuscript and about Adana Moreau and Maxwell Moreau and how trying to find the theoretical physicist was an effort not lacking in all kinds of difficulties. In addition to spending countless hours online, he had emailed other theoretical physicists, but the only responses he did receive were not helpful. No references to other family members besides Adana Moreau could be found. He contacted the publisher of *A Hidden Multitude*, but the only mailing address they had for Maxwell was at the Universidad de Chile. They did have a university email address for him, but a "mailbox full" error bounced back when he tried to send a message. He even talked to the, thankfully, bilingual executive assistant to the dean who had originally sent the package back, but she only reiterated that nobody at the university, not even the chair of the Physics Department, knew where he was. He retired, she said, and left the city.

So, said Saul to Javier, the only thing that makes sense to me is that I still need to find Maxwell Moreau. The manuscript was meant for him, not me, I only found it by accident. Javier nodded, thinking, his eyes on his daughter, Maya, a skinny girl with long black hair who had just been frozen. Well, pana, I still want to read it, said Javier, by which Saul understood with some amusement that he wouldn't read it and that at some point he would have to tell Javier, chapter by chapter, the plots of both *Lost City* and *A Model Earth*. So, the question is, said Saul, where did Maxwell Moreau go? But the question hung in the silent humid air without a response because Javier was already walking toward Maya, who had been unfrozen by a new player, a small boy nearly a head shorter than her, and had then slipped and fallen and scraped her right palm and was just then shedding tears while the pair of little girls stood on a rubber hill, watching her like bored sentries.

As Javier tended to Maya's right hand, it occurred to Saul that he had been around Maya's age when he had taken the long transatlantic flight with his grandfather to Chicago. Like Maya, he was an immigrant. He wondered if she saw her new country as he had seen it, under a glaring unfamiliar light, everything preceding her arrival fading to a daydream. In fact, she might not remember anything at all or, like him, images of her previous life might slip through when she least expected it, images of high plateaus and endless markets and pleasant courtyards and colonial ruins, while closing her eyes on a train platform or gazing at a summery dusk, during a thirty-minute lunch break at her work desk or, like her father, while wandering a foreign city like a sleepwalker under petrified yellow dust clouds.

Afterward, they walked back to Javier's house and watched episode after episode of a cartoon about a type of postapocalyptic Candyland, until sometime later Marina came home from work. She was wearing light blue scrubs and when she saw Saul she smiled and hugged him. While Javier prepared dinner, tamales in banana leaves and roasted chicken in red mole sauce, Marina put Maya to bed. For a few minutes, Saul could hear Marina reading Maya a lyrical children's book about a 17th century winged-man who flew like a bird from the top of Galata Tower in Constantinople to Doğancılar Square in Üsküdar, only to be exiled to Algeria by the fearful Sultan Murad Khan.

During dinner they talked about Maxwell Moreau, about his status as a genius or a madman, about the innumerable gaps in his biography. Then Javier asked Saul to tell Marina and him, chapter by chapter, the plot of *Lost City*, something he was, of course, happy to do.

★ ★ ★

When Saul finished, Javier said, damn, pana, and Marina said, que a toda madre. Then she paused, finished off her drink, and added that something in the story, something like a sense of departure of the *self* or maybe an extirpation of the *other*, in any case, a sense of *those who leave and those who stay behind* had reminded her of her childhood home, a village on the coast near the city of San Pedro Pochutla. Bizarrely enough, even the "immense creature with a sword-like beak and black wings," as Saul had put it, had reminded her of something that had happened to Javier and her during their honeymoon there. Then she went on to explain: Javier and I got married in Mexico City at my uncle's house under the cover of night, as people used to say during confession, after we had known each other for only two months. Not many of my friends or family had even met Javier, not even my mother, which is why the following morning we borrowed a car from my uncle, a green 1986 Volvo, I can see it perfectly right now, and left for my childhood home, a village that had once existed but due to NAFTA didn't exist anymore, even if my mother still insisted on living there. Anyway, we left Mexico City in that battered tank of a car first thing in the morning and drove thirteen hours straight to San Pedro Pochutla.

For the entire trip a terrible notion ran through my head, the notion of filicide. I knew that my mother would take one good look at my new husband, an Ecuadorian gringo, and just kill me because *what sinvergüenza daughter of mine marries a man after just two months*. But here's the kicker, after thirteen hours in that battered tank, my mom wasn't even home. So, all we could do was wait in her house, a small, humid, and airy house which had a ghost-like quality about it, not haunted in the supernatural sense, I don't believe in those things, but memory-haunted, as if its floors and walls and altars and shelves full of figurines and letters of those who had left contained the entire memory of the abandoned village.

But that was only half-true. My husband, as you know, Saul, is prone to journalistic suspense. Yes, it's true that there are people from that village who died, and my mother spent some years collecting mementos of them. All that explains the ghost-like quality of the house. But there are many others who are still alive and who have ended up in other places, especially the United States. When there are people like that, said Marina, when there are *refugees*, because that's what they truly are, refugees not illegals, like everybody in this country obsessed with barbarism says, when there are refugees there are disseminated memories, tendrils of memories like octopus ink, orphaned memories, fragments of memories like pages of a half-burned book. All of those memories are still living.

Anyway, in the end, we decided to wait for her in the house, too exhausted to do much of anything besides cook a small meal, beans and fish, before going to bed.

The next morning, Marina continued, we woke early, cooked breakfast, and sat outside on my mother's little porch, which had a view of the Pacific Ocean. Since I was sure that my mother wouldn't be coming home that morning, we went to the beach to watch the black-eyed turtles, which arrived every month by the thousands to lay their eggs. As we walked along the beach, careful not to step on the turtles, I told Javier how the turtles were hunted, their eggs collected and sold, and how the federal government had recently passed laws to protect them. Many locals, including my mother, were angry about the laws and had started a black market for turtles and turtle eggs.

I was right in the middle of telling Javier the history of the turtles when a gap in the beach opened up, a gap that suddenly revealed an immense creature with a sword-like beak and black wings the size of a small plane, just like in the Dominicana's story. At first, we had no idea what we were looking at. We just stared dumbstruck at the immense, terrifying creature about to take flight.

After overcoming the initial shock, we realized it was only a *replica*, if a rather imposing and impressive one, so we walked closer and saw a short man in a Panama hat waving at me. He walked right up to me and said, "You're Juana's daughter, right?" and I nodded. Then he grinned and told me that Juana was a good woman. "She's a one-woman rebellion," he said. Then he asked us if we liked the Quetzalcoatlus. That's the word he used to describe the creature, *Quetzalcoatlus*, after the Aztec god Quetzalcoatl. We said we did and that for a split second we had thought it was real.

He began to talk with fondness about the prehistoric creature's feeding habits, its terrestrial habits, its sleeping patterns, its ability to fly thousands of miles all over the planet, its ability to obscure the sun when in flight, like an eclipse, a nerve-wracking experience for any creatures below, especially, for example, newly hatched turtles like the ones under their feet, and, finally, he added with the melancholy of a time-traveling Don Quixote, its eventual extinction at the end of the Cretaceous Period.

But, said Marina, he refused to answer any of our questions about how or why he had built the replica of the Quetzalcoatlus in the first place, because it was entirely clear to us by then that he had built it. Instead, he just smiled and explained that there was nothing else like it in the world and that it didn't matter why he had built it, in fact, he hardly knew himself, the only thing that mattered was that it existed again.

And what about your mom, asked Saul, did she return, did she want to kill you? Yes, said Marina, she returned the following morning, and, yes, after meeting Javier, she really did want to kill me. In fact, she refused to talk to us for three days. It was the worst thing ever, even if I had in some ways anticipated my mother's silence and the silence of that house, which, when I walked from room to room, felt like I was walking through a cemetery at night. But then, on the morning of the fourth day Javier went into the kitchen where my mother was silently preparing breakfast and he handed her a perfectly white turtle egg and said, señora, you don't have to say one word to me, but I want you to teach me how to cook breakfast for your daughter. My mother took the turtle egg and turned it over and over in her hands. Then she smiled, like she had just received the prized possession of the town idiot, and said, mírame. For the next three days, they barely left the kitchen, she said, and Saul and Javier laughed.

Some weeks later, in early July, Saul went to his grandfather's two-story greystone on Humboldt Boulevard to finish packing. The second-to-last things he packed were his grandfather's historical artifacts: a railroad spike, a 17th century Spanish map of the New World, the single leather shoe of someone who had been killed (or so his grandfather had once casually remarked) during the Haymarket riot, the letters and diaries of WWII soldiers and nurses, a melodramatic and kitsch Cold War propaganda poster of an atomic blast, among many others. The manuscript of *A Model Earth*, he thought with some curiosity, was in all likelihood just another one of his grandfather's artifacts, each one of which formed an infinite and unmappable branching of causality. How could anyone even be a historian? he thought as he packed. These artifacts were only a tiny fragment of the lives, thoughts, and actions of real people, living or now dead and inexorably forgotten. It was a losing battle. But, still, he couldn't help but wonder, how had his grandfather gotten a hold of the manuscript in the first place? And, along with *Lost City*, had it somehow consoled him during his final days? Of course, Saul had no way of knowing these things, even if he was still responsible for delivering the manuscript. After packing his grandfather's artifacts, he labeled each box Future History, a reference, he thought with a sad smile, to Isaac Asimov's Foundation series, which he had read with his grandfather as a child.

The last things Saul packed were the books his grandfather had written. Once, when he was twelve or maybe thirteen, a graduate student in the University of Chicago's Department of History, who was corresponding with his grandfather for his thesis, came to dinner and asked his grandfather if he considered the books he wrote "a connecting thread between the living and the dead." The academic was serious, thin, and in his early twenties. Maybe too serious and too young to study history or to have lost any loved ones in his life, thought Saul. Maybe not. In any case, his grandfather had liked the young academic, even if Saul could tell he didn't like his question. He responded, "History books are *not* a connecting thread between the living and the dead, but they coax us into thinking they are because the dead are already us and we are already them."

At that time, while sitting at that dinner table, Saul hadn't fully understood what his grandfather had told the young academic, who, to give him a little credit, had then nodded seriously in agreement. But then, years later, when he was eighteen, Saul understood those words more clearly when he read them word for word in his grandfather's book *October Rising*, a type of historical narrative that follows the lives of seven people during the Russian Revolution, including the life of his own father, a translator and tailor from Vitebsk who Saul was named after. History, like fiction, was illusory, if not an outright lie, but we still existed because of it and it existed because of us.

The U-Haul truck moved through the dense traffic on North Sacramento Avenue in starts and stops. At some point Javier rolled down the passenger's-side window and located the cause of the traffic. A group of people in black T-shirts with the words NO MORE DEAD was walking down Division Street. They held posters that read: WE CAN END GUN VIOLENCE. And:

STOP POLICE BRUTALITY. One man moved between the protesters, playing a sad song on a cuatro, paying no mind to anyone else, as if adrift in a somber ocean. A group of policemen watched the protest from under the shade of a green ash tree.

With a quick nod to Saul, Javier got out of the U-Haul truck, and approached a woman and a man, a couple in their fifties, and talked to them briefly before they rejoined the others. Once he was back in the U-Haul truck, Javier explained that the protest was to demand transparency in the investigation of a thirteen-year-old boy who had been shot and killed by the police. Some minutes later, the traffic started moving and they set off west down Division Street toward the direction of the self-storage facility, even as Javier continued to watch the protestors in the rearview mirror as they marched east, toward their uncertain refuge.

They were unloading boxes into the self-storage unit when Saul remembered something Javier had said to him about protests once. He had called from Buenos Aires one late December night in 2001, when he was reporting on the Argentine Great Depression.

I joined a street demonstration that the Argentines call a cacerolazo and it turned brutal, pana, Javier had said. I joined the demonstration, even though I knew I wasn't supposed to, maybe because I have never really fought for anything in my life, at least not like you, pana. Saul's immediate thought that night was that Javier was confessing something between the lines but he wasn't sure what. Something more had happened, something unpleasant or something he couldn't mention on the phone during that volatile time in Buenos Aires. But Saul didn't press him further.

After Javier's half confession, their conversation began to flag and he didn't say anything else about the matter. Some minutes later, they made tentative plans to talk again in a few weeks and hung up. The next day, Saul read Javier's report on foreignpolicy.com about the clashes between demonstrators and police in the Plaza de Mayo. Several people had died. Had he witnessed those deaths? To what extent then had Javier been involved? Saul asked himself.

Something even more puzzling had stood out during that phone call: Namely, what had Javier meant when he said, "I have never really fought for anything in my life, *at least not like you, pana*"? What the hell does he think I've fought for in my life? he thought with a slight shock. To rid myself of the stench of orphanhood? To be an American? A life just inside the margins? Endless time to wait for those who would never return, for those irreplaceables who only remained on this Earth as five photographs wrapped in scraps of black Egyptian linen?

Later, after they locked up the storage unit and dropped off the U-Haul, they walked east down Division Street, just as they had done as teenagers, talking nonstop about the cuatro player, exoplanets, Simón Bolivar's once-stolen and later-returned sword, the laying of fiber-optic cables under the Atlantic seabed.

One night in August, Javier invited Saul to his house for drinks. Saul hadn't heard from him in a few weeks since he had been in Mexico City tying up loose ends with work and the move to Chicago, so his call had been a little unexpected. Bring the manuscript, he said, Marina is working a night shift and Maya is already in bed, so I got nothing else going on tonight.

Some hours later, after Saul had finished telling Javier the plot to Part I of *A Model Earth*, he yawned and said, it's late, we should stop here. But Javier said, absolutely not, pana, I want to hear more, keep going, I'll make us a strong pot of Cuban coffee, adding some seconds later as he took out a canister of expresso grounds, anyway, if you stop now, pana, you will never finish.

At the end of Part II, Javier went to the refrigerator, took out a carton of eggs, and cracked some into a pan. For some reason, pana, he said, while you were telling me that last part, especially the part about the resistance fighters on a parallel Earth, I remembered something your grandfather said to me once, "Every telling of an event is a portrait of the teller and not the event itself." Saul thought that Javier might say more, but he didn't. He poked the eggs with a spatula. He's remembering something, thought Saul. And he's unsure how to proceed.

I'm not sure I understand you, said Saul, when did he say that to you, when was the last time you spoke to him? Then he thought too that Javier's voice had unexpectedly taken on a more gravel-like and reflective tone, very much like his grandfather's. I think what your grandfather meant, continued Javier, was that each witness gives a unique account of an event, but more than anything that account is a *self-portrait*. It's not a document: it's an image of the person doing the telling. Then Javier plated the eggs.

Your grandfather's history books present portraits of people rather than accounts of events, said Javier. What do people think? What makes them happy? What do they fear? What stays in their memory? What is lost or concealed just beneath the surface? It was, I think, his greatest strength as a historian and, at the same time, his greatest flaw. Javier handed him a plate. But I'm talking too much, he said. Let's continue, pana. Tell me more.

Saul's grandfather too had always been insistent about hearing more. To him, a narrative path was to be followed even if it split off into another path and then another. After all, each path carried the probability of all the others. It was an Old World Jewish trait, thought Saul, in which survival depended on navigating forking or converging paths adeptly. His grandfather could be assertive, even a little pushy. He would raise his hand and say, "Don't stop, go on, there's always more, what else happened to you, Saul?" and yet at other times he would be uncomplaining and calm. "Don't rush it, Saul, gather your thoughts, the past or a version of the past will all catch up to you, let's wait here until it does." Two months before his grandfather's death and just before he stopped recognizing himself, both in mirrors and in his own thoughts, Saul spent an afternoon with him helping sort through boxes of small cassettes that contained thousands of hours of interviews with politicians, entertainers, surgeons, teachers, factory workers, and activists that he had conducted over his career. Even more abundant were the impromptu interviews he recorded with strangers in grocers, bars, currency exchanges, department stores, parks, backyards, alleys, and rooftops, interviews that he had collectively called "Vox Humana," the human voice, and in which he had—for the most part—remained silent but in which Saul could still occasionally hear his grandfather's gravellike voice behind the clamor of an L train or the white noise of a bar: "Talk more about that year, do you think it could happen again, yes, yes, I remember that summer night in 1968, how did the strike end, why do you think they lied to you, why do you think they let him suffer, who else did she love, what else do you remember about that day, that night, that year, that decade now almost forgotten, what else, what else can you tell me?"

That afternoon, his grandfather was sitting on the cheap Turkish rug with those boxes of small cassettes stacked in front of him, hands at his sides, like someone who waits impatiently for the day to begin—and now and then he would pick up a cassette, place it in the player, and put on large headphones. After some minutes, during which Saul thought his grandfather had forgotten he was in the room, he would stop the cassette player, choose another cassette, and the process would start over once again. It was a long, aggravating process, distressing at times, but Saul never suggested they stop.

At some point that afternoon, after Saul had started to feel invisible, he asked, who are you listening to now? His grandfather squinted and said, what? Push the stop button, tateh, he said and was surprised just then that he had used the old Yiddish term for father. His grandfather nodded and pushed the stop button. Who's on the cassette, tateh? he asked. Maria Hitzig, he replied. Saul had never known a Maria Hitzig. Who's that? he asked. Who do you think it is, Saul? his grandfather said. Then Saul shrugged and said, I'm sorry, tateh, I don't know anyone named Maria Hitzig.

Still, his grandfather looked taken aback, sure that Saul had known her. Then he said, of course, Saul, how should you know her, she was a cleaning lady I met years ago in a bar off Rush Street called The Trap. It was nothing more than a dark room with booths, a counter, and, if you were lucky, a pianist. When I walked in she was arguing with two German men sitting at the bar. She was a fat, pretty woman and her voice was like a brass instrument. She was in the middle of telling those two German men she was from the Kingdom of Prussia and they kept telling her that the Kingdom of Prussia didn't exist anymore and that she was a crazy hag, even though she really was quite pretty and smarter than them. I recorded some of their argument before talking to her alone. Anyway, that's who I was listening to, he said.

Why did she tell them she was from the Kingdom of Prussia? asked Saul. His grandfather took off the headphones and his eyes contracted and became clear once again.

Well, he said, for one, she really *was* from the Kingdom of Prussia. She was born there in 1910, some eight years before the German Revolution replaced the imperial government. That's what she told me too when I pushed her a little about her origins. It's all on the tape. "Don't be stupid, Ben. Listen to me. I'm from Šilokarčema in the Kingdom of Prussia and if anybody says I'm from Heydekrug they have shit for brains." Later, after a little digging around, his grandfather continued, I found that Šilokarčema was the old dialect name for a town the Germans called Heydekrug and which is now called Šilutė in Lithuania. Three tongues for just one town. That was a common thing in those old Baltic towns which got used to changing hands and names, especially during an era when nations would appear and disappear with a simple stroke of a pen.

But why did she insist that her town not be called Heydekrug? asked Saul. Try to connect the dots, Saul, his grandfather said patiently. She was raised during a time when Germans went about erasing as much history of the Kingdom of Prussia as possible. In a later era and in another nation, when Soviet orthodoxy was once again forced onto Czechoslovakia, the historian Milan Hübl said, "The first step in liquidating a people is to erase its memory. Destroy its books, its culture, its history. Then have somebody write new books, manufacture a new culture, invent a new history. Before long the nation will begin to forget what it is and what it was. The world around it will forget even faster." This was true for the Kingdom of Prussia too, said his grandfather. The Germans erased their history and with it the names of streets and towns and books and people. Maybe those new Germans really did want to liquidate the Kingdom of Prussia or maybe they wanted to create the illusion that only Germany had ever existed and would exist for at least another thousand years. Nationalism always works overtime to create its own reality.

But Maria wasn't going to let those two German men erase the name of her town, just as their ancestors had done, or make her forget the Kingdom of Prussia of her childhood, the one that still existed unchanged in her mind. In her own way, he said and smiled, Maria Hitzig was a rebel. But, of course, she's dead now. Long dead. So is the Kingdom of Prussia, or rather, it's just beneath the soil in Germany and Poland and Lithuania and Russia and Denmark and Belgium and the Czech Republic. The garbage of the Kingdom of Prussia can still be found almost anywhere you dig, he said and then fell silent.

But you have her voice on that cassette, said Saul, that's not beneath the soil. Yes, that's true, see, you're connecting the dots now, he said and laughed a little. Then, after a moment of thought, he said, for some people, Saul, an entire place or an entire nation can't just disappear in a lifetime, let alone overnight. Especially when that place is home.

His grandfather did not speak of Mary Hitzig with a wistfulness common to men of his age when they spoke of long dead acquaintances or friends, but rather with such a deep and vivid fondness that he wasn't so much slipping into the past but visiting Maria Hitzig in that Rush Street bar again. Her voice, hermetically sealed on that cassette, was instead a type of time machine. This was true for each interview, each voice in his "Vox Humana," yet, there is always a moment, sooner or later, when one comes upon a voice that carries the weight and sadness and joy of all the others. Though neither his grandfather nor Maria Hitzig could have possibly known she would be so one day, she was his last voice.

Yes, Javier—and not him—shared that trait with his grandfather, thought Saul as he poked at his eggs. They were both men who insisted that others tell their stories, however long or short, however superficial or far-reaching, and almost everyone loves a person who loves to listen. Listening—even more than telling—was a type of gift that both men offered others.

You never answered my question, said Saul eventually, breaking the silence. When was the last time we spoke, Javier reiterated. We spoke last in November, pana. In fact, we spoke at least once every month for a few years.

Saul looked away from Javier and glanced at the manuscript. I didn't know you two spoke while you were *away*, he said.

I'm sorry, pana, Javier said. I tried to tell you that night in the bar after you told me he had already died, but it wasn't the right time, we hadn't seen each other in ages and maybe I was a little shocked. In any case, I called him first a few years ago, somewhat out of the blue since—to be honest—I wanted to see how you were doing. For a time, we just talked about you. I suppose that it was unfair not to tell you, he said.

What do you mean, "how I was doing"? asked Saul. We spoke on the phone. We emailed. You knew how I was doing. Javier fixed his eyes on Saul like an interrogator. Yes, there it was, thought Saul, that same gaze which saw right through him, that same gaze which now said: you know exactly what I mean, pana, I had no idea how you were doing, you never really told me more than "I'm fine" or "Everything's fine" or "Everything's the same," like a tiresome teenager.

Sure, said Javier, I was in the Amazon and the Andes and those foreign cities falling apart before my eyes, but you were the one who was *away*, pana, you revealed so little about yourself during these past ten years, you told me next to nothing at all, so, of course, I spoke to your grandfather, but don't think for a second that I took our friendship for granted.

At some point, continued Javier, your grandfather and I got to talking about other things, about traveling, about his books, about the other foreign correspondents I knew who were either pompous little gods in foreign lands or who were talented and penniless. Then I started seeking his advice, especially when I ran into roadblocks on certain pieces.

Saul nodded. There was nothing to do to change the fact that they had talked about him without his knowledge. Which pieces did he give you advice for? he asked. The BBC piece on the Tepito Market in Mexico City, for example, said Javier, and another one was a profile on José "Pepe" Mujica and the Movement of Popular Participation in Uruguay. He suggested that I follow "Pepe closely since he had a talent for dissent." His exact words. There were quite a few others actually. He even gave me advice during my coverage of the Argentine Great Depression. I learned a great deal from your grandfather, pana. He taught me that journalism, like history, is an apparatus of justification. Your grandfather and his books also taught me how to ask people questions that meant something to them and how to urge them to reveal things they wouldn't otherwise reveal and sometimes the things that others didn't want them to reveal, which can be dangerous, both for them and the listener. Maybe, pana, I never told you how much I admire his work, he said and took a quick bite of the eggs, which by now were pale and in all likelihood cold. I should've, he added, it's stupid that we only say these things after someone is gone.

Saul nodded. I'm sorry I didn't tell you right away when he died, Javier, I know it must have been a painful shock when you showed up here, he said thoughtfully. Anyway, it all happened so fast, even though I was waiting for it to happen, he said. Does that make any sense?

Javier hesitated. It does, to a degree, he said. But we can't spend our days and nights waiting for things to happen, either. Anyway, to answer your original question, pana, that November day we spoke about interviewing taxi drivers in Mexico City for a piece about the long shadow of the Zapatistas. I spent a lot of time in taxis, but it was a shit piece. Later that night, continued Javier, he got a hold of me again, an unusual thing for him to call twice in one day. He wanted to know if I would ever visit Chicago again. I told him I was sure I would visit, but I didn't know when. Without really listening to my response, he then told me he could make a call to an editor he knew at the *Chicago Tribune* if I ever decided I wanted to move home. From what I could gather, the editor was a granddaughter of one of his old friends. I never expressed to him an interest in moving back to Chicago, said Javier. But maybe, that night, I did in fact get the idea to move, or maybe I had already been thinking about what Maya's future in Mexico City might be like. Maybe I was just tired. I don't know. In any case, I didn't need him to call an editor at the *Chicago Tribune* or anything of the sort, but I didn't say that to him. I could tell it would make him feel useful to make that call on my behalf. In the end, he made the call and I took the job.

A suspicion suddenly crossed Saul's mind. Did you know then that he was dying? he asked. It occurred to him that the story of his grandfather's life and death didn't belong to just him anymore. It didn't belong to anyone. It would be told for a few years by others like Javier who still remembered him and then, eventually, it would dissipate like clouds over a cemetery.

No, said Javier, I suspected something was wrong, but I didn't know what and I didn't ask him anything specific on the phone. Later that night, in bed, I told Marina about our conversation and I remember she said that he might not have that much time left and that I should call you. She's rarely wrong with these sorts of things. She has gut instincts about the sick and the soon-to-be sick and the dying. It makes her quite a good doctor. So, yes, I suspected something and I did in fact call you. I left three messages that you never returned, but that's okay, in the end how can we really know what's going to happen while we're away? If we knew all those things, pana, there wouldn't be anything left to tell.

You sound exactly like him, said Saul. Then he shuffled the pages of the manuscript, took a short deep breath, and began again.

My sense is that in her own way Adana Moreau was thinking about the end of history, said Saul quite unexpectedly after finishing Part III and without adding anything further. Then, after a short silence, he nodded at the kitchen window and said, look, it's morning.

Javier leaned back in his chair and gave out a long, contented sigh. Saul could tell just then that Javier felt, more or less, the same sense of wonder and exile he had felt after reading *A Model Earth*.

Then Javier held up his pointer finger and said, just one more thing, pana. He reached into his back pocket, smiling from ear-to-ear now and with his eyes wide like a boy about to play a trick, but also that same boy's father who hoped the trick went smoothly and that nobody got hurt in the process. Then he handed Saul five sheets of paper, folded three or four times into one small flat rectangle, and said, so, I found Maxwell Moreau.

For a while, Saul sat on a park bench in Palmer Square Park reading an article entitled "Un ojo gigante en desierto solitario" which appeared in *El Universal* on October 15th, 1999, and was written by a Mexican reporter who had gone to Chile to cover a small group of elderly women who had spent the better part of two and half decades combing the Atacama Desert for the preserved remains and bone fragments of their husbands and children "disappeared" by the brutal Pinochet regime.

The article, which had been translated by Javier for Saul onto those five sheets of paper with the title "A Giant Eye in the Lonely Desert" and which was now spread on his lap, proceeded in five stages: First the Mexican reporter went to Calama, Chile, to interview the group's organizer, Victoria Ortiz, a sensible and assiduous woman "like a Flemish painter," who in 1979 had watched helplessly as her son was taken away by DINA, the secret police under Pinochet, never to be seen again. Then the reporter recounted her experiences traveling through the Atacama Desert with the elderly women as they drove in two large white pickup trucks from the little town of San Pedro de Atacama with just two telephone lines and one gas station to the edges of a long-abandoned town even deeper in the desert, a "surreal trip," according to the reporter, full of stony "Mars-like" terrain, sand, salt lakes, felsic lava flowing toward the Andes, pre-Colombian rock carvings made by shepherds ten thousand years earlier and preserved almost flawlessly by the desert's extreme hyperaridity, and even visible land mines planted decades before by the Chilean military.

Then the reporter explained how she helped the elderly women as they combed one hundred square yards of red and yellow desert "like archeologists" until it was too hot and they had to retreat to the shade of their white pickup trucks, where they talked about the fate of the "disappeared," about which next to nothing was known. They reviewed old rumors and gossip, compared anecdotes and possible bone fragments (phalanges, femurs, a mandible), and speculated about the whereabouts of their loved ones' remains—thrown into the sea or buried beneath the sands under their feet. And finally they returned to San Pedro de Atacama and ate lunch in a small nameless restaurant with a "tall, enigmatic, and easygoing old man with immaculate gray and black hair," a professor of theoretical physics from the Universidad de Chile who was setting out afterward into the expansive plateau at the bottom of the Cerro Chajnantor in order to camp for a few days and "read the night sky," which was, according to the reporter, "a strange way to put it," and also take measurements for research groups who were planning on building the world's largest and most powerful radio telescope. Because of its sheer height, dryness, and translucent sky, the Atacama Desert was the perfect place for such a telescope.

The Atacama Large Millimeter/submillimeter Array or ALMA for short, as the telescope would be called, would allow astronomers to glimpse the very first galaxies that formed and even register light produced by the Big Bang. "A giant eye in the lonely desert," the theoretical physicist said in a casual and elegant Spanish, "gazing into the very origins of the universe."

Later, when the professor asked the women what they were doing in the Atacama Desert, they told their stories just as they had told the reporter. The professor nodded solemnly while they talked, but didn't say anything. Later, as they walked the bright, arid streets of San Pedro de Atacama, Victoria Ortiz and the professor exchanged contact information in case he happened to find any remains during his trip. Then, as the two large white pickup trucks wound their way from San Pedro de Atacama to Calama, the road empty save for a shepherd sleeping in his dilapidated truck, the elderly women turned their conversations to the living, to their grandsons and granddaughters, to their neighbors and friends, who all wanted them to "get on with their lives."

At some point, the reporter finally asked Victoria Ortiz the question she had meant to ask since the beginning of their trek. Why did they keep returning to the desert again and again when only fragments of their loved ones remained? What did they hope to prove or change? Instead of Victoria Ortiz answering her, another elderly woman sitting shotgun, who, up until that moment, had said little, looked at the reporter in the rearview mirror as if analyzing a missed exit and said: I think for the same reason that the professor we met today comes to this desert to "read the night sky." Memory is a gravitational force. It is constantly attracting us to the past, even if we shouldn't stay there for too long. Those of us who have a memory are able to live in that fragile space between the past and the future. Those of us who have none are already dead.

On the last page of the article, there was a yellow Post-it note with Maxwell Moreau's telephone number and an address for him in New Orleans, given to Javier by Victoria Ortiz. Through an online Mexican newspaper archive, Javier had managed to find the article and then he had tracked down the Mexican reporter. Through her he was able to speak to Victoria Ortiz, who had developed a close friendship or maybe even more than a friendship (it was hard to tell) with Maxwell Moreau since their initial meeting in the Atacama Desert and had kept in regular contact with him until he left Chile in late March 2003. After that, she told Javier on the phone, she hadn't heard from him again until April 2004 when he sent a postcard from New Orleans.

Saul took out his cell phone and called Maxwell Moreau's number. After ten or eleven rings, he hung up. Then he called again, but there was no answer.

★ ★ ★

That same night, at 7:15 p.m., Saul left The Atlas and walked down the street to the twenty-four-hour FedEx. The FedEx employee took the newly sealed box that contained *A Model Earth*, but then she glanced at the mailing address and told Saul that she couldn't send the package. He then told her that this was the second time he had been unable to mail the package and she checked the computer to see if there were any errors, but there were no errors. No packages were being sent to New Orleans or really anywhere in the Gulf Coast that day and possibly even the following day due to the approaching hurricane.

Later, Saul, Romário, and two awestruck guests of The Atlas watched the Weather Channel on a lobby television as a meteorologist explained that there were mandatory evacuation orders in effect in coastal Mississippi, Alabama, and large areas of southeast Louisiana, including the city of New Orleans. Saul started to say something about Maxwell Moreau, about the package he still had to deliver, but then he fell silent, as did everyone else, when the screen switched from the meteorologist to a NASA satellite image. For two or three minutes, before the guests left The Atlas and Romário changed the channel to a sitcom, they all gazed silently at the approaching hurricane, at the swirling, hypnotic winds and the hopeless vacuum of the fatally becalmed eye.

THE LAST PIRATE OF THE
NEW WORLD

September 1930–July 1933

On September 7th the pirate arranged a funeral for Adana Moreau, which was attended by twenty people at St. Augustine and followed by a mournful but, at times, serene dinner at the house on Melpomene Avenue.

After his mother's funeral, Maxwell began to wander farther and farther away from home. Sometimes, in the morning, he would start out walking toward school and end up somewhere completely different, oblivious as to how he had gotten there, like he had walked through a portal.

In late November, he stopped going to school altogether. Other times, he wouldn't come home for two or three days, after which his father would interrogate, scold, and then starkly warn him that white men wouldn't heed any of his reasons, justified or not, for wandering alone. Mostly he walked, but on certain occasions he hopped a train out of Algiers rail yards. On one such occasion, the train stopped near a pier on the Mississippi River and Maxwell got off the train and sat on the pier and watched workers dismantle a ship for scrap. On another occasion, he ended up in Baton Rouge, which Maxwell thought was a strange name for a city since it meant *red stick* in French. He walked around the city and when he was tired he sat on a bench near a large Creole Catholic church. After some time, a Creole woman in a blue and yellow floral summer dress stopped and gave him two slices of bread and a can of mackerel. He said thank you and ate quickly as the woman watched.

He then hopped a train on the west side of the river and got off in a small town. He roamed the town for a few hours, but found nothing of immediate interest. He then followed a dirt path, which led to a worn plantation house near a sugarcane field. The field was sparse and dry and there were a few shacks scattered among the dying crops, in addition to a handful of old army tents. Maxwell guessed that transient men lived there, and before long he saw a small group of white men come out of a shack and peer west, in unison, like meerkats looking for prey. Maxwell avoided them and walked along the perimeter of the sugarcane field until he came to a half-collapsed wooden fence. He climbed over the fence, careful not to cut himself on rusted nails, and walked down a slight hill until he found a river. Maxwell crouched down by the river and washed his face and drank from its water, which was clear and sweet. He then followed the river east for an hour or so, thinking vague and sorrowful thoughts about his mother, until he came to a house on stilts on the bed of the river. After deciding that the house was abandoned, he entered through the front door, which hung loosely from two broken hinges.

The house was disheveled. In the front room, there were two wooden chairs, a table turned on its side, a cabinet stocked with canned food, and a fireplace filled with ash. In the back room, which smelled moldy, like a cave, he found one empty bed. The bed was narrow and hard. A kind of yellow and green weed stuck out of a crevice between the frame and the mattress. He also found a mirror on the floor. For a long time, he looked at himself in the mirror, as if looking down into a sunken lake. At first, he didn't recognize himself. His black hair was tangled, his face thin and gaunt, his eyes vacant and wet. That's me, he thought, but he knew it could have been anybody. He picked up the mirror to get a better look and cut his hand on the edges. He watched as six or seven drops of blood fell onto the mirror. Then he went looking all over the house for something to wrap up his bleeding hand and that was how he found Marie Brown's *The Imaginary Life of the Son of Kanada* in a small closet lined with rotting magazines and books.

Maxwell wrapped his hand in his shirt and sat near the river-bed, half-naked, with the novel. This is what he discovered: In the spring of 612 BCE, Kanada's son is born in Prabhas Kshetra. At the age of five, his parents take him to the coast near Dwarka, where he almost drowns in the blue sea. Shortly afterward, his mother gives birth to a baby girl, who, his father tells him, is a gift of beauty and possibility. In his first act of rebellion, he refuses to admit his sister's existence. In the years 599 BCE to 595 BCE, his father teaches him his life's work, the Vaisheshika School of Philosophy, which proposes the idea of the paramāṇu, an indestructible and eternal particle of matter—the *thing* which cannot be divided up further. A paramāṇu, his father tells him, is like the smallest grain of rice or a speck of dust trapped in sunlight.

The Son of Kanada is a good student; however, he's much more interested in sensible matters: sword handling, the accumulation of wealth, how to seduce foreign women. At the age of eighteen, in his second act of rebellion, he renounces the Vaisheshika School of Philosophy. Then, in his final act of rebellion, and against his father's deepest wishes, he leaves Prabhas Kshetra. He travels west through new empires, dying kingdoms. He briefly joins the remnants of a nomadic tribe, but is captured by the Babylonians and sold as a slave to a rich trader. In captivity, while crossing the Euphrates River, he watches helplessly as a yellow and black tiger hunts, kills, and devours a farmer. In a market in Babylon, he learns three modern languages and one forgotten language, taught to him by an old Theban poet with one black eye, one leg. In 590 BCE, he escapes and wanders north along the Tigris River, as if lost in the dreams of another man. While living like a street dog in the lonely ruins of the royal palace at Nineveh, he unearths twelve damaged clay tablets on which is written *The Epic of Gilgamesh*. The story gives him an unusual and acute joy, which he will preserve in the face of idleness and horror for the rest of his life.

In the spring of 587 BCE, as a soldier of Babylon, he witnesses the siege and fall of Jerusalem. In the fall of 583 BCE, in a suburb of Jerusalem, he sees a total lunar eclipse and remembers his sister for the first time since leaving Prabhas Kshetra. I was wrong, he thinks with remorse. She existed and still exists and will continue to exist. She was a gift of beauty and possibility and her face is just like the red face of this moon. Some years later, he starts a prosperous business as a trader on the island of Cyprus, in the Kingdom of Salamis. In 569 BCE, following the conquest of Cyprus by Amasis II, he falls in love with the widow of a Greek mercenary. Over the next ten years, he fathers three children with her, two girls and one boy, and transcribes *The Epic of Gilgamesh* with moderate, local success. Afterward, he donates one-third of his wealth to a public library and subscribes to various schools of philosophy in Salamis and Amathus. His efforts at philosophy are sometimes admired, sometimes held in ridicule.

More than a few times, he dreams about a burning landscape full of towers and yellow and black tigers hunting men, men hunting each other. Still, he wakes early every morning and sees to his family, his business accounts, and his sailors who, as they unload wares, talk about women, magic, and a spring of clear water to the east which gives men immortality. In the evenings, he visits the public library and speaks with a priest who has studied in Athens and who dreams of returning one day. He reads and reads, his eyes in constant motion, like insects eating other insects.

One morning in the fall of 550 BCE, while bedridden due to a strange feverish sickness, he glimpses a dizzying halo of dust forming over his nose and he sees in the dust *irrefutable proof*, as the Greek priest likes to say, of the paramāṇu. At first, he is speechless. He shivers with joy. Then, in his mother tongue, which he has not spoken since leaving his childhood home, he professes the Vaisheshika School of Philosophy. His youngest daughter overhears him and starts laughing. What are you saying, Father? she asks. With great effort and happiness, he calls her over and explains to her the *thing* which cannot be divided up further. Hours later he dies, but he doesn't know that he has died or that many years later nothing will remain of his life except a book written by his youngest daughter.

Maxwell read *The Imaginary Life of the Son of Kanada* from beginning to end in one sitting, sometimes aloud, sometimes laughing or yelling at the top of his lungs. When he finished, some long hours later, he dove into the river and swam to its silent depths, and if he hadn't remembered to go back to the surface to breathe he would have stayed there forever, contemplating, like the Son of Kanada, the little green rocks and the black water with little paramāṇu-like particles of black mud, and planning his escape from New Orleans.

Later, at dusk, as he walked back through the dying sugarcane field with the book under his arm, Maxwell thought about how satisfying it would be to get home and sit with his mother at the kitchen table and tell her all about *The Imaginary Life of the Son of Kanada*, but then he remembered this was impossible.

★ ★ ★

On no few occasions, the pirate went looking for his son. The old mad pirate was convinced that the boy had a wandering disease, much like the mourning Sumerian gods or the 3rd century Chinese poet Pan Yue, who, the old mad pirate explained to the boy's father one night at the kitchen table, paced *to and fro amidst the graves and tombs.*

"He misses his mother is all," the pirate said and looked down at his knuckles.

Then the pirate asked the old mad pirate how he had survived the death of his son.

At first, the old mad pirate didn't say anything, but then he exploded into a fit of laughter, slamming his fists against the table so that it shook like a small earthquake, nearly coming to tears. Then he told the pirate that he hadn't survived the death of his son. He said nobody ever *survived* grief. Then he said a few strange things about grief. He said that grief was an immortal samurai endlessly stabbing himself in the abdomen. He said grief was a sea-green forest in France. He said grief was Odysseus' dog, Argos, waiting for his master to return, lying in a pile of shit.

One morning in March, the pirate and his son rose before dawn and drove to Lake Pontchartrain. At the shore they noticed a group of fishermen who were gazing into the sky as a small flock of gray herons were flying north, like a squadron of planes, maybe toward Mandeville; some of the fishermen pointed with their poles, then drew signs or letters in the air with their poles, communicating, imagined Maxwell, with the gray herons. Where are the fish? they asked. Why the hell should we tell you? replied the birds, Look how far you've already come on this planet. A logy heat moved sluggishly over the lake, but otherwise the water was still. The pirate and his son walked in silence together along the shore.

"I have to leave to find work, mijo," the pirate said finally.

For a few seconds, Maxwell was silent. Then he said, "So, take me with you."

"I can't," said the pirate.

"Why not?" he pleaded. "I've been to Baton Rouge, and farther than that, too."

"There's no work for you out there," said the pirate.

In the distance, the fishermen pushed off into the water, their nets and tackle boxes slung up in the boat. As they walked, Maxwell lifted his gaze, and what he saw suggested the unknown world that existed beyond the city and the lake, beyond the marshes and the sand-colored horizon, a world inexplicably turned outward, a world with borders on the brink of conversion, erasure, and violence. Maxwell felt as if he could cry, but he didn't want to in front of his father. At some point, the pirate drudged up a few bills from his pocket and gave them to his son. Maxwell shook his head and said he didn't need the money.

"Keep it, mijo," said the pirate, "you have to take care of yourself now."

Maxwell nodded and put the bills into his back pocket.

On their way home, they stopped by the cemetery where Adana Moreau had been laid to rest. They stood in front of her small plaster and brick tomb, where, surprisingly, someone had laid fresh yellow roses, in all likelihood an admirer of *Lost City*, possibly even Afraa. The pirate and his son were vaguely embarrassed, but also glad someone else had thought of her. For fifteen or maybe twenty minutes, they stood there in a silence fraught with memories of the Dominicana and questions about the boy's future that not even the insects of the cemetery could disturb.

So, in the spring of 1931, the pirate left New Orleans and Maxwell went looking for a job. At first, he walked around the Barracks Street Wharf, where he hoped he could get a job on a fishing boat, but a skipper who smelled like sweat and clay told him that there were no jobs and then chased Maxwell away with a fisherman knife when he asked again. On Dryades Street, he found a run-down YMCA where a group of stone-faced middle-aged women told him the best they could do was feed him, after which they handed him bread and a bowl of tomato soup. In the French Quarter, he ran into a group of older boys, who were all immigrant and first-generation Sicilians but who had taken on the air of Americans, an air of baseball games, gangsters in tight suits, and early risers, older boys who, thought Maxwell, dreamed of newspaper empires and leather suitcases stuffed with green cash. They took one obstinate look at him and told him "good luck and fuck off," and in that order, because even luck, they explained to Maxwell, was something that eventually ran out.

A few days later, after some careful pleading on Maxwell's part, the old mad pirate found him a job at a speakeasy called the Three Junipers on the chaotic corner of South Rampart Street and Perdido Street. The speakeasy's owner, Salvatore, was an ex-sailor who had dark tattoos running along his arms and neck and who had served in the Great War on an L-class submarine, which, according to the old mad pirate, had basically done shit-to-shit and had been ordered to wander the deep waters of the Skagerrak Strait looking for an enemy that never materialized. In short, Maxwell was hired because Salvatore owed the old mad pirate a favor.

"The most valuable thing in the world," the old mad pirate explained to Maxwell, "is a favor. Better than cash or gold."

In the mornings, after breakfast with the old mad pirate, Maxwell went to the library to search for other books by Marie Brown (there were none) or sit at a long, crowded table to read *The Great Encyclopedia of Astronomy and Physics*, which, to his irritation, didn't include any entries on Kanada, but did, to his utter and happy astonishment, include entries on Hypatia, Ibn al-Haytham, Kepler, Einstein, and Schrödinger. Afterward he worked ten-hour shifts at the Three Junipers, dusting, mopping, and helping weathered men unload boxes and barrels of whiskey, gin, and sacramental wine. As they worked, the men talked about types of swamp birds, films, "Blonde Bombshell" Jean Harlow, Marlene Dietrich as Lola-Lola, mistresses, detectives who moonlighted as whores and whores who daylighted as detectives, the failure of politics, the brutal events taking place in Berlin, murder, illusions, work, and waiting for the vague, dense redemption of work. Sometimes, they told Maxwell that a mixed black boy like him was lucky to have a job, even if it earned a pittance, an opinion the young introspective Maxwell listened to, his sweaty hands on a barrel, without saying a word. Still, on some nights after finishing a particularly grueling job, one of the men, usually a younger Creole man but sometimes an older black man who said his name like his father, called Maxwell over and slid a dirty coin into his palm.

Sometimes, his shifts at the Three Junipers coincided with one of the illicit meetings Salvatore kept throughout the neighborhood in order to keep his speakeasy running smoothly, and then he would ask Maxwell to watch over the place for a few hours, almost always without advanced notice. The only advice Salvatore ever gave Maxwell about running the speakeasy was this: *regulars come here for two reasons: a good drink and a silent listener.*

For the most part, the regulars viewed Maxwell as an improvement over Salvatore, some because they could convince him to pour stronger drinks, after which the speakeasy would take on the voracious qualities of a bar before Prohibition, and others because unlike Salvatore he actually followed Salvatore's bartending words of advice.

One of the regulars who took an instant liking to Maxwell was a legless man named Laszlo. Sometimes, he sat on a stool or rolled around the floors of the speakeasy on a platform with wheels, drinking bourbon and talking nonstop about a girl named Ana who didn't love him or who had loved him once and then never again, and who, in any case, made the legless man so enraged that, as the night and his drunkenness progressed, he would yell, "Tear out my fucking heart, kid! Do it now before I'm dead!" and then bring his fists down on his stumps like a hammer and wince in pain too, and cry out.

Regarding his unrequited love for Ana, naturally, Laszlo had a few ideas. Either Ana's heart was an artificial heart, like the ones the Russian commies in the papers always threatened to invent, or Ana was like his own hypothermic, opium-addicted mother, able to love, but not able to love him. It's not true that a man lives in the shadow of his father, like everyone says, Laszlo explained to Maxwell one night, but rather in his mother's dreams and later her nightmares.

"Don't you agree, kid?" said Laszlo.

Maxwell, of course, said nothing, but not because of his bartender vow of silence. He sincerely didn't know. No matter how hard he tried he couldn't remember if his mother had ever told him about any of her dreams and that troubled him greatly.

On better nights, the legless man asked Maxwell questions about his own life. What did he want to do when he grew up? What did the future look like to him? Did he ever think about temptations? Did he ever think that the world they lived in was just someone else's dream? Did he ever think about the past, the Incas, the Mongols, the Romans, or the British, all of them civilized, all of them bloodthirsty assholes?

Of course, Maxwell never answered the legless man's questions, at least not directly, but he did think about them before falling asleep, generally long after a white tropical moon had risen above his house on Melpomene Avenue. He didn't know what he wanted to do when he grew up, but he already saw the future as a passageway through which people stumbled blindly.

Yes, he thought about girls, especially the ones he saw in thin blue and green summer dresses on South Rampart Street, and he thought about the sweet, hard sips of whiskey he snuck when

Salvatore was gone. He thought about the letters his father sent him from places like Fort Worth, St. Louis, and Kansas City; he thought about the violent stabs of loneliness he felt when reading them and the humid, indistinguishable days between the arrival of one letter and the next. He thought about the letters he would write back to his father, letters that he never sent because they would just get lost in the mail or because he decided that they wouldn't make any sense. Every day, he thought of leaving the city and finding his father. More than once, he thought about tearing up his father's letters or burning them in a small blue fire.

Yes, the world they lived in was the Son of Kanada's dream as he wandered north along the Tigris River in 590 BCE. And what he thought of the past was easy. On one hand, the past was *starlight*. On the other, there was no such thing as the Incas, the Mongols, the Romans, or the British. Only variations of the same bloodthirsty assholes repeated through time. The past was a cemetery, a half-buried or drowned maze, claustrophobic. None of his ancestors were buried there or, if they were, they were nameless. You got lost in it for no reason at all.

Still, Laszlo liked to talk to Maxwell about the past, especially his own. When he was much younger and had both his legs, he told Maxwell one night, he had been a circus strong man and a wrestler with the stage name Cronus. For years, he traveled the country challenging rivals with names like Horned Viper, Judas, Cyclops, Jesus "The Beast" Field, Grendel, etc. For a period of time, he was even undefeated. Then, inevitably, one night in Nashville under a black and red tent, he was defeated by a man called Djinni, an Arab who had fashioned himself after a supernatural warrior-poet and who, under his real name, Mahmoud Yaseen, had written forty dime novels about the desert, some of which he sold at matches, and all of which essentially followed the same plot: a wandering man in the desert falls in love with a woman, in order to make the woman fall in love with him he searches for and then unearths a magical artifact, the man then uses the magical artifact and the woman suffers a death or something like a death, a disappearance, imprisonment in an asylum, or a transformation into a desert breeze that carries the seeds of an iris flower.

"I was fucked over twice," said the legless man, "first, by Djinni, or rather by Mahmoud Yaseen's novels, which taught me the true cost of love. And then by Ana, who I love more than myself, but who's dead to me."

Of course, upon hearing about Mahmoud Yaseen's novels, Maxwell broke his bartending vow of silence and asked Laszlo if he had any copies he could borrow. He said he used to have a few, but he sold them all to replace cracked wheels for his platform. Sometime later, the legless man stopped coming to the Three Junipers and Maxwell never heard from him or saw him again.

In October a letter arrived from a ranch outside of Fort Worth. In the letter, his father described his new job. He repaired farm equipment, put up fences, and took care of horses, but occasionally there were other things which involved driving to the city. He wrote that Texas was very different from Louisiana. The sunsets in Texas were endless, but during the day the sky was empty, and this produced a sense of abandonment and plunder.

In February, another letter arrived from the ranch. The letter was short and uneventful, but the envelope included a money order worth two months' wages and a photograph of his father saddled on a horse. The horse was sinewy and stiff, its hooves firmly planted in the dry earth, the opposite of manning a boat, thought Maxwell, which explained his father's apparent unease.

Three months later, Maxwell received a letter, unexpectedly, from St. Louis. His father described an uncertain scene in which the owner of the ranch had refused to pay his black and

Mexican ranch hands, followed by a brawl which left one ranch hand with a broken arm and another with a bullet wound in his right leg. There were no jobs in St. Louis. The pirate wandered the city from day to night. Occasionally, he took refuge at a damp and run-down hotel where guitarists from Kansas City played until dawn.

In July, a postcard from Cedar Rapids, Iowa, arrived, but nothing was written on it. On the front of the postcard was an illustration of a green tractor, framed by a blue sky and a yellow field of corn. In October, a money order arrived with thirty-five dollars, a fortune to the old mad pirate and Maxwell. Shortly afterward, a letter arrived from Dubuque. In this letter, his father wrote about long lines outside a factory, frostbite, the terrible drone of machinery, his wages, and his nostalgia for the sea. But nostalgia, he advised near the end of the letter, is a terrible form of amnesia.

In February, Maxwell received a two-page letter postmarked from a hotel in Chicago called the Jonava. The city was immense, awe-inspiring, and lonely, especially in the winter. Toward the end of the letter, as a way of explanation, he wrote, *I miss your mother, mijo.*

In April, a few days before his thirteenth birthday, Maxwell received a large manila envelope containing a letter and a crisp star map of the northern constellations. His father wrote that he was going to take a good job with a shipping company and that he should have enough money saved up by July for Maxwell to come live with him in Chicago. After he finished reading the letter, Maxwell imagined, at the speed of light, his father and himself living in an apartment in Chicago, going to the market and then an enormous library on an enormous street. He imagined riding a crowded subway, standing side by side, and nights together, eating in diners, then reading the northern sky and its starlight as it led them home with infinite joy. No other letters arrived at the house on Melpomene Avenue.

★ ★ ★

In late June, Maxwell quit his job at the Three Junipers. When he told Salvatore, he looked at the boy for a few seconds, rubbed his tattooed neck, and said, "You sure, kid? You got a good gig here." Maxwell nodded and said he had to leave the city, after which Salvatore dug into his trouser pockets, handed him three extra days' worth of wages, and said, "It's probably for the best. Nine states already ratified the 21st. Prohibition is as good as dead anyways."

After his final shift, the old mad pirate met Maxwell in front of the Three Junipers. Maxwell gave him his extra wages and then they went on a long walk through the city. They walked first along Perdido Street and then along Carondelet Street, as blithely and happily as they had walked those same streets together when Maxwell was a little kid, which, to Maxwell, was a long time ago, an entirely different life altogether, but which to the old mad pirate was only yesterday, and this wasn't due to the fact that he was mad, he explained as they walked, but due to his old age.

"Mas sabe el Diablo por viejo que por Diablo," he said and then he laughed like a madman. Maxwell knew that this was something people from his mother's island (and the surrounding islands) said about growing old.

When the time came for him to go, he left alone. In an old Army canvas backpack, he carried a few items of clothes, his father's letters, a flashlight, the star map of the northern constellations, a pocketknife, a few sandwiches, and two books: *The Imaginary Life of the Son of Kanada* and one of the three remaining copies of *Lost City* in the house on Melpomene Avenue. He took the ferry to the Algiers rail yards and found a train marked with the Illinois Central logo, IC. A few bullmen patrolled the tracks and held rifles, but Maxwell was careful not to be seen. When the train jerked alive, he ran alongside an empty boxcar and then hopped on by grabbing a low handle. Once in the boxcar, he jammed the door open by bashing a rail spike into its track. Then he smiled and wiped his face, which was covered in coal dust, and watched the scenery pass by slowly. Later, the wheels of the train spun still faster, hitting their joints, and he heard the train's whistle, like a song, he thought, a train song, familiar, relentless.

Outside of Natchez, the train changed conductors, and a large group of transients hopped on. Most were boys a few years older than Maxwell. Some looked as if they had marched through a malarial jungle, while others looked like they had been living in a cave. One transient, a Choctaw boy with dirty-brown hair and a sallow face, told Maxwell that he should get off the train. In a nearby town, it was rumored that a young white girl had been raped and the town's patrolmen were looking for a Negro from New Orleans. Rumor was he was riding boxcars. Maxwell told the boy he was only thirteen and just heading north, toward Chicago, but he immediately regretted telling the boy anything at all.

"Doesn't matter," the boy said, his expression impassive, "you're tall, like you're sixteen or something, and they're all looking for a tall Negro, any tall Negro to lay blame and hang, and you sure as shit look like one. If I were you, I'd hop off."

It wasn't until hours later, as he walked on a path leading through a cypress-tree forest, which eventually opened onto the countryside and a solitary road in the distance with men carrying torches, that he realized the Choctaw boy with dirty-brown hair and a sallow face had probably saved his life.

In Natchez the next morning, Maxwell hopped a train with *Morell's Pride—Ham—Bacon—Canned Meats* stamped across its boxcars. The train passed through Louisiana and parts of Arkansas. At a stop in El Dorado, two boys joined him. The smaller one kept his back to Maxwell, watching the stark green pine forests and yellow farmlands as they passed by, coughing for minutes at a time. Sometimes, when he coughed, he clenched his torn, bloodstained shirt, which was much too big, thought Maxwell, and looked like an insult to him.

"My younger brother, Thomas," explained the other boy, who had an ash-colored scar along his right temple and who spoke with a thin German accent. "He's just sick." He then told Maxwell that his name was Adel and they were heading toward Colorado and then California, where they could ride out the fruit-picking season and hopefully make a little money. Maxwell didn't know anything about Colorado or California, so he didn't say anything. "Where you headed?" the boy asked.

"Chicago," said Maxwell.

The brothers looked at each other and laughed.

"You're on the wrong train, comrade," said Adel.

That night Maxwell dreamed about his mother. She was standing in front of a library in New Orleans with a man dressed like a 17th century cartographer. His mother scolded him for losing her son in the dry folds of a map the exact same size as the Earth. At some point, Maxwell woke up and couldn't fall back asleep. He was hungry and sensed that the dream had made him melancholy and homesick. What happens to you as you travel farther and farther away from home? he thought. Where does one life begin and the other end? At the same time, he wasn't unhappy as a traveler, wandering great distances in a matter of days. He gazed northeast, toward where he imagined Chicago to be, but he didn't see anything, just a moonless black landscape evaporating into the horizon as the train sped west. Slowly, his eyes adjusted to the darkness and then he saw farmhouses, short and boxy, and monotonous fields. In one of those fields, he saw a camp full of half-starved drifters, some men, a few families, all sitting around a small fire. He saw red and blue trucks on distant roads. He saw small towns and lines of trees and rivers. He saw other trains like enormous black millipedes. Overhead, the sky was full of burning stars and he could immediately recognize two or three constellations from his star map. This felt inevitable to him, like finding his father waiting for him at the Jonava or a math problem stretching into eternity. Later, although Maxwell couldn't tell how much later, dawn crept into the sky from the far side of the Earth, and he saw dead yellow fields, as yellow as anything he had ever seen before, and red dust clouds aflame in the light of the sun. At some point, the brothers joined him. They both stood on the edge of the boxcar, like sentinels in some distant war.

"Kansas is dying," said Adel. Then his brother sighed deeply, without coughing for once, lit a cigarette, and handed it over to Maxwell. "Take it," said Adel, "it helps when you're hungry."

Some hours later, the train slowed near a remote stop in Great Bend and the brothers told Maxwell they were going to get off and head into town to look for food and shelter for a night or two. Maxwell's plan was to get off as well, but then wait for a train heading east or north. Still, when they asked him to go with them he said yes.

As they crossed an empty dirt field, Adel told Maxwell that they were from a small town in Pennsylvania, but that they had both been born in Cologne, Germany, a great fortress city on the Rhine River that he could still see with his eyes open or closed, even if his poor brother remembered very little.

In town, just off the main road in a one-story redbrick building, there was a Salvation Army where a small woman with small blue eyes told the boys that they could stay for three meals and one night as long as they attended a sermon. In a crude chapel in the back of the Salvation Army, the boys sat on a long pew and listened to a stocky man with charcoal hair and a croaky voice as he preached about buffalos and oil and savage Indians who had been sacrificed at the foot of something called *the Altar of Fate*. Afterward, in the adjoining room, where the boys ate potato soup and bread, Adel said that the sermon had been confusing.

"What the fuck is the Altar of Fate anyway?" he said.

Then he asked Maxwell if he was religious. At first, Maxwell made a gesture with his left hand that could have meant anything. Then he said:

"Sometimes yes, sometimes no."

Then, after a long interval, he added: "No."

"Me either," said Thomas and he smiled a little, first at his older brother, and then at Maxwell. Only then did Maxwell realize it was the first time he had heard him talk.

Later that day, Thomas developed a fever and he lay on an Army cot in a cramped dark room of the Salvation Army, coughing blood and soot for minutes at a time, until he fell asleep. His brother sat on the cot with him, his eyes full of tears, while Maxwell sat silently on the next cot over, thinking about his mother and the abyss of sickness, both listening to Thomas as he said incomprehensible things in German during a type of fever dream, things, Adel later confessed to Maxwell, about their baby sister, an uncertain trip west, and Germany, an invented Germany from 1926 or 1927 his brother couldn't possibly remember, but one which still stole into his brother's fever dreams, sometimes taking the form of a shitting crow perched atop the twin-spired Cathedral of Cologne and other times taking the form of a black rock, disintegrating little by little into black pebbles, at the bottom of the Rhine River.

Maxwell had a light meal at the Salvation Army and then went to a small pharmacy down the street. He greeted the pharmacist and then described Thomas' symptoms. The pharmacist, who at first thought Maxwell was an errand boy, asked him a few questions about Thomas, most of which sounded contradictory and vague to Maxwell. Still, he answered them the best he could. In the end, the pharmacist suggested aspirin for the fever, painkillers, and Vaseline, which should be generously rubbed on the boy's chest. When it came time to pay, Maxwell said he didn't have any money.

The pharmacist let out a long sigh and said, "Well, what do you have then?"

Maxwell opened his old Army canvas backpack and took out his flashlight, his pocketknife, and *The Imaginary Life of the Son of Kanada*.

"I can't take any of this," he said to Maxwell, slowly.

Maxwell nodded.

"I have a boy around your age," said the pharmacist as he handed Maxwell the medicine.

Later that night, Thomas' fever subsided and he slept soundly. To pass the time, Adel and Maxwell played solitaire, told jokes, and talked about their families. Adel's little sister made fake silver bracelets out of paper. His parents had once been factory workers, but they were laid off after the Panic. Now they were something else, something he couldn't quite figure out anymore. When Maxwell told Adel that his father was the Last Pirate of the New World, he shrugged and said he'd heard stranger things. In the morning, when Maxwell woke, the brothers from Germany were gone.

It was around this time, as the train sped north under clouds streaked with flashes of heat lightning, that Maxwell remembered his mother's manuscript *A Model Earth*. One morning, after his father had rushed off to buy replacement typewriter ribbon while his mother slept, Maxwell found the pages on the kitchen table and read them in one long sitting. Later, after the manuscript had been destroyed and his mother had died, the figure of the Dominicana, who, he imagined, had the same beautiful, almond-shaped face of his mother, blurred, twisted, and faded away into something remote and unrecognizable, a disfigured shadow, a fragment of a fragment, a parallel universe.

In North Platte, the train stopped for a crew change and Maxwell hopped off. He was hungry and worn-out. The sky was blue and the train yard was empty. On the outskirts of the train yard, he saw tents and a group of men in tattered clothes. A few of the men played dice, others took turns shaving in front of a mirror tied to a tree branch, and still others sat in a semicircle, eating soup from tin cans. Maxwell watched the men for a long time and he imagined that they were the sad ghosts of a retreating army. At some point, a man about sixty with a beard approached him.

"Don't go into town, son," he said, squinting in the sun. "The rat people who live there chased away the Negroes a few years ago. Better to get back riding the rails."

"But I've never met any rat people before," said Maxwell, and they both laughed.

"Where you headed?"

"Chicago," said Maxwell, "but I think I'm lost."

The old man picked up a stick and drew a few directional symbols into the dirt.

"Well," he said, "you can find an Illinois Central in Omaha, straight to Chicago. But listen, son, if I were younger, like you, I'd head west instead of east. I'd head all the way west and barrel right into the Sierra Nevada and pilfer it for all its worth. I'd dress in a suit of gold and live in its rocky veins and drown in its rivers."

In Omaha, at night, while waiting for an Illinois Central freight, Maxwell took out the final letter his father had sent to him and read it again and again. *Meet me at the Jonava in July*, his father had written at the end, very carefully, thought Maxwell, because the letters were facing forward, as if trudging into a risky crosswind that could scatter them like particles of ash across the flat Nebraskan plains.

Somewhere in Iowa three older boys, maybe fifteen or sixteen, hopped the train with him. One of the boys was shoeless and had dried blood on his face. He looked like he had been in a fight the night before but had forgotten about it. Another boy handed Maxwell a long stick of beef jerky, but for the most part they kept to themselves. Occasionally, the train passed a solitary prairie house or a solitary town. Some of those towns were completely dark, like black holes, and above others there were fireworks, at first aflame against the black sky, then falling, sickly and dim, into the fields. At some point, while watching the fireworks, the older boy with dried blood on his face said, "Happy birthday, shithole."

On the third day of traveling, just before dawn, the train reached a river and turned south along its shore into the downtown of an enormous city, where the lights of a thousand and one buildings—warehouses, factories, stone mansions, and skyscrapers—quaked faintly like faraway constellations. In one of those buildings, thought Maxwell, was his father. At some point, the train blew a sharp whistle and pulled into a busy train yard just north of a tall brick building with an even taller clock tower. The time was 5:03 a.m.

When the train came to a full stop, a bullman and a police officer were waiting for them. The bullman was short and broad backed. He wore black overalls and his expression was ambitious, even happy. I've been waiting all day for this shit, it seemed to say. The police officer, regardless of the humidity, wore a thin black wool coat over his uniform. He was tall and blond; his expression was bony, impassive. In fact, Maxwell sensed that he wasn't even thinking at all. Then the three older boys from Iowa hopped off and ran full speed into the train yard, each in a separate direction and each running in his own way, like dusky fugitives who had long ago arranged a secret place to meet up and plan their next futile crime.

Maxwell watched them run away with a sense of betrayal, realizing much too late that they had used him as a red herring. When the bullman climbed into the boxcar and lunged at him, he felt anger, of course, but stronger than anger was shock. Half-stunned, he managed to shove the bullman. Then, as the bull-man fell over backward into the train yard, and the police officer pulled a long black truncheon from under his wool coat, Max-well slid the boxcar door shut. When they manage to open it, he thought, I'll take off like the others. Yet, some seconds later, he heard something like a bark that he only later understood was a kind of laugh, and the boxcar door locking shut. Then there was total darkness. Maxwell took out his flashlight, and in the dust trapped by the white beam he too saw irrefutable proof, as those ancient Greeks liked to say, of the paramāṇu.

LOST CITY

October 2005

We have plowed the sea, said Javier quite out of the blue or possibly as a continuation of things already said. Then, without explaining what it was he was trying to say, he looked in the rearview mirror at the shrinking city and then at the highway stretching out into the southern distance ahead of them and added, I-57, right?

That morning, as they passed Champaign Urbana and then Humboldt in an old black Cadillac borrowed from Romário, they discussed Adana Moreau and her life, about which, like the lives of those Chilean "disappeared" during the brutal Pinochet regime, next to nothing was known. Then they speculated again about the whereabouts of Maxwell Moreau and about the motives that might have compelled him to either evacuate or stay in New Orleans during those last days before the Storm. For six weeks, as Javier and Saul planned the trip to New Orleans, they searched countless online Missing Persons boards, forums, and lists for news about Maxwell Moreau, but he wasn't mentioned anywhere. They also left countless posts, but nobody responded. An area of disaster, Javier explained a few miles outside of Champaign Urbana, takes on an attracting force for all those people who benefit from historical uncertainty, and an expelling force for many others, especially for those who are cheated or forgotten and end up as displaced, as desplazados.

I think I understand what you mean, Saul then said to Javier, that I should prepare for the possibility that we might not find Maxwell Moreau. That he might even be dead. I've read reports that bodies are still being found every day, he added, but they both already knew what those reports contained. Javier nodded several times, without saying anything, and Saul was abruptly aware of the futility of their search.

Then, almost without thinking, Saul said, what did you mean earlier when you said, "We have plowed the sea"? I've never heard it before, but it still reminds me of something my grandfather might say.

I don't think I've ever heard him say it, said Javier, but it does sound like him, doesn't it? It's rumored to be Simón Bolivar's last words. I think I first saw it in a newspaper in Peru or maybe on one of those walls in the outskirts of Quito that are plastered with cheap revolutionary slogans and old indigenous proverbs, walls at war with one another come to think of it; in any case, it's something I find myself repeating when I close my eyes or when I can't afford to blink, when looking for someone who has left behind only a few traces or maybe none at all.

In Effingham, they stopped for breakfast at a small diner on Avenue of Mid-America. Saul ordered a ham and cheese omelet and a cup of coffee. Javier ordered a corn beef sandwich, fries, and a cup of coffee. Javier talked about his job at the *Chicago Tribune*, which was, in his opinion, going well and about one of his coworkers, a half white, half Guatemalan reporter in her twenties who had learned Spanish not from her parents, who were told by a white 1st grade teacher to stop speaking to their children in Spanish, but by watching old movies on Univision after they had gone to bed. Then Saul talked about his favorite childhood movie, *Godzilla*, and its unknown actresses, cities in flame, overcrowded hospitals, and irradiated children, a movie that in 1954 had made Japanese WWII veterans leave the theater before they were caught weeping.

After breakfast they got back in the car and sped south down I-57. They passed Mount Vernon, West Frankfort, and Future City. Just after Future City they crossed a bridge over the Mississippi River. At some point, Saul fell asleep and dreamed of an elevator building itself, slowly, straight out into space. When he opened his eyes, the sun was bright and they were on another bridge crossing the Mississippi River again. They gazed at the tall trees that lined the muddy riverbank and beyond that, to the southeast, the yellow-burned paper skyline of Memphis. To the northeast was an enormous bronze and glass-glazed pyramid. The pyramid looked outlandishly foreign on the banks of the Mississippi River yet at the same time furiously (even a little desperately) American, a copy of a copy of a copy.

Saul then thought of the ancient city of Memphis. The Memphis submerged under sand and stone. The Memphis undeniably wiped from the "slate of time" as his grandfather might say. Then, unexpectedly and all at once, he was struck with the memory of his grandfather telling him that his parents had once gone to Egypt. They had taken a flight from Tel Aviv to Cairo in 1971 or 1972. This happened before I was born, so it didn't happen to me, he thought as the car sped through half-empty streets, I didn't see anything, I didn't walk through the arid cranial streets of Cairo with them, I didn't travel with them down lonely desert roads in a white taxi to visit the clustered and interminable pyramids surrounding Cairo, I didn't listen to my parents' voices as they haggled in the Khan el-Khalili bazaar for those scraps of black Egyptian linen with which I had at some point after their deaths wrapped those five photographs before placing them in a small wooden school box. Did any of that even happen? he then thought. The trip to Egypt? His grandfather's telling of the trip? In what version of the past had his parents taken a flight from Tel Aviv to Cairo in 1971 or 1972? In what permutations of the past were they now being arranged as shadows or ghosts? He would never know. There was no one left to ask.

Some minutes later, they pulled into the parking lot of a Walmart. They purchased flashlights, jugs of distilled water, dehydrated food, a single burner propane stove, snacks, two first aid kits, an emergency hand crank radio, two coolers, a camping lantern, antiseptic cream, and water boots. The supplies were for those residents of New Orleans who were starting to trickle back into the city.

For the first time in my life, Javier said as he picked up a package of three flashlights, I'm not going somewhere for the disaster but for the recovery, at which point he fell silent.

Since the National Guard was enforcing a sunset curfew in New Orleans, they decided to spend the night in Memphis. As Javier drove to the Sheraton Memphis Downtown Hotel, Saul called Maxwell Moreau's number. The landline was still dead. Since the Storm he had called it three or four times a day, but it was always dead.

After checking into the hotel, they wandered the city on foot, talking nonstop. In the course of nearly two hours, observed Saul, Javier repeated the words *piranha* twice, the word *earthquake* three times, the word *misinformation* three times, the words *Lago Agrio oil field* four times, the words *Ryszard Kapuœściński* twice and the words *George W. Bush* five times.

Without meaning to, they ended up in front of Sun Studio, an unremarkable two-story brick building, where, so the building advertised, rock & roll had been born. We don't have to take a tour, said Javier, I just want to see it. For a few minutes, they stood under a giant yellow guitar fastened to the side of the building and watched as couples in elegant faux-cowboy boots passed by. Later, as they drank beer and ate catfish, hushpuppies, and coleslaw in a crowded restaurant, Javier admitted to Saul that even though he had only been away for ten years, the United States was *unrecognizable* to him. Maybe, it was the fake pyramid or the big box store (the colors too bright or somehow wrong), or the giant guitar or the lonely prisons along the side of the highway. Or maybe it was something else entirely. He didn't know.

Once, while in a small dive bar in Quito, he met an Ecuadorian ecologist who had studied in Boston and they started trading notes about the United States. I don't remember anything I told him, said Javier, probably something stupid about pleasure or capitalism, but I do remember exactly what he told me. According to the Ecuadorian ecologist, the United States was, in fact, a hysterical reality show that took place entirely in a giant marble room where four hundred naked and oiled billionaires took turns fucking each other over and over again, sometimes with deep, green-eyed affection and other times as a form of earth-shattering vengeance, but always against a grotesque altar of iron and gold. And no matter how much your people suffer, he told me, they can't keep their eyes off them. Your country, your empire, is going to entertain itself to death.

Saul said it was a little different for him. Something Kafkaesque had happened to him, but that was a cheap way to put it. In any case, at some point, something hornet-like had burrowed under his skin so quietly and so slowly that he hadn't even noticed until one morning he woke up, looked in the mirror, and saw that he was an American.

★ ★ ★

They passed Crystal Spring, Bogue Chitto, and Amite City. The sun was white and volatile, like camphor. At one in the afternoon, they passed Ponchatoula. Then the highway began to climb before turning into a series of long bridges that shot straight through a half submerged, half wild landscape full of waterways and dark green islets and swamps with colossus cypress trees broken like toothpicks and shacks in various stages of ruin. On the half-sunken tin roof of one shack, an egret stood motionless, its spear-like beak aimed at something below the still surface of the water, its hesitance and vulnerability constituting a state of grace. To the south, power lines ran through the swamplands and parallel to a rail line, where it was possible to make out the silver flash of an Amtrak train. At some point, they merged onto I-10 and joined the flatbed trucks and work vans and emergency vehicles all heading east, toward the swaying, rippling city of New Orleans, like a procession of sad caravans.

They did not look back at the combat-armed National Guardsman who waved them through the checkpoint with an impatient, even skeptical, flick of his hand, nor did they look in the rearview mirror at the deserted street blanketed in greenish-yellow film or the long snake-like roots of fallen oaks or the magnolia trees stripped of their flesh like skeletons wandering a wasteland as dreamed by Bosch, nor did they every so often gaze up at the white ballistic sun shining through the dusty car windows; instead they stared wordlessly ahead as the car teetered and swerved among potholes and piles of debris. They passed rows of abandoned cars that looked like strange and shattered undersea vessels run aground, and they saw rows of homes that were now just ruins casting shadows of their own destruction before them, fractured shadows creeping imperceptibly toward sidewalks and streets filled with bulging, sickening refrigerators and flood-soaked furniture and shattered porcelain and rusty pipes and rusty bicycles and drywall covered in black mold and dark green mold and clothes and CDs and DVDs and television sets and moldy curtains and moldy rugs and shoes and children's toys, cracked and peeling, painstakingly abandoned during those last hours before the Storm.

And yet, thought Saul, fairly shaken, there were no people. He felt as if he were seeing things in a daydream or in a half-awakened state; there were no people at all, only streets and streets of desolation. Javier, however, radiated enviable calm, his hands resting carefully on the wheel, his lips turned slightly outward like he was about to smile or say something conclusive, his eyes fixed on the road ahead and shining with the serene intensity of an explorer. Then, suddenly, he slammed on the brakes, and right in the center of South Telemachus Street or what remained of South Telemachus Street, they finally saw a person—a man walking a dog and holding a machete. As he passed the Cadillac, he raised the weapon with a vigilant and hermit-like air, somewhat startled by the sudden presence of others. Then, as he continued to walk, he turned to face them, smiled, raised the machete higher still, and then waved it back and forth, back and forth, as if to say bienvenidos to the end of the world. A few moments later, the man and the dog disappeared back into the ruins of the city.

We made a mistake coming here, said Saul to Javier as he stood paralyzed by the sight of Maxwell Moreau's two-story cottage on 209 South Telemachus Street—the address Victoria Ortiz had given Javier in mid-July—to which Javier responded by placing a hand on his shoulder, saying, it's too late for that, pana, and heading up the five steps to the front porch. Before following him, Saul blinked, closed his mouth, and held his breath for a few seconds to shut out the swarming flies and the smell of rot enveloping the neighborhood like a toxic fog that had drifted in from another dimension.

★ ★ ★

Maxwell Moreau's two-story cottage was painted a light but vibrant blue. The narrow front yard was tangled with dying grass and dying exotic plants and a somehow still-thriving banana tree. At some point after the Storm, someone had spray-painted a large X with an indecipherable array of numbers and letters on the façade. The front door was half-ajar. Inside, the walls were marked with green waterlines and blooming with black mold and peeling as though suffering from leprosy. The hardwood flooring was caked in mud and warped. On one side of the living room was a moldy couch, overturned chairs, and a flaking coffee table made from old railway ties. On the other side of the living room there was a huge hole in the wall, through which long vines, like tentacles, had entered the house.

He did not go into the kitchen. From the threshold he could see a small rotting kitchen table set for one and a green glass vase holding the stems of dead flowers, a sad still life, thought Saul, that touched him deeply because of the loss it radiated.

Upstairs there was a sparse office with a floor lamp, an old bookcase stacked with used books, and an ornate oak desk in front of a boarded window. On the floor of the office were notebooks full of indecipherable (at least to Saul) equations and diagrams and a photograph of a group of young men and women in a desert, tired and happy, dressed in beige and red shirts and with large backpacks placed at their feet like they had just ended a long trek. Although the desert was unfamiliar and the people in the photograph strangers, Saul suddenly longed to join them. On the back of the photo, in pen, someone (in all likelihood Maxwell Moreau) had written *Atacama Desert, 1999.*

Javier called to him from a balcony off the bedroom. On the balcony was a pile of dirty clothes, a sleeping bag, a red folding chair, half-empty jugs of water, canned food, and a single propane stove. I checked each room, said Javier, and even the attic. Thankfully, there are no bodies in the house and it looks like he camped out on the balcony after the Storm. Don't worry, pana, maybe he left at some point and is still planning on coming back.

Of course, thought Saul somberly as he stared down into the ruins of South Telemachus Street, there were other possibilities: maybe he hadn't survived the Storm and someone had already removed his body, or maybe he had escaped to Houston or Atlanta and then took a connecting flight to Santiago or Madrid or any of the other vast old cities across the Atlantic Ocean that Maxwell Moreau had visited throughout his life, biding his time until he could return (if he could even return), his once immaculate gray and black hair now unkempt, with only a notebook full of equations to his name, like one of those 16th century astronomers condemned by the Holy Roman Empire and exiled to spend the rest of his years in the dark green and ice-blue forests of Denmark or in one of those ancient frontier villages in Lithuania, places diffused by rain and snow and clouds like ground glass, in other words, fractured, impossible places to study the stars. Or maybe it wasn't like any of that at all, thought Saul. Maybe Maxwell Moreau was just simply visiting someone, maybe an old German physicist living in Berlin or Vienna who would chuckle at the sight of his long-lost friend as he walked through the arrival gates.

In the office, they wrote a note with their contact information and placed it on the oak desk in the hopes that Maxwell Moreau would return and find it. Afterward, they went for a walk around the neighborhood, half expecting to see a tall theoretical physicist emerging from the ruins of the city. They walked through a twisting maze of streets blocked by debris and wreckage, passing one-story shotgun homes and vacant lots out of which every so often there rose half-stripped oak trees and abandoned dogs, half-feral and shy, hurrying under homes or down old railway tracks.

At some point, near the banks of a low-lying bayou which

ran through the neighborhood, they came across the wreckage of a red helicopter. At the end of the bayou, there was an empty post office, a flatbed truck full of scrap metal, a blue tent, and three black sleeping bags. On one of the sleeping bags was a high school literature textbook, its cover full of random words of poetry in cursive and illustrations of old men with white beards, suggesting ridiculously, thought Saul, that literature had somehow only emerged from the fog of the Renaissance. Pickers, said Javier, who probably just arrived here from who knows where to rummage through the remains.

Javier picked up the book, opened its cover, and read a name on the inside. Rosa Salinas, he said, at which point Saul envisioned a picker named Rosa Salinas defiantly hitchhiking through the swampy fields of Louisiana, bowed by the happy weight of a literature textbook stuffed into her backpack.

Farther south, near a red pickup truck parked in the middle of the street, they came across a small group of workers who were cooking vegetables and chicken on a portable grill, the smoke hazing across the street. Javier spoke to them in Spanish for a few minutes. Later, as they walked back down South Telemachus Street, Javier told Saul that the workers were undocumented Hondurans and that they had already been in the city for a few weeks. They found work gutting and repairing homes. The money was good, but the city was not what they had expected. What had they expected? asked Saul. An American city, said Javier.

On South Telemachus Street, on the dilapidated front porch of a half-gutted sea-green shotgun house, they saw a bald man in his seventies wearing cargo pants, work goggles, and a half-mask respirator. The man, who waved the moment he saw them walking by, lost no time taking off his goggles and pulling the half-mask respirator down to his neck before introducing himself. Aaron Douglas, he said with a smile. Wasn't there a painter named Aaron Douglas? asked Javier, careful to step around a pile of moldy drywall. Right, the bald man said, a distant ancestor and one of my mom's favorite artists. Javier then introduced himself as a reporter from the *Chicago Tribune* and explained that they were looking for a friend who lived nearby, a retired theoretical physicist, and then he gave the bald man Maxwell Moreau's description and address.

And you thought you'd find him back here? said the bald man. There's nobody else on this entire block except me, a few stray dogs, and those fool kids with M-16s driving around in National Guard Humvees. He said, I'm sorry, truly sorry you came all this way, but there are a lot of missing people these days. I wish I knew him so I'd have something to tell you. I wish I knew the fate of everybody on this godforsaken street, he then added with a tone of sadness.

Javier pulled out a small digital recorder. He then said, is this okay? The bald man looked at them with a thoughtful curious smile, and then he said, that's fine, I could use a break anyway. It took Saul a moment to understand that Javier was implying that the bald man tell his story of the Storm. There was nothing Saul could do to change the topic or stop it. So he waited and watched them in silence, listening at first to the noises that seemed then so unexpected on that otherwise terribly silent street: a song playing on a distant radio, the low grumbling of a tractor nearby, a solitary bird of paradise trilling from an exposed roof beam.

Aaron Douglas shared his story. He was from New Orleans and had worked for a long time as a bartender, first in run-of-the-mill neighborhood joints, and then, when his kids were a bit older, at a few lavish restaurants in the French Quarter, until he decided to go back to school to be a lawyer, which had been his original idea all along. After law school, he served as a public defender with some success for nearly two decades before retiring in late 2001. His wife, Eulalie, was originally from a small town in Kansas and had taught music in an elementary school for some thirty years before retiring in 1998. For the most part, they could be found in New Orleans, but sometimes they spent their summers in Seattle with their daughter and grandkids. But this summer they hadn't gone anywhere, at least not until they were forced to leave the city by gunpoint. Yes, they stayed. They were holdouts. They found safety in a neighbor's second-story duplex.

The Flood was like a slow-motion nuclear bomb. You could feel the end from a mile away. Afterward, when it was clear the city was destroyed and had started to drain, soldiers started showing up in Humvees right through the water, pointing guns at people, making those who had stayed leave their homes. A boy, nineteen or twenty, with a cleanly shaved head pointed an M-16 at him, then his wife, and told them they had to evacuate within three hours. Instead of food, water, medical attention, and buses, they sent soldiers. Like in Baghdad. Because the American government only knows how to respond to a crisis in one way, whether in Baghdad or New Orleans.

Still, they were more fortunate than others. A lot of people died here, he said, and many more are still forced to live like refugees in their own damn country. *Refugees.* That's what all the major television networks said about us. Refugees. Tax-paying citizens, black folks, refugees. They couldn't say it enough.

We plan on staying with friends in Baton Rouge, said Aaron Douglas, but as soon as this house is ready we're moving back. You know at first, I didn't want to return, I wanted to stay in Seattle where we have family and where we could start over. Why the hell return to any of this? But my wife wanted to. She said we didn't have a choice. We fought for weeks and weeks about it, he said—isolated in his own words—and I came to finally remember and understand one singular fact about my wife: she was a little girl during the Dust Bowl. Her earliest memories are of vast clouds of dust, horizons of dust, dust in her eyes and layers of dust under her small fingernails, in the lining of her mouth and nostrils, and even in her dreams. Dust that brought hunger and dust that even took her baby sister's life one August morning. Something like that happens to you as a child and it becomes almost impossible to separate yourself from the event. It lives and breathes in your bones and blood, and you live in its memory, if that makes any sense to you, Javier. My wife's family eventually left Kansas and they never returned because there was nothing to return to. Sure, my family suffered through a few hurricanes, but the city always endured. Maybe this time it won't. I don't know. None of that matters right now. What matters is that I finally came to understand that my wife would never be chased out of another home for as long as she lives.

When they got back to the car, Javier said he had to meet up with a colleague. They drove to a bar called Molly's in the French Quarter. The bar was long, dark. On the bar and at each table, there were candles burning. There were six other people, none of whom, thought Saul, were Maxwell Moreau. On a bar stool near the front doors, Javier saw his colleague. They shook hands and then he introduced himself to Saul.

The photojournalist's name was Roberto Herrera and he was originally from Santa Fe, but hadn't been back in some time. For the foreseeable future, he would be staying in New Orleans. It was a welcome change of pace. His previous assignment had been to follow troops fighting insurgents in the Euphrates River valley in Iraq. The photojournalist's face was thin and long, his short black beard giving him a serious look, yet he was dressed like a tourist who was taking a hiatus from a very serious life.

Over beers, Javier and Roberto talked about a colleague of theirs who was stuck in an impossible situation in Mosul. When they were all finished, they went outside and unloaded the supplies from the Cadillac to Roberto's jeep parked out front. Afterward, the photojournalist took out a cigarette and handed one to Javier, who lit it with a small lighter. Saul couldn't remember just then if Javier smoked or not. When the photojournalist tried to hand one to Saul, he shook his head and said, no thank you. Then the photojournalist lit a cigarette and blew smoke rings, bluish nimbuses that dissolved in the fading yellow light of that long colonial street. I have to quit this shit, he said to Saul and raised his hand in a gesture of surrender. Then at some point Javier told Roberto that they should get going if they were going to drop off the supplies and get a little work done before the curfew. They both got into the jeep and Javier said, alright, pana, we'll be back in a few hours, then we'll call it a day. The jeep sped down the street and Saul spent a few seconds gazing after it, thinking the whole time that he should've taken the cigarette from the photojournalist, then, later, as he sat at the candlelit bar reading an old, yellowed copy of the *Times-Picayune*, the words, at times, floating weightlessly above the pages like a hologram of granulated ash, thinking that it actually didn't matter one way or another.

A few hours later, just after sunset and the city-wide curfew, Javier returned alone and they drove to their hotel in the Lower Garden District through streets flanked by old Hellenistic buildings, most of which were empty and dark, but a few of which were lit with red or pale yellow light bulbs on the front porch or lit dimly inside with candles behind half-parted window curtains, as if it were another century, the 16th or the 22nd century, a sclerotic century, burning at its edges, encased rib cage–like in disaster.

The hotel, Javier explained as he drove, really wasn't a hotel at all, but a large Victorian home owned by a famous music producer whom the photojournalist had put Javier in contact with and who had temporarily converted the building into a type of communal space for volunteers and journalists.

They took a small clean room on the second floor equipped with two air mattresses. A second-story balcony was accessible by a door painted green and purple. Javier stretched out on the air mattress nearest the balcony and closed his eyes.

Saul took a very cold shower. In a small shaving mirror in the shower he caught a glimpse of himself and noticed that there were semicircles under his eyes and that he had black stubble. I don't look like myself, he thought. His gaze was, at any rate, strained, surprised, and slightly helpless, as if he had not quite yet grasped that something elemental, something quantum, like the direction of wind, had changed since his grandfather's death.

What other probabilities and selves run in my veins? he thought.

Later, as he dried off—the rotting smell of the city still clinging to him—he thought of those other versions of himself: one who had presumably died with his parents on bus 311 traveling to Tel Aviv, one who still lived in Israel and corresponded with his American grandfather through postcards, another who was a solitary but otherwise untroubled hotel concierge in a foreign country, and yet another who hadn't listened to Javier when, some weeks earlier, he had convinced him that they should come to this half-drowned city in a futile search for Maxwell Moreau. Maybe, he then thought, those still-living Sauls also sometimes think of me. Maybe not. By the time he returned to the room, Javier was already fast asleep.

A muffled noise woke Saul and he saw a flicker of movement—the movement of a floating ember—and realized that Javier was smoking just beyond the threshold of the balcony door. What time is it? he asked, yawning. Javier turned around, a little surprised, and said, shit, pana, sorry, I didn't mean to wake you. It's okay, he said, what time is it? It's 2:00 a.m. or maybe 3:00 a.m., I don't know. Saul got out of bed and went to the porch to join Javier. I woke up to take a piss and couldn't fall back asleep, said Javier. For some reason, I was just lying there in bed and I was struck with the strange urgency to call your grandfather and ask him something about his World War II book. *On Dreams and Tombs*, said Saul without much surprise, especially now that he knew his grandfather and Javier had shared a close-knit—even collaborative—friendship. Yes, that one, he said and fixed his eyes on Saul. Anyway, he continued, I suppose it's quite a normal thing to want to do, especially in the middle of the night. To call the dead? said Saul and he smiled a little to tease Javier and to help ease his mind. He then made a corresponding gesture with his hand to indicate that he would like to take a drag from Javier's cigarette. Javier handed him the cigarette. Saul leaned against the porch, one elbow propped on the railing, and took a small drag.

It's really quite a normal thing to want to do, he thought, in the middle of the night or even during the day, in fact, he too sometimes wanted to call the dead, his parents for one, whose voices he could never remember, voices as foreign to him now as a sprawling city in the desert. And, yes, he also sometimes wanted to call his grandfather, whose impatient gravel-like voice had filled his childhood like a long soliloquy.

After a short silence, he said, what did you want to ask him?

I wanted to ask him about the Sicilian soldier he interviewed for the book, said Javier, do you remember him? I wanted to ask him how he got that Sicilian soldier to talk about the war. The soldier had kept silent his entire life about the war. He didn't share any details with his wife, his siblings, his children, though we end up telling our children so little, even now I spend my days and nights thinking about what to tell Maya and what not to tell her, pana, there are far too many consequences for even the smallest things you tell or don't tell your kids. He served in Sicily in the Italian 6th Army under Alfredo Guzzoni and then later immigrated to the States, first to Cleveland, then Chicago, and telling anyone anything would've risked rebuke or even implication, especially from Americans who had served or lost loved ones during the war, it would've risked friendships and jobs, even though in the end he had done so little during the war—he admitted to killing a British soldier, if I remember correctly, but he wasn't a war criminal by any stretch of the imagination—and was by then an American citizen anyway.

Still, his silence was completely understandable. You can't blame him. I've met people like that Sicilian soldier all over Latin America, he said.

The streetlight flickered and the air began to buzz, like a swarm of insects was surrounding the house. It's been doing that all night, said Javier.

I might have an answer for you, said Saul suddenly and then he smiled. Yeah? said Javier, lifting both of his heavy eyebrows.

Giorgio de Chirico, said Saul, or, rather, one of his paintings, *The Anxious Journey.* That's how *we* got him to talk about the war. What? said Javier and he fixed his eyes on Saul with bewilderment. Yeah, I played a small accidental role in that interview, and I remember it exactly too, said Saul. I went with my grandfather to Park Ridge where the Sicilian soldier, or, rather, ex-soldier, lived. I think I was eight or nine. And you're right about him by the way. He *was* afraid of rebuke, and also wary of the way Americans might perceive him. In short, he was nervous about the whole thing, even though my grandfather and him had already been friends for a few years. But just imagine, said Saul, you're an ex-Axis soldier and a Jewish American historian shows up with his orphaned Israeli grandkid and asks you to violate a promise you made to yourself to keep silent. Then he added: and all just for the sake of a history book only a few people would read anyway.

Exactly, said Javier, that's the puzzle to me.

Well, said Saul, by then it was the fifth time my grandfather had paid a visit to the Sicilian ex-soldier with the intent of asking about the war, but this was the first time he had brought me. He offered me cookies and Coke to make sure I was comfortable. It's really strange how adults treat orphans, said Saul, as if, somehow, they were also at fault for their orphanhood. And, come to think of it, maybe he was at fault for someone's orphanhood since, as you said, he had killed a British soldier.

He showed us pictures of his family, his elderly parents in Sicily, his daughter who had recently graduated as a lawyer, and his son who worked in a small theater in the city. He was very proud of both of them. He also showed us his shop in the garage where he tinkered with old neon signs and computers. Of course, he was stalling. Anyway, at some point, I asked about a framed print of Giorgio de Chirico's *The Anxious Journey* hanging in the garage. I didn't know the name of the painting at the time.

The Sicilian ex-soldier smiled and explained that it was a print he'd bought at the MOMA just a few years back during a trip with his wife to New York City. *The Anxious Journey* was a claustrophobic, surreal painting of an ominous locomotive behind a brick wall in the background and in the foreground a series of colonnades *which led to nothing and opened onto nothing*, which is exactly how the Sicilian ex-soldier described it. He clearly respected the artist, a fellow Italian, greatly, and these were the exact words about the painting my grandfather later recorded in his notes, but I don't think they appear in the book. His editor must've cut it or maybe he did later, I don't remember, which is why you wouldn't know about the painting anyway.

My grandfather then said, Saul here likes the print, and I do too, Carlo, but what compelled you to buy it out of all the other posters at the MOMA gift shop? As if jolted suddenly by a brief electric charge the Sicilian ex-soldier started talking about the war. During the evacuation of Sicily in the summer of 1943, he had been separated from his battalion for a day and a night. It was a real mess, he told us, especially as the Allies under Patton moved toward Messina. Exhausted and fearful of the advancing Allies he sought safety in an abandoned town on a large hill with a steep winding descent toward a shore full of drying seagrass and corpses of starfish and men tossed up by the waves. The town was really just collapsing buildings and empty streets and stray wolfish dogs, like here, said Saul, come to think of it, like this city.

In any case, said Saul, he walked around the town for some time like a sleepwalker and he began to admire all the still-standing doors which had once given purpose to now ruined buildings—"doors which led to nothing and opened onto nothing and which gave me the terrible sense that I was lost inside of something monstrous, inaccessible, and withdrawn from the rest of the world." Those were his exact words and that is what my grandfather recorded and later quoted in the book.

Later that night, continued Saul, the Italian soldier ate the last of his rations and slept in an empty niche in a cemetery bordering that town and another, dreaming of a dark, pristine forest in the north of Italy and a wolf wearing a medieval suit of armor, which is where the title of the book, *On Dreams and Tombs*, actually originated. The Sicilian ex-soldier never said it outright, but it was perfectly clear to me even at that age that *The Anxious Journey* by Giorgio de Chirico and that one day and night during the evacuation of Sicily were the same in his memory. That's why he used the same words to describe both, but only my grandfather and I would ever know that.

With that one accidental question he granted my grandfather and me a little trust. In turn, my grandfather was able to get him to talk. It was like that with so many people he knew and interviewed. People loved to tell him everything, even at their own peril, said Saul and he laughed and handed the cigarette back to Javier.

The next morning when Saul woke up, Javier was gone. On the dresser there was a note that said, *back later, I'd check the train station and the Red Cross in the French Quarter.*

Saul went to the kitchen where he sat at a small rectangular table, sipping coffee. He then left the house, carrying the manuscript for *A Model Earth* in a backpack, walking first along Prytania Street, then Jackson Avenue, and finally along Simón Bolívar. The city at that hour, like no other city he had ever been to, was hollowed-out, blurred, and utterly empty, as if he were walking through the sulfurous vapors of another Earth. An Earth, in fact, as imagined by Adana Moreau. Then he thought of what little remained of her, if anything, in the ruins of the city. He thought of her exile, her stillness and dissension, her grace, and her total abandonment to science fiction, and he felt a surge of affection for her traveling back through the years, to 1929. Time—and all the killing hours it contained—had erased his parents, but it hadn't yet erased Adana Moreau or his grand-father, incredibly too, it hadn't yet erased the manuscript that somehow linked them and which he now carried like a porter through an extraterrestrial landscape.

At the train station, he stood near the Amtrak counter and watched for Maxwell Moreau in the small crowds of passengers disembarking. He saw a distressed young woman with an army backpack hurrying up the platform. He saw a cheerful-looking office worker with rolled up shirtsleeves approach another, older man, who looked as if he hadn't slept in days and who began openly to cry. He saw a volunteer carrying a box marked *donations* in large black letters. Above the Amtrak counter the hands of a giant stainless-steel clock were frozen at 4:30.

On Canal Street he talked to two busy Red Cross volunteers who didn't have any records for Maxwell Moreau, but who took Saul's contact information and Maxwell Moreau's address, in case anybody knew his whereabouts.

In a small bookstore on Chartres Street, he looked through a collection of magazines and newspapers. First he looked through stories of evacuees and then the stories of those who had stayed behind, then the death notices. Nothing about Maxwell Moreau.

Afterward, he talked to the owner of the bookstore, a fatigued and sympathetic man who explained that he had returned to the city as soon as possible to keep the bookstore going and who apologized to Saul. He didn't know any theoretical physicists named Maxwell Moreau but would keep his eye out for him. Saul thanked him and bought a copy of *The Invention of Morel* by Adolfo Bioy Casares, a novel about a fugitive hiding on a deserted island somewhere in Polynesia who discovers a machine capable of reproducing reality, a novel he had already read and liked some years earlier, but which, right then, in the cavernous blue light spilling in through the front glass windows of the bookstore, seemed entirely new to him.

Later, for lunch, he ate a turkey sandwich purchased from a small, busy corner store called Verti Marte. While he ate, he sat on a curb across the street and watched people go in and out of the corner store, a figure wearing a hazmat suit and a Darth Vader helmet, strippers in high heels and floral skirts and the off-duty military men following them, and the dazed volunteers who, Saul thought with a sense of fatalism that surprised him, had probably arrived just before nightfall from Seattle or Denver or Cedar Rapids and would return the following week.

Later still, as Saul stood in front of a hotel on Royal Street, gazing at hundreds of Post-it notes, notecards, notebook paper, and ripped pieces of cardboard taped onto the hotel's front window and scribbled with the names of missing family members and friends, he had the terrible Schrödinger-like sensation that Maxwell Moreau and, by the same logic, all those missing, were simultaneously right in front of him and somewhere else entirely; they were both at once lost and already found.

The following morning, Saul woke early. Javier was fast asleep in his clothes, a single blue bedsheet crumpled near his feet. Saul thought about waking him, but quickly decided against it.

Later that afternoon, after Javier had left yet again, Saul received a phone call from a professor of mathematics at the University of California who had seen Maxwell Moreau's name and Saul's contact on the Red Cross Missing Persons website. The mathematics professor, whose name was Robert Walsh, was originally from New Orleans. He didn't have any information for Saul but was eager to know if he had found Maxwell Moreau. Unfortunately, I still don't know where he is, said Saul.

Then, as if he had been caught in the middle of a hoax, Saul confessed that he had never actually met Maxwell Moreau. The story struck the mathematics professor as amusing and he asked why Saul wanted to find Maxwell Moreau in the first place. On the other end, there was the silence of someone between breaths, waiting for an answer, but Saul didn't say anything. It's okay, the mathematics professor said finally and with a little laugh, I get it, I once sought him out, too.

The story he then told, in short, was as follows: In 1980 when he was twenty and studying mathematics and physics on a study-abroad scholarship in Cambridge, a friend gave him a copy of *A Hidden Multitude*. He read it over the course of a single day, entirely awestruck, even if he understood little of it at the time. Still, he could sense even then that there was a *hidden center* concealed beneath the book's mathematical models and theories, just as the title suggested, and that the theoretical physicist who wrote it was struggling against something vast and terrifying. In other words, he was blazing a path into the unknown and the young student wanted to be a part of it. He didn't know it at the time, but there were many of them, young students—mathematicians and theoretical physicists alike—reading *A Hidden Multitude* as a rite of passage and defying their mentors and professors, who were unscrupulous in their feelings that they had already figured everything out. By the end of the '70s, physicists had very accurate theories of three of the four fundamental forces of nature, and there were prospects for merging quantum physics with

Einstein's theory of the fourth force, gravity, and then pulling everything together into what would be called the Theory of Everything or the Final Theory.

Many physicists and students were attracted to the idea that a Theory of Everything could unify all of physics. But, according to Maxwell Moreau's book, they were like intelligent fish in a pond who thought the entire universe was completely filled with water. Of course, from that day on the young mathematician was an enthusiastic supporter of Maxwell Moreau. So, when Robert Walsh heard that he was speaking at a physics conference in Brussels that summer, he saved and borrowed money to go. The conference itself was a type of ecology the young mathematician was unfamiliar with, and for the first two days he went from panel to speaker to meal with a trudging melancholy. But on the third day he went to see Maxwell Moreau speak in a small lecture hall at the Free University of Brussels and things started to pick up for him. From what he could tell, the audience in the lecture hall was divided between the old guard of physicists and the new, with which the young mathematician had already aligned himself. As he listened to Maxwell Moreau's lucid, remarkable lecture on parallel universes it seemed to him that the limits of physics had suddenly dissolved or that reality had imperceptibly changed and that he was one of the first to witness it.

After the lecture, when the young mathematician was finally able to introduce himself to Maxwell Moreau, he mentioned that he was from New Orleans and the theoretical physicist took an immediate interest in him. Afterward, they went for a walk through the Ixelles Cemetery. They did not talk about New Orleans, but as they walked the cemetery's calming and elegiac energy seemed to be a type of shared remembrance of both the bodies interred there and the distant crescent-shaped city itself. Instead they discussed a letter that Maxwell Moreau had recently received from a colleague with whose work the young mathematician was somewhat acquainted, a strange letter about the mathematical curiosities surrounding black holes and theoretical wormholes, which he then described in great detail.

He gets drunk and writes me letters, explained Maxwell Moreau and he laughed and the young mathematician laughed too, a cautious laugh, like he had not yet realized that great theoretical physicists were people made of flesh and blood and enamel, too.

Then they went into a bar and Maxwell Moreau ordered two beers and a plate of fries. As they drank and ate, the young mathematician talked about summer in Cambridge, which was an illusion of summer, and for some reason he talked for a long time about his charming yet turbulent father who had dropped out of high school to work on Gulf Coast oil rigs, and about his relationship with his girlfriend, which was, if he had to admit it, a type of prolonged distraction for both him and her.

In short, he talked about the life of a disoriented American student living abroad. Really, what he wanted to ask in that bar in Brussels but couldn't find the courage to ask was what Maxwell Moreau thought about all the rumors that he was a madman. Afterward, in front of the bar, they shook hands and the theoretical physicist went back to his hotel, somewhere in the north of the city, and the young mathematician decided to ditch the last night of the conference and he went to the Brussels Central Station and took a train to Antwerp instead.

The second and last time the mathematics professor saw Maxwell Moreau was during an international symposium in Los Angeles celebrating the 100th birth anniversary of Srinivasa Ramanujan, a famous self-trained mathematician from India. This was in 1987. He saw him in a muggy, crowded hallway outside of an auditorium talking to two mathematicians from New Delhi who had been invited to give speeches.

He recognized the theoretical physicist immediately and before he could think about what to do next, Maxwell Moreau had spotted him and was already walking over. They shook hands and he said, I heard you were teaching nearby, so I was hoping to run into you. The mathematics professor nodded and said, I didn't know you would be here, too.

By then, a good portion of Maxwell Moreau's work was beginning to circulate widely, especially by members of the new guard who considered it a type of infrastructure for their own work. So, in that crowded hallway full of detractors and admirers, the mathematics professor hadn't expected to be remembered. He hadn't expected anything to really happen at that symposium. Then Maxwell Moreau invited him to meet the two mathematicians from New Delhi, after which they resumed a conversation about infinity. Really, their conversation was a type of ode to Ramanujan.

As Walsh listened in silence, he started to feel worse and worse about standing there, like he was an imposter, and he excused himself and went to the bathroom, which was too bright and too small and smelled like cologne, piss, and fresh paint. The exact opposite of infinity, he remembered thinking. By the time he returned, the two Indian mathematicians were gone and Maxwell Moreau was standing by himself reading an old mass-market paperback with a cover of a cobalt blue, mineral green, and black nebula, like an immense burning tapestry, which the mathematics professor immediately assumed to be a book on cosmology or astrophysics, but which Maxwell Moreau explained was a novel called *The Seas of Eternity* written by Tomas Flores, a Mexican American science fiction writer who had died in obscurity in Nevada in 1977. He then told him it was a novel about space pirates.

Maxwell Moreau explained that his father had been a pirate in New Orleans. One of the characters in the novel reminds me of my father, he said. The mathematics professor tried to imagine his own drunken father standing at the helm of a ship with a great black flag, a surprisingly easy task. Shit, maybe my father was a pirate too, he said and they both laughed. Some minutes later, the two Indian mathematicians returned and Maxwell Moreau left with them. He never saw the theoretical physicist again.

Did you ever read *The Seas of Eternity*? asked Saul. Yes, said Robert Walsh, as it happened, some weeks afterward a package from Maxwell Moreau containing the novel arrived at my office at UCLA. Was it any good? asked Saul. The mathematics professor couldn't say. He wasn't familiar with science fiction. He had never read anything like it before. He then explained: there are star systems and landscapes as seen through spectral prisms, Euclidian landscapes, and wormholes and nameless galaxies where nameless creatures the size of planets roam the peripheral edges of solar systems, and there are irreconcilable time and space wars between three empires vaguely resembling the United States, the USSR, and Mexico, and also space pirates with synthetic eyes, synthetic penises, synthetic fever dreams, with an aura of feverish humanity who are forced to negotiate between life and death on a massive scale.

Toward the end of *The Seas of Eternity*, he found equations written in dark pencil on sheets of folded notebook paper. He wasn't sure if Maxwell Moreau had wanted him to find them or if he had forgotten all about them. In any case, he checked the equations night after night for nearly three sleepless months. It was a time in his life, he recalled, which seemed to pass through him like a rush of cool night air. Those equations, he said. They were all beautiful.

That night, when Javier finally returned to the house, Saul decided not to tell him about the mathematics professor. Instead, after Javier asked him if he had found anything new, Saul just shook his head no. Some seconds later he added: why are we still even here, we should go home, but Javier didn't respond.

Later, as Javier lay on the air mattress, gazing indistinctly at the ceiling with his arms crossed over his chest in a type of cryo-genic silence, Saul realized that both of them for some days had been reluctant to admit what sooner or later they would have to admit: that they would not find Maxwell Moreau and that Javier had used this trip, this false quixotic journey, entirely as a pretext for traveling to yet another ruined city. In the end, it hadn't been Saul's idea to come to the city. It had been Javier's because—as Saul understood more fully now—he wasn't driven by friendship, not by an interesting story about a recovering city that could be parceled, packaged, and sold to the highest bidder, or even a persistent, adolescent search for freedom, but rather by a *yearning for disaster*, a need to see himself and others at the imminent end of the world.

Disaster as obsession or addiction, thought Saul. Disaster as a symptom of something uncanny at work in the world: the Lago Agrio oil fields in Ecuador, the Tepito neighborhood of Mexico City where Javier went looking for Marina and her sick patients, the collapsing financial center of Buenos Aires, the aftermath of the great deluge of New Orleans. Disaster as the infrastructure of the world. Disaster as jet-black liquid enveloping his skin like oil. Disaster as guilt, self-reproach for earning a salary from disaster while in other places, other people with his same fore-head, earlobes, teeth, skin, and voice were invisible—displaced from time and history—as if a thousand-mile fog had settled over that southern continent.

But did he have any right to be angry with Javier? If he were to be honest with himself, or, at the very least, half-honest, was he any different? Didn't his own mind tunnel ceaselessly back to abandonment and disaster, to landscapes of the dead, to endlessly repeated images of a Kalashnikov rifle, his American mother, his foreign father, smoke, flesh, filth, bullets, an incinerated bus? Didn't his own mind also tunnel incessantly forward to all those vast and synthetic skies as imagined and portrayed by Isaac Asimov, Samuel R. Delany, Ursula K. Le Guin, William

Gibson, and, now, even Adana Moreau, skies set in motion by modern-day harbingers of disaster, skies awash in the mingling of human grays and dead alien stars?

My feeling is that you're addicted to disaster, said Saul after a long silence, and then, not being able to determine if Javier had heard him or was fast asleep, he went to the porch and looked out at the flickering streetlight, under which a rooster was moving in slow oracular steps, before adding rather more quietly, but I'm hardly one to talk.

You're probably right, pana, said Javier, after a long pause. Then he joined Saul on the porch, put both hands on the railing, and said, we're both a little fucked, aren't we?

The photojournalist and I found a corpse, he said, like the words were poisonous to him. A man, he said, young, or I think he was young, like us. We were taking photos in the Fairgrounds, a neighborhood northeast of Maxwell Moreau's house, and we came across an overturned canoe in a backyard full of high grass and weeds. The photojournalist turned the canoe over and there was the dead man, lying faceup. Both the severe humidity and time had already taken its toll, said Javier, his skin was blistered and already greenish-blue from decomposition, his abdomen swelled like a fat man, and dried blood covered his face. He smelled even worse, like a rotten egg. It was just shit, pana. There were no forms of identification. Maybe he died there or maybe the flood had placed him there. We don't know. But it was clear that he had drowned and that, at some point, someone else had covered him with the canoe.

I've seen similar things before, in other cities, in Mexico City and Buenos Aires, for example, but those places and events now suddenly feel like a daydream or like it happened to another version of me on a parallel Earth, just as you always say, pana. In any case we tried to call the morgue, then Kenyon International Emergency Services, the fucking failure of a disaster-relief company hired by the state to care for the dead, and even the police, but we couldn't get through to anyone.

We waited on the dead man's front steps. The sky was yellow and orange and violently red, like something, I remember thinking, out of a Neruda poem about an Aztec garden. In the end, nobody came for the dead body.

It's strange, pana, how all stories about the apocalypse are essentially the same, which is why I always end up writing the same goddamn story. So, yes, you're right in thinking I'm addicted to disaster. In fact, it comes with the territory. The whole fucking media is addicted to disaster and the money that comes pouring in during one. Not only that, but we are complicit in creating audiences with powerful addictions to disaster, to fear, self-righteousness, outrage, and vitriol. A real apocalypse would be the most cosmically lucrative reward for the media.

Or maybe, what I'm trying to say, pana, is that my job has taken its toll on me. On my family. Especially Maya. I know so little of my daughter and I can tell she already suspects that this is the case. It's even taken a toll on our friendship, hasn't it?

For a while neither of them said anything, both waiting expectantly for the other to speak, both listening to the erratic sounds of night—the occasional solitary footfalls, the faint insect-like buzzing of the single working streetlight, the distant and languid clip of sawteeth on lumber. It was a quarter to midnight and even from a distance Saul could tell that whoever was sawing would be doing so well into the night, until his eyes were cloudy with specks of light and dust, until his joints were stiff and his limbs like paper limbs, sawing, sawing.

This is the second or third time you've brought up Buenos Aires, said Saul finally. What happened there? Before, you told me you joined a street demonstration that turned brutal. I read your report on foreignpolicy.com that protestors were killed that day. Am I right to think that the dead man you found made you remember something terrible about Buenos Aires? Am I right to think your addiction started or ended there? Who were you with? asked Saul. What happened that day?

While covering the Argentine Depression toward the end of 2001, Javier began, I was invited by a senior editor at *Clarín* to take a tour of the Navy Mechanics School (ESMA), which was used as a secret detention center during the Dirty War. I told the editor it sounded interesting, but that I was running two dead-lines and it would have to wait. He just said, "Listen, Silva, the past devours the future, as you norteamericanos always say in your novels. I've already made the arrangements, so it's the least you can do. It's not a church. You don't have to cross yourself when you enter or leave."

Two days later, I went to ESMA. I was surprised to see gar-dens and walkways and colonnaded whitewashed buildings with red-tiled roofs. But, then again, pana, the State often conceals acts of treachery behind elegance, doesn't it? At some point, I was approached by a man in his late twenties. He introduced himself as Alejandro Marías, a taxi driver and occasional fixer for foreign journalists. Our mutual friend from *Clarín* had been unable to make the appointment. He had a touching smile and wore his hair to his chin, like someone out of an American film from the seventies, all of which contributed to his resemblance to "Che" Guevara, but the comparisons stopped there.

As we walked around the compound, Alejandro explained the similarities to the Terezín Nazi camp; some prisoners worked and were even entertained, especially when foreign journalists visited, while nearby others were tortured and killed. At ESMA, he told me, the prisoners were kept hooded and chained in tiny cells. They were tortured with water and electric cattle prods or taken on vuelos de la muerta, during which prisoners were drugged, weighted, stripped naked, and thrown from a plane into the ocean.

"So, they were disappeared," I said.

"Yes," he said, and his voice sounded very close, like an echo, and also very gentle, "into the abyss."

At some point, we went to the basement of ESMA. From outside I could hear the sound of high school kids playing in a nearby field.

"Also like Terezín," said Alejandro, "prisoners were forced to contact family members and tell them they were being treated well. There was a monitored telephone booth in the entrance. I remember just such a call from my mother."

I didn't say anything or ask anything just then. I suspected this was the story the senior editor at *Clarín* had wanted me to hear in the first place.

"We only spoke briefly," he said. "She asked me to tell her about my day and the days before that. I was eight at the time. I was staying with my grandmother. I'm sure I spoke of soccer, school, and cartoons. Then she told me about her days. She told me she was happy and watching good films and reading a lot. She was writing poems like she always did, and she promised to show them to me when she returned home. At some point, my grandmother heard me talking and came into the kitchen and took the receiver from me. My mother and grandmother spoke for a short time. After my grandmother hung up the phone, she told me that my mother was having 'a nice visit in Mar del Plata.' But then she sat at the kitchen table and started to weep inconsolably into her palms. Everybody, I remember thinking then at supersonic violent speeds, was lying to me."

"My mother, Sol Marías, stopped being a poet at ESMA," said Alejandro, sometime later as we walked the streets of San Telmo, a neighborhood I often visited during my trips to Buenos Aires, but, on that day, I felt like I was visiting it for the first time. Alejandro's parents had been organizers for a Marxist off-shoot of the anti-government Peronist movement. At that time, his father was in exile in France and his mother was a celebrated poet in underground circles sympathetic to that movement. I asked him what her poems were like.

"She wrote about eclipses of the sun, semblances, spectacles of entertainment in the face of political incoherence, impulses being starved of expression. They were modern poems and some of them even had drawings and were quite funny—she was a disciple of Nicanor Parra—but according to the regime they were seditious poems, they were reason enough to arrest her. She was seized midday as she walked to a corner grocer while passersby turned their heads."

We walked in silence for a few minutes and then we went to a narrow bar tucked into a building with a crumbling façade. We ordered beers and talked for some time about soccer and my great-uncle, the poet, Medardo Ángel Silva. As we paid our tab, Alejandro confessed, a little drunk, that when he told his mother at the age of fifteen that he wanted to be a journalist, she just looked at him, as if spitting out a mosquito, and said, "Avoid any profession involving printed words at all costs, mijo, before it's too late."

Shortly afterward, he quit school and started a type of poor man's apprenticeship with our mutual friend from *Clarín*, who was familiar with his mother's past and whose articles con-demning the Dirty War he had read in secret as a kid while sitting on a lonely curb outside a café long ago frequented by Borges.

I hired Alejandro as a fixer, continued Javier, and over the next two months he helped me set up interviews with laid-off teachers, waitresses, oil workers, two priests from the church of San Cayetano who were helping the unemployed, and a night watchman for a bank who told me he kept all his savings in a small lacquered box along with his great-grandmother's glass eye.

All over the city, like a shared dark secret, people were afflicted not only with the python-like constrictions of austerity, but also by fears of a literary and political nature. That is, pana, they were fears that afflicted both the self and the body politic, so that a person had trouble distinguishing one from the other. Fears of the self, a self *clothed* in the flesh of the State. As people waited in long bank lines or struggled to feed their families, they were once again asking themselves: Could I really push an enemy of the State from a plane into the bloodless sea? Could I risk being disappeared for my beliefs in a better life?

One afternoon, we went to a Chinese restaurant where he introduced me to three former oil workers who told me about the oil towns scrapped and abandoned after the privatization of the state-run oil company YPF in June 1993.

I asked them what they thought of the future of the country. One of the former oil workers said, "A better question is—in what kind of country are we living in right now?"

"A country full of orange-faced chantas like Menem and de la Rúa," said the man to his left, "*hollow men* willing to sell anything they can get their hands on."

"A country half in love with Peronism and half in love with death," said the man to his right.

"A labyrinth with no center," said Alejandro, quickly.

"See?" the former oil worker said to me. "How can we talk of the future when this is a country with no future, a country entirely dependent on the false myth of inexhaustible wealth, just like your country, che, a wealth once so great that my dad who worked the pampas his entire life told us as kids that you could kill any cow you wanted out of thousands just to eat the tongue."

Some days later, Alejandro invited me to go with him and his family on a day trip to San Antonio de Areco, just seventy miles outside of the city. His wife, Edin, was tall and had big green eyes and shoulder-length black hair combed straight. She drove and Alejandro sat next to her. I sat in the back seat with their three-year-old daughter, Sophia, who wore large round black sunglasses that hid her eyes and half her forehead, like a Mexican actress from the sixties. We headed northwest, through the empty pampas. To pass the time, Edin told jokes that stretched like rubber bands until, at some point, Alejandro and Sophia would explode into fits of laughter. I remember thinking then (or maybe I'm thinking it only now, pana) that this is what happy families did as they drove long distances, they told jokes and invented stories that made sense only to them, creating a rarified sense of space and time all their own. By comparison I felt rootless, mute.

We checked in at an estancia, a cattle ranch, just a few miles west of San Antonio de Areco's main plaza, and spent the afternoon with a few other families watching horse races and a gaucho sport involving crossbeams and small rings called corrida de sortija. Afterward, we bought ice cream bars and walked around. There was an outdoor pool, a playground, a large ringed barbecue pit, and a small lagoon crowded with noisy migratory birds. As we walked, Alejandro held his daughter in his arms and talked to her about the things they had seen that day. Despite all the excitement or maybe because of it, she fell asleep, still holding, but loosely, the small wooden stick from her ice cream bar, her head resting on the crook of Alejandro's sunburned neck. Alejandro kissed her forehead, which was damp with sweat. The sky turned violet and there were prairie shadows toward the pampas. On the shores of the lagoon, we listened to the migratory birds as they called out to each other, one by one.

On December 19th Alejandro and I drove from supermarket to supermarket in Buenos Aires, documenting as best we could what other foreign correspondents had by then already started calling *looting*, but it wasn't looting, pana, people were exhausted and starving and on the brink of something, yet, at that time, I couldn't figure out what, maybe—I thought as Alejandro drove and as I stared out the car window at people gathering on streets as if on the proscenium of a great theater, at helmeted officers firing tear gas, at dark buildings, at orange and red fires in the street that had been set ablaze, I suspected, by piqueteros—maybe they were on the brink of something like the destruction of a machine.

The following morning, after a quick breakfast, Alejandro and I made plans to visit Plaza de Mayo, where protestors were converging, in direct violation of the state of siege declared by De la Rúa, which suspended constitutional guarantees, and where the Federal Police would no doubt meet them in full force.

We parked Alejandro's taxi on the corner of Estados Unidos and Piedras, just south of the neighborhood of Monserrat. We walked north along Piedras, past closed storefronts covered in bright graffiti, car parks shaded with blue tarp, the Argentinian Puppet Museum, and apartment buildings with narrow, wrought-iron balconies packed with onlookers.

In the middle of Venezuela and Piedras there were burning tires and a man holding a sign that read PATRIA O BUITRES. Near the church of San Juan Bautista, we saw a man lying in the middle of the street while another man, possibly an emergency worker, placed a thin cloth over his mouth and then gave him CPR. Nearby, we ran into our mutual friend from *Clarín*. He was bent over and sweating. When he saw us, he held up his hand and said, "Ah, good, you two." He then told us the rumors that De la Rúa was "disconnected from reality" and that one of his ministers had found him just that morning in his office watching cartoons. "Fucking cartoons, che," he said and then waved us along.

We headed east down Avenida Hipólito Yrigoyen, avoiding

a knot of shirtless men wearing bandanas over their faces. At some point, we crossed a street flooded with chanting protestors, workers, and students banging on pots and pans, all marching toward Plaza de Mayo in a general atmosphere of festivity, as if they were in a carnival procession. As we neared the plaza, someone handed me a pot and a large wooden spoon.

A cacerolazo, said Javier some seconds later, is a sound. Let me put it another way, pana. To understand a cacerolazo, don't read about one. No, there are never enough words to tell the whole story. And don't look at photographs or watch a broadcast of one on a news channel. Images lie by what they omit: protestors being dragged away like pigs by riot police, even as they chant *we are not animals*, or lying on their backs in the street with blood pooling in their mouths, ears, and eye sockets, a burning car in the street, banners with red paint reading NO CAEMOS, NOS LEVANTAMOS, a small anemic sun made anemic by yellow-black smoke and acrid tear gas.

So, yes, pana, a cacerolazo is not a half-told story or a false image or a five-second news clip, which will only disappear in the audience's mind ten seconds after they have been entertained with visions of joy or violence, but rather a city-resounding *sound*. It is the rock-soft sound of hooves on streets when there are police horses and the crunching roll of tires when there are armored vehicles. It is the heavy thud of stone hitting bank doors, riot shields, jaws. The flushing sound of water hoses like shitting leviathans, the hypnotic blades of helicopters, hellish sirens, the crackle of blazing tires and effigies burning to ash, the violent cartoonish pop emitted from tear gas guns and the screeching tear gas canisters arcing the yellow-white sky. The weeping of a father, who, during those nightmarish years of the Dirty War, lost his only child. Rubber bullets hitting soft flesh with a terrible thump. The sad crack of a police club on a skull. The thunderous voices of those singing the "Internationale." Feverish footsteps, the drum of running away. The sickly scraping sound of metal barricades and raw skin being dragged against hot asphalt. The primordial rawness of a scream.

But finally, pana, through it all, the heart of the cacerolazo itself, thousands of pots and pans banging.

I took the pot and the large wooden spoon and joined the cacerolazo instead of following it from a short distance like I normally would, after which Alejandro just looked at me and said, "¿Vale la pena?" Then he smiled and started chanting with others.

Some minutes later, we reached Plaza de Mayo and saw the May Pyramid and the Casa Rosada, where De la Rúa, according to our mutual friend at *Clarín*, was busy watching "fucking cartoons," maybe, I thought with disdain, Bugs Bunny or Popeye.

At some point, a line of police advanced toward a jagged crowd of protestors. Some of the police were holding wooden truncheons, others carried tear gas guns. A few were on horseback. To my right were forceful chants of *the whole world is watching*, yet, I thought with gut-wrenching sadness, just months after the events of September 11th it was, in fact, very doubtful that the world would be watching.

Despite the tear gas, the protestors advanced against the police. To my surprise, Alejandro took off his shirt, wrapped it on his face, and joined the protestors. My eyes were burning with tear gas and my ears rang with the noises of the cacerolazo now beating steadily. Alejandro's face was one of hallucinatory calm. There were a few seconds when I could've saved him and didn't, pana. Some yards away, several more tear gas rounds fell.

Later that night, continued Javier, when I didn't yet know that Alejandro would die, I sat in a waiting room in Hospital J. M. Ramos Mejía watching a television clip of De la Rúa escaping the Casa Rosada by helicopter.

Other looped images followed: cheering crowds in Plaza de

Mayo, a bloody fat shirtless man being dragged down a street, the burned husk of a neoclassical building, men and women dancing in the streets—disjointed and juxtaposed images that would only lie to millions of viewers, that would only show them a fraction of the story. But I didn't give a flying shit, pana. None of it mattered to me then. How could I report any of it? What was the point? Just one hour earlier a tired-looking doctor told me that Alejandro had suffered an acute subdural hematoma, in all likelihood due to a police truncheon striking the side of his head. He was in a coma.

"I'm so sorry," the doctor said. "I know he's a friend of yours." He rested a hand on my shoulder then added: "He's not the only one like that tonight."

Sometime later, I saw Edin and who I assumed correctly to be Sol Marías, a thin, elegant woman with bird-like shoulders and sharp gray curls, like someone fleetingly imagined by Luis Buñuel, talking to the same doctor at the end of the hallway, a hallway, I remember thinking, like an underground tunnel dissolving inch by inch into nothing. As Edin listened to the doctor's words, she stood motionless with her arms folded, staring at something directly over the doctor's right shoulder, her big green eyes frozen in disbelief. At some point, Sol stopped listening. She sank into a nearby chair and without saying anything to the doctor or her daughter-in-law began to weep. Afterward, I left the hospital and walked to a small bar on Avenida Belgrano, where I called you, pana, but you already know that part.

And telling you all of this finally, pana, I can't help but now think: What had Sol Marías escaped when she decided to stop being a poet at ESMA? What lives had she inextricably erased with that decision, including her own son's? Pana, let me ask you of all people: On how many Earths is Sol Marías an exiled revolutionary, a corpse, a madwoman, a teacher, an accomplished busy poet who visits Nicanor Parra every spring in Valparaíso?

On how many Earths had the dictator Jorge Rafael Videla been murdered in his sleep or disappeared into a bloodless sea? On how many Earths, pana, had he, as an ugly gangling boy, secretly admired the dissident authors of the German Exilliteratur instead of Hitler? On how many Earths had he rejected instead of embraced Plan Condor and Nixon and Kissinger's violent clandestine warfare on Latin American people? On which Earth—if there could be at least one—had Jorge Rafael Videla tripped on a sidewalk crack and fallen headfirst into a streetlight, turning him into a happy idiot savant (and Sol Marías into a happy poet) who drew skillful and obscene cartoons in small notebooks instead of a murderous general who *disappeared* thirty thousand political enemies?

But, pana, I also can't help but wonder: What the hell is the point in thinking about all those other Jorges or Sols? On this Earth, the only Earth you or I will ever know, Sol Marías is a former poet who was cruelly blacklisted and tortured at ESMA. That simple fact determined her. It silenced her. It left her wordless. To think of all those other Sols on Earths we can never see is to relinquish her history, no matter how terrible. It denies her existence on this Earth. It erases her and also the memory of her son.

In a fit of grief, continued Javier, I spent an entire week looking for her lost poems. I searched online, rifled through countless bookstores, visited dozens of those newspaper stands that still sold books of poetry. But I never found anything. In truth, Sol Marías and Alejandro have already been erased off the face of this Earth. Javier shrugged miserably, yawned, then glanced at the two air mattresses on the floor of their small, sad, clean room, before saying, in any case, you're right, pana, there's nothing here at all for us, tomorrow we should go home.

The following morning, since they didn't have anything to do except make final arrangements to return to Chicago, they decided to check in on Aaron Douglas. The front door was wide open, so they stood carefully on the dilapidated porch and called his name into the dark, gloomy house. A few moments later, an older woman came to the threshold. Her curly dark hair was gray at the roots and pulled loosely behind a half-mask respirator, which only accentuated her postapocalyptic appearance.

You must be Eulalie, said Javier. Yes, she said as she pulled the respirator down, and you two must be those boys from Chicago my husband was telling me about. Javier and Saul nodded, both smiling somewhat self-consciously at her use of the term *boys*. He's out scavenging some lunch, she said, but should be back in a bit.

Then she explained that her husband had already talked to her about the matter of the missing theoretical physicist and that she did, in fact, know him in passing. Is there anything else you can tell us about him? Saul asked. He's easy to spot from far away since he's very tall, she said, like a trombonist I used to go with before Aaron. She laughed and the respirator trembled like a necklace. But what I want to say, she then said, was that I told a good friend of mine about the matter too, a bookseller in the Marigny who's known by everybody's mom and them as Ms. Zora, and she told me that she'd seen him just the other day.

Saul and Javier drove to the address Eulalie had given them, a large yellow shotgun house in the Marigny neighborhood just outside the French Quarter. A small wooden sign on the front door read: *New Orleans Rare Book Center.* They were received by a thin, upright boy no older than thirteen or fourteen by the name of Junior. When he disappeared into a back room, presumably to get Ms. Zora, it occurred to Saul that he might be the youngest person in the city. As they waited they looked at framed photographs on the wall, the meticulously organized bookcases, and the elegant mirrors that seemed to reflect the bookshelves endlessly. But Saul and Javier were much more interested in the photographs, which were all of writers standing with a beautiful and modern woman at various ages of her life.

My grandmother, Afraa Laguerre, knew all the writers who passed through this city some way or another, said Ms. Zora, and they all loved and respected her, even if a few of them mistakenly felt as if she broke their hearts into a thousand and one glass shards.

Ms. Zora wore a floral blouse and a black skirt. She bore a striking resemblance to the woman in the photographs. So, she continued, gesturing toward the wall, here we have Eudora Welty with my grandmother, William Faulkner with my grandmother, Nelson Algren with my grandmother (whose heart she really did break), Tennessee Williams with my grandmother, Arna Bontemps with my grandmother, Andrei Codrescu with my grandmother (very near the end of her life), William Burroughs with my grandmother, Lillian Hellman with my grandmother, Daniel F. Galouye with my grandmother, Alice Dunbar-Nelson with my grandmother (very near the end of Alice's life), Shirley Ann Grau with my grandmother, and Jean Toomer and Nina Pinchback (his wife of some years, a New Orleans native) with my grandmother. Saul didn't see any photographs of the only writer from New Orleans that really mattered to him.

Are there any photos of Adana Moreau? he asked.

Ms. Zora shook her head. But I know of her well, she said, my grandmother and Adana were close friends, if briefly, and she spoke of her more than a few times when I was a kid. She told me about a lot of the writer friends she made through the years. To her, they were all companions in one long, thrilling, and happy journey. From somewhere in the house came the muted strains of a reggaetón song. Then they talked about Afraa Laguerre and Adana Moreau in what might be called abstract terms, speculations on the nature of their lives and close friendship that, according to Ms. Zora, inevitably led to *Lost*

City, Afraa's exodus from Port-au-Prince as a young woman, Adana's exodus from Santo Domingo as a teenager, Afraa's flight from New Orleans to San Francisco during the Great Depression and her return some long years later to open the New Orleans Rare Book Center, and, finally, Adana Moreau's death in 1930, an untimely death, according to Ms. Zora, that could still sink her (a *reader* before anything else) into a deep sense of melancholy. What if, what if, what if, she said with a sigh. The Great Depression, like this Storm, she said, was a rupture in time and we'll never know what we've lost. She looked at them and smiled. But, she said, I understand you're looking for her son.

They drove west on River Road, an empty prehighway connection to Baton Rouge that wound along the Gorgon-like tail of the Mississippi River. They passed antebellum plantation houses and battered cottages with rusted tin roofs that, according to Javier, were reminiscent of those found in Ecuadorian villages tunneled out of the tropics. There were also some fields with rows of sugarcane that reached ten feet and swayed in the wind, filling the air with the smell of molasses. A daytime moon, nearly full, silhouetted the blue sky, *an orphan moon*, according to Ms. Zora, since only orphans looked up during the day.

While they drove, Ms. Zora and her son talked to Javier about life after the Storm, a type of survivors' carnival, Sisyphean and tragic, exemplified for them by the apoplectic voices and weeping they heard from their front porch at night. Saul half listened, preoccupied not only with the box containing the manuscript of *A Model Earth* resting on his lap and the unaccustomed sense of autonomy he felt as they drove through that remote place, but also with the paralyzing horror that came over him when confronted with the traces of destruction reaching far back into the centuries that were evident in those antebellum plantations and sugarcane fields, overshadowed only for seconds at a time by the encroaching insensate petrochemical and oil refineries on the banks of the river.

Sometime later, as Saul was lost in these thoughts and others too, thoughts of the science fiction novel *Neuromancer* and its toxic Sprawl and the unfamiliar smell of burning sugarcane, of burning oil, of metal dissolving into the thick air, of a remote place that produced a sense of pyromania and unease, the black Cadillac pulled into the parking lot of a Quality Suites motel.

A lot of people came here after the Storm, said Ms. Zora, nodding at the busy courtyard of the motel where a group of teenagers stood talking and laughing. Junior joined them. We came just three days ago when we found out that a few of Junior's friends had made it out okay and were staying here. They spend their days and nights exchanging survivor stories and searching for lost friends and family members online. That's how we ran into Maxwell.

Saul and Javier followed her up a staircase, ducking under clotheslines. They passed people fidgeting with cigarettes and cell phones, and motel room windows taped over with graded homework and crayon drawings of prehistoric creatures and rescue boats crammed with stick figure people, and submerged houses, where still other stick figure people stood on rooftops. From behind a closed door, Saul could hear the faint sound of laughter. From behind another, he heard the sounds of a trumpet, sometimes louder and sometimes softer, like an exchange of faraway shouts, not of sorrow or joy, but of pure self-consuming energy. Ms. Zora stopped at Room 307 and said, right here. For a few seconds Saul didn't move. He stood there, breathing deeply, his right hand clenched in a fist inches from the motel door. He glanced at Javier, who shrugged and said, all you, pana, and then Saul knocked.

FROM VITEBSK

July 1933–October 1933

Long after the white beam of the flashlight had faded and died, Maxwell lay on the floor of the boxcar, half-asleep, sweating in the claustrophobic heat and gazing into a type of darkness that both aggravated his sense of fatalism and fear, but also, at the same time, induced a happy dream in which he found a book covered in moss in an Isleño shack, a book written in Spanish that for some strange reason he couldn't read, but which he still thumbed through slowly, page after unintelligible page, until, at some point, he heard someone pounding on the boxcar door and then a voice.

Maxwell stood up, a little shaky, and yelled back. Then he heard the door unlocking and sliding away.

"How long you been in here, kid?" a bullman asked.

Maxwell rubbed his eyes and then looked up at the hazy, dark sky, the pale half-moon, and the burning lights of the city just beyond the train yard. "I don't know," he said.

"That goddamn piece of shit Friedrich could've killed you," said the bullman. Then he gave a long sigh and told Maxwell to leave the train yard, no other questions asked.

Maxwell followed a street bordered by warehouses and factories and smokestacks. He walked by pawnshops and hotels and late-night diners and tattoo parlors and theaters that lit up the street. On one of those theaters was a painted mural of a man holding a sledgehammer in one hand and the Earth in his other. Some minutes later, he found himself in a neighborhood full of tenement buildings, where people walked up and down the sidewalks in constant motion. Avoiding their wary gazes, he walked through an empty alley. Under the lonely light of a single dim light bulb, he pissed and thought about his dream.

The following morning, first thing, he went to a Sinclair gas station to ask for directions to the Jonava. He chose the Sinclair gas station over others because out front on a thin strip of dying grass was a green model Brontosaurus, maybe six feet by ten feet, and it fondly reminded him of the library book *Dinosaurs and Flying Reptiles of the Jurassic and Cretaceous Eras* that his father had once read to him when he was a child.

Inside the gas station, an attendant with dirty-blond hair and owl-rimmed glasses told Maxwell that a map of the city was a nickel. Maxwell eyed the brightly colored maps near the cash register, then he turned to leave.

"Wait," said the attendant, "where are you going?"

"The Jonava."

"The Jonava? In Jewtown?"

"I think so," he said, "I don't know."

"Some people call it that," said the attendant, by way of explanation, "some people call it Maxwell Street Market. Regardless, it's my old stomping grounds. I'm a Jew on my mother's side, which means I'm bona fide, but don't tell the bonehead owners outside. They think I'm Catholic, which, for them, is a small step up and better for business. I'm like a false medieval convert. A modern-day Marrano. Don't tell them, and I'll give you a map. Deal?"

"Okay," said Maxwell, nodding, a little confused, but still taking the name of the market as another good sign.

At the Jonava—a cramped four-story brick building near the center of an open-air market crammed with pushcarts, kosher meat stands, bakeries, and shops—a febrile, green-eyed, and overwhelmed hotel clerk told Maxwell that he wasn't allowed to say one way or another who was staying at the hotel. Maxwell took a deep breath and explained that he had come all the way from New Orleans to meet his father, Titus Moreau, who had written him a letter *telling him* to meet there in July. All he needed was a room number, nothing more, after which the hotel clerk said there was no one staying in the hotel with that name. He would've remembered a name *that* ridiculous.

Some minutes later, while the hotel clerk was helping a guest with his suitcases, Maxwell snuck behind the front desk and started flipping through the pages of the guest register, landing on February 1933, the same month his father had sent his first letter from Chicago. When he saw his father's name, halfway down the page under Room 42, Maxwell started shaking. He thought about his new life with his father in Chicago, but then the hotel clerk saw him behind the front desk and told him in a calm voice (but a voice with traces of violence, like a claw) that if he didn't leave the hotel that second he would personally take him out back into the alley, if the *boy* understood what he meant.

But a young maid who had heard the hotel clerk ran into the lobby, glared at him, and said, "Nobody's taking nobody out back, Mr. Walker." She then touched Maxwell's back with her long fingers and said, "What's wrong, child?"

"My father's in Room 42," he said carefully.

"Okay then," she said.

The maid and Maxwell went up four flights of dimly lit stairs and she asked questions the entire time: where are you from, child? how old are you, child? are you hungry, child? her voice like low-lying waters running through a cypress grove, and Maxwell knew that she had children or badly wanted children of her own. On the fourth floor there were yellow light bulbs hanging by wires and whitewashed walls and rows and rows of doors, multiplying in the hallway, all black, like portals.

They came to Room 42, and the maid knocked. When no one answered, she opened the door for him with her keys. The room smelled musty. In one corner stood an iron bed with a paper bag hanging on one of the bedposts; in another, a cheap wooden wardrobe and a desk. Above the desk hung a faded painting of a prairie with a man and a woman on horseback and a white prairie schooner being pulled by two pairs of large oxen. A small, filthy window overlooked the alley below. There were no signs of his father, or anyone really.

"Lots of men come through like ghosts," said the maid.

Afterward, for hours on end, Maxwell stood alone under the red and white awning of a large bargain store across the street from the Jonava, watching for his father in the crowds lining the sidewalks or in Chryslers and Fords on Halsted Street, watching for his tall self-assured gait, his sharp jaw, his weather-beaten forehead, his air of grief (just like Maxwell's air of grief) but all he saw were semblances, men who *seemed* but never were. Something is wrong, he thought. The crowds were part of the same world he lived in and yet not one person could take his arm and say, "I knew you when you were born" or "I knew you before everything changed" or "I am your father."

Later, after her shift had ended, the young maid saw Maxwell still standing under the awning of the bargain store. She approached, looked him in his eyes, which were full of tears, and said, "Oh, child."

That night, after the young maid bought Maxwell a hot dog, she took him to a Roman Catholic orphanage for boys on West 15th Street. The director, a serious and obtrusive, if baby-faced, nun asked Maxwell if he was Protestant, on account of him being a Negro. After which Maxwell, instead of explaining that his mother had emigrated from the Dominican Republic, a country so Catholic the old mad pirate had once told him that even the Pope avoided visiting it, he just shook his head and lifted his gaze toward an immense and brightly colored mural of boys marching through a wheat field under a blazing sun, at the center of which was—impossibly—a wooden cross. The boys were German, Irish, and Italian immigrants (that much was clear), but their translucent white skin, the wheat field, and the sun were all hyperbolically American. Then, Maxwell imagined the boys marching beyond the wheat field, through towns with Indigenous and Spanish names that rose from rust-colored lands like hallucinations of towns, without stopping, until they came to the sea (a sea they feared because of the unknown boys on the other side), a perfectly gray sea, utterly gray and still.

At that moment, which hardly lasted a second, Maxwell decided that he didn't want to be an orphan, but at the very same moment the director handed the young maid a paper and told her to sign. Now he was an orphan.

At 5:26 a.m. every morning, a young bird-like nun wielding a radiator brush woke the boys in Maxwell's dormitory and for twenty minutes they performed military calisthenics—jumping jacks, push-ups, and sit-ups. After washing up, they were given a piece of bread and led single file to a church adjoining the orphanage, where they sat on long pews and listened to a deacon with a strange, sometimes incomprehensible sense of humor, as he delivered homilies about the Trinity (which later, in Maxwell's mind, took the shape of a Pythagorean pyramid).

Most of the boys in the orphanage did not talk to Maxwell. Behind his back, one flat-faced kid, thirteen or fourteen, even gave him the nickname Kerchak, after the "savage king ape" who killed Tarzan's father. He didn't know Maxwell's real name. Maxwell didn't know his real name, either. The nuns didn't call the boys by their names, but rather by their orphan case number followed by their dormitory. The flat-faced boy's name, for example, was 23-7. Maxwell's name was 72-9.

In the afternoons, after lunch, they were led single file to an outdoor playground, or to a classroom, where they sat silently under the smoke-eyed gaze of an old nun, filling out reading and math workbooks, which, to Maxwell (if to no one else in that classroom) were far too easy.

More often than not, dinner was bread, cheese, and salty tomato soup. Occasionally, after dinner, the young maid stopped by the orphanage to check in on Maxwell. Once or twice, he saw her from the distance talking to the director. He could see that the young maid, in turn, was watching him out of the corner of her eye, her look betraying an unfulfilled urgency, as if sunk in a well of compassion, until she stopped coming altogether.

At night, in the dark, he lay on his cot in dormitory number 9 still as a stone statue, thinking of the unknown whereabouts of his father and carefully planning his escape from the orphanage to find him.

A few weeks later, Maxwell had his chance. One afternoon, after lunch, the old smoke-eyed nun didn't show up for their lessons. The boys, who assumed the nun was either dead or dying, her soul either floating upward like cigarette smoke, or, in all likelihood, being pulled quicksand-like into the hellish core of the Earth, marched up and down the classroom like they had scorpions in their pants, stood on their desks, threw paper balls, told dirty jokes, and even planned to strap the wooden cross over the blackboard to 65-9's back.

During the commotion, Maxwell left the classroom and went to his dormitory to gather his belongings. The front doors were blocked by two nuns quietly talking, so he began to search for another way out, and that's how he found the hiding place.

The hiding place was extremely simple, a small alcove converted into a janitor's closet with a metal storage cabinet, a washbasin, and an old wooden door that looked like it had been taken from a confessional. The alcove was wide enough for Maxwell to crouch in the center with the door closed. While he waited, he stripped and washed his clothes in the washbasin. At some point, he heard the nun in charge of his dormitory yelling at a few boys in the hallway. "Where is 72-9?" she screeched like a hawk that delights in its territory, to which there was jittery silence, followed by the sylph-like sounds of the radiator brush smacking across a boy's cheek.

Some hours later, long after his clothes had air-dried and the boys and nuns had gone to sleep, Maxwell left the janitor's closet and snuck into the cafeteria, where he took two apples and a box of oatmeal. Nourishment, he thought. Then he walked out of the orphanage through the front doors without once looking at the immense and brightly colored mural above.

At night, in an alley next to the Jonava, Maxwell slept on a piece of cardboard. During the day, he wandered the market, searching for his father.

From time to time he stopped to examine a shop through a window or a stand brimming with novelty displays: Civil War pistols, salves in green-tinted bottles, ivory-handled knives, crates of liquor sold out of the trunk of a Ford, ornate iron birdcages, and blankets and rugs with designs of golden insects.

On one occasion, he stood for hours near a vendor selling fading antique maps of the New World in the hopes that it would attract his father's attention. Once, exhausted by his search, he spent an afternoon mesmerized by an old musician wearing black slippers who sang and played from a dented black guitar. Some of the musician's songs were familiar to Maxwell, Southern songs about riverboats, blue skies, and lost loves, joyful and melancholic in turn, but some of his other songs were new and strange to Maxwell, songs that recounted violent love affairs and shattered landscapes and memories of home that were like burning fires, so, in one sense, these new songs ached and throbbed and bled (as his mother might have said) like Prometheus' liver, but they also gave a sensation of regeneration, a tingling, cooling sensation like the cellular division and regrowth of Prometheus' liver, which was the sensation of returning to a place never seen before but somehow still remembered.

I don't know what I'm doing here, Maxwell said to himself after he'd been searching for his father in the market for two weeks. He said it at night in the alley next to the Jonava while trying to fall asleep on the piece of cardboard. But by then he had already twice seen the Jewish boy who had told him not to leave the city yet.

The first time was during a particularly cool morning when Maxwell was looking through an old geometry textbook at a bookstall. The Jewish boy, who was a full head shorter than Maxwell and who had black curly hair and long wiry arms, was inspecting a milk crate full of old magazines and talking confidently to the owner in a guttural foreign language. Then, for some reason unclear to Maxwell, the Jewish boy turned to *him*, smiled (an awkward electric shock of a smile), and told him in English he was having a hell of a time that day looking for werewolf stories in old issues of *Weird Tales*. He'd already been to three other bookstalls that morning, to no avail. The first one he had ever read was a novella entitled *The Werewolf of Ponkert* by H. Warner Munn in the July 1925 issue, and this led him to the short story "The Werewolf of St. Bonnot" by Seabury Quinn in the May–July 1924 issue.

Some months later, in the April 1926 issue, he found an unexpected werewolf story by C. Franklin Miller entitled "Things That Are God's." Then, following this logic he also found *The Wolf-Woman* by Bassett Morgan in the September 1927 issue. After scanning a few more issues in reference to both werewolves and women, he realized with some melancholy that he had come full circle, more or less, with *The Werewolf's Daughter* by H. Warner Munn, a novel in entirety spanning three issues in 1928 from October to December. The year 1929, he observed, was suspiciously absent of werewolves and he suspected that this had something to do with the pale and predatory men of Wall Street who had caused the Panic and were probably werewolves themselves and now trying to hide the fact, but he didn't have proof, at least not yet.

After the boy stopped talking, he let out a deep sigh of resignation, waved goodbye to the shop owner and Maxwell, who was by then a little stunned, and left.

The second time Maxwell saw the Jewish boy was a few days later, when he went to a grocer on West 14th Street to look for his father. It was getting dark, but Maxwell could still make him out standing under the globular lights of a delicatessen next door. He was wearing a large sandwich board with the words *Only the Best on the Planet.*

When he saw Maxwell, the boy waved him over. Then he took off the sandwich board and took out a cigarette to share with him. Since Maxwell didn't know what to say, he nodded and took the cigarette. The boy smiled and, without skipping a beat from a few days earlier, started to explain that since the last time they'd seen each other he'd visited the editorial offices of *Weird Tales* on 840 North Michigan Avenue, where none other than Mr. Wright, the editor of *Weird Tales*, had told him that there was a very good reason for the omission of werewolves in the 1929 issues, a reason he couldn't just tell anybody off the street, but one that could still in all likelihood be rooted out from a dime novel published that same year called *The Werewolf of New York City* by Margaret Bok.

It was a blood-soaked and uncanny dime novel which had taken him nearly two days to find if only four hours to read and which was about a solitary wealthy banker who, at night when the moon was bright and full, metamorphosed into a werewolf and prowled tenement buildings of the Lower East Side looking for unsuspecting, newly immigrated, and impoverished victims, all of which not only proved his theory correct but also gave an entirely new historical significance to *the Panic of 1929.*

"I don't believe in conspiracies all the time, Joe," he said, "but I had to tell someone."

Maxwell and the boy passed the cigarette back and forth.

"So, Joe," he said, "what brings you here? You need any more math books?"

Maxwell told the boy that he was looking for his father. "I was supposed to meet him at the Jonava, but I don't where he is," he said. Then he added: "I think I'm going to go home."

"Where's home?" the boy asked.

"New Orleans."

The boy took one final drag of the cigarette before snuffing it out on the curb. He then put the cigarette butt in his front right pocket. "Shit, Joe, don't leave just yet," he said, finally. "I'll help you look for him. Meet me at the bookstand tomorrow morning."

Then they said goodbye, but not without first introducing themselves:

"My name is Benjamin Drower," the boy said, "what's yours?"

He told him it was Maxwell Moreau, after which the boy said,

"Like the market and the doctor. Got it." They shook hands and went their separate ways.

All of this Maxwell recalled as he tossed and turned on the piece of cardboard in the alley next to the Jonava, unable to sleep. What was it about the boy that made Maxwell tell him about his father? Was it his short height, his vague foreignness, the fact that unlike anybody else in the market he had talked to Maxwell, or even the sudden impression that, like an impossible perpetual motion machine, he had never stopped moving? And he wondered again: I don't know what I'm doing here, should I return to New Orleans? is there an unopened letter from my father waiting for me there? would I even know him if I saw him again after all these years? Finally he grew tired of all the questions and he focused instead on the unequivocal shapes of a geometry problem floating like dust under his closed eyelids, and fell asleep.

By the time Maxwell went to the bookstand the following morning, Benjamin was already there waiting for him. Wandering the market, they questioned vendors like detectives. Had they met a man named Titus Moreau from New Orleans? they asked. Had they met anybody staying at the Jonava looking for work? Had they seen a man writing letters or *reading the sky*? Had they heard any rumors about someone called the Last Pirate of the New World? Etc., etc. To which some of the vendors looked askew, and to which others simply said, "Some men might have a name like that," or "Lots of men from the South here," or "Lots of people from everywhere here."

In any case, the vendors, many of whom Benjamin knew personally, knew nothing. Two or three times, he fell into heated arguments with the vendors in the same guttural foreign language Maxwell had heard him speak earlier. Maxwell didn't ask what language he and the vendors were speaking. But later, Benjamin explained to him, a little frustrated, that it was next to impossible that nobody in the market knew anything, but the problem was that the vendors thought and often spoke in Yiddish, a language that, at least according to his father, a tailor originally from Vitebsk, suffered from a sense of Weltschmerz, which was the melancholic suspicion that there was never enough knowledge or reality to go around.

Later still, as they sat on a curb in front of the delicatessen on West 14th Street, sharing a sticky bun Benjamin had purchased and watching the coral sunset as it swirled above the market stands, Benjamin asked Maxwell where he was staying.

"I was staying at the Catholic orphanage," he said, "but I snuck out."

"Why'd you sneak out?" asked Benjamin.

"They're Catholics," he said, "they wouldn't let me leave."

Benjamin laughed. Then he told Maxwell he had an idea.

"Follow me," he said.

They hopped the metal bumper of a streetcar heading west and then another heading south. They passed through several neighborhoods and a park with worn-out tents surrounding a steadily burning fire in a steel drum. Some minutes later, they hopped off the streetcar and walked a few blocks west until they reached a limestone building. Out front, a group of older boys stood talking with two middle-aged men wearing black suits and black hats, one of whom, Benjamin whispered to Maxwell, was his rabbi. As they walked by, an obstinate silence descended inexplicably over the quartet.

They entered the limestone building and climbed five flights of stairs until they reached a locked door to the roof. Benjamin took out a key and opened it and they walked outside. The sky was black and the lights of the endless city were like thousands of incandescent anemones floating on the surface of a black sea. At the far end of the roof stood a small storage shed. Inside was a bookshelf, lined with dime novels and old issues of *Amazing Stories* and *Weird Tales*, and a single, spotless cot in the center. On the cot was a wool blanket, a flashlight, and a black skullcap, which Benjamin picked up and put in his back pocket.

"Sometimes, when I want to get away to think or read," said Benjamin, smiling, "I come here. It's a regular goddamn Babylon."

It didn't take long for Benjamin's father, Saul, to find the boy on the rooftop. The first time he saw the boy he was fast asleep on the cot in the storage shed on the roof. He didn't wake the boy or wonder where he had come from. He guessed correctly that his son, who was prone to avid, sudden friendships (a Russian habit really, he thought), had met the boy in the market and invited him to stay with them. Soon afterward, there was a decrease in the amount of food in the apartment, due, the father understood immediately, to the boy staying on the roof. Some days later, he prepared three modest plates of rye bread and gefilte fish, and sat at the circular table in the kitchen that served as both desk and dinner table. He then waited for his son to come home from the market. Around 6:00 p.m., his son arrived.

"Did you go to synagogue this week to study?" he asked his son, knowing full well that he hadn't.

"Yes, tateh."

"There is a boy sleeping on the roof?"

To which Benjamin slowly nodded.

"Yes, tateh."

"How long?"

"A week now, no more."

"Just a week?"

"His name is Maxwell."

Saul folded his hands and waited for his son to tell him more.

"I'm helping him look for his father in the market. He's an orphan. I don't think he has a mother."

The father winced and looked into his son's eyes. They were

dark, with a thin vein of hazel, the eyes of Vitebsk, he thought sadly, and they told the truth.

"He's a Negro, Benjaminas," he said, using his son's given Old World name, "this will cause commotion for us."

"What does that matter? Who likes Jews but other Jews? And not even half the time at that."

"We don't have much, Benjaminas," said the father, "only a few people come to the tailor shop now and it is less every day."

"I know. But I'm working now, too. We have enough, tateh."

So, for a second time, Saul went to the rooftop, and he saw the boy there, reading one of his son's dime novels. The roof, thought Saul, was real solitude. He understood why his son spent so much time there. He cleared his throat and when the boy turned around he asked him if he would like to join him and his son for dinner. The boy nodded and then followed Saul down to the apartment.

After dinner, Saul opened the front door and a window in the kitchen to create a draft in the humid apartment, and then he got out a deck of playing cards and placed them on the kitchen table. He asked the boy if he knew the basic rules of poker, a game his own father had forbid when he was young, and the boy nodded and said that he had played a few times with customers when he worked in a speakeasy called the Three Junipers in New Orleans. Saul smiled and handed out poker chips, which were small pieces of paper torn from a newspaper.

As they played, he told the boy that he was originally from Vitebsk, which was in the Liteh or what some Americans now called Jewish Lithuania. He then talked about Vitebsk, a stunning city, which rested on the banks of the Dvina, Vitba, and Luchesa—rivers, he had imagined as a young man, with the names of three beautiful and heartbroken sisters who rebelled against the Torah and snuck out at night. Then he said that when he was homesick, which was not often, but often enough, he dreamed about the three sisters. He said he dreamed about dancing with them over the city at night, a promenade in the sky.

"But Benjaminas' mother and I had to leave Vitebsk in 1920 because I got into some political trouble," the father said. "A dear friend of mine helped us escape. To this day I'm sure he saved our lives. In Italy we boarded a ship and crossed the Atlantic to America. It was like a nightmare. But Benjaminas was born on that ship. In the heart of some nightmares, there are also gifts."

Maxwell nodded.

"His mother and I often joked that Benjaminas is a true Jew. He doesn't have a nation. The ocean is his nation."

"Yes, yes, tateh," said Benjamin.

"Maybe I am embarrassing you?"

"No, tateh. I know where I was born."

"I'm sorry, Maxwell. This must be boring. You've come from far away and shouldn't have to listen to another family's stories. Of course, you have your own," said Saul.

"I'd like to hear more," said Maxwell, thinking then of the old mad pirate and his long stories.

Saul collected the playing cards and made two small piles. He then folded his hands on the table and thought for a moment. "When I was a boy," he said, "we told stories all night sometimes. But now, with radio and movies, it's different. We don't talk or listen in the same way. Still, maybe it's time I told the whole story."

He then regarded his son.

"It's okay, tateh."

Saul then told his story.

I left Petrograd the summer before the October Revolution in 1917. I had just finished my studies. Like many from my generation, I studied philosophy and languages. In addition to my native Yiddish and Russian, I became quite fluent in German, Polish, and Italian. One of my older cousins, who had immigrated to New York City in 1912, wrote me before I started my studies and suggested that I also study English. In his letter, he said that it was the language of gold.

As a student, I participated in the February Revolution. I confess now: when the revolution started I didn't understand much about what was happening. Of course, there was a savage global war and there were signs of it everywhere, but my studies still kept me busy. Yes, I was hungry. But I grew up with hunger. It was something I understood. I worked under the distinct, possibly naïve, impression that all students on Earth went hungry. It was a price to be paid.

Overall, I kept to myself, somewhat out of necessity, since I was a Jew living in Petrograd—I had to pretend to be a servant in a doctor's house in order to avoid the residence restriction— and somewhat because that was the type of person I was then. My day-to-day life consisted of studying, writing letters to my family back home, and, when I had a moment to myself, wandering the streets of the city.

Then, one day in February, the streets filled with tens of thousands of starving soldiers, students, and factory workers, a spontaneous city-wide protest led by women workers from the districts of Vyborg, Liteiny, and Rozhdestvensky. The next day, I joined a massive march, maybe more out of curiosity than anything, or maybe I didn't have a choice. I don't know. So much of what we consider free will is subject to fleeting moments transmitted from one person to another like conduction. Maybe, we don't have any individual free will at all. Maybe, those crowds and the revolution was a sort of collective will charged with electricity. In any case, we marched to Nevsky, the extravagant city center, under red banners, through streets lined with mounted Cossacks and snow piles, shouting for bread, for an end to the war, for an end to the monarchy itself. And since the Petrograd police had blocked the bridges to Nevsky, thousands of us descended from the embankments and walked across the frozen face of the great Neva River itself.

On the thick ice, a young man introduced himself to me. He was tall and he had a trimmed black beard. He looked to be in his mid-twenties, yet, by the way he spoke and by his posture, he could have been somewhat older. He carried an old sword from the Turkish War, which was a short-lived but significant war for Russia. The sword had been his father's. He grabbed my elbow and said, "You study languages, correct?" I nodded.

It seemed strange that he knew me since I was sure that I had never met him. But it was a strange day. He introduced himself as Alexander Sidorov, a metalworker and Bolshevik activist, and then he asked me if I could help him edit and translate some letters and leaflets. It was obvious to me that he was in charge of some sort of operation. He said my talents were needed and that he would be sure I was well fed. I agreed to help. Maybe, I was hungrier than I had thought.

Before I knew it, I was in a small apartment in the Vyborg district with Alexander and a few of his associates, furiously translating a variety of foreign letters and leaflets. Much of the writing felt spontaneous and vague—eager appeals for exiles to return, feverish calls to soldiers for mass desertion, and fiery debates between Bolsheviks, Mensheviks, and the Socialist Revolutionary Party—but it was clear to me that something serious was happening. I returned to that apartment again and again. While I worked on translations, I could hear the boisterous shouts of workers striking, the coughing of machine gun fire followed by howling, hundreds of soft footsteps trudging through snow, the stricken silence of night. The rest is a hypnotic blur, and even today it is difficult to tell the part, if any, that I played in the February Revolution. It was chaos in the flesh and I remember imagining that a great beast, an old coiled dragon, had been suddenly ripped apart. Before we knew it, the Czar abdicated and the Petrograd Soviet and Provisional Government, under

Prince Georgy Lvov, was set up. For the first time in my life, I felt as if something was happening for a reason.

That was the beginning and the end of my involvement, though. I finished my studies and some long turbulent months later Alexander visited to warn me that my name was on a list being put together by a dangerous coalition of counterrevolutionaries that included landowners, capitalists, and the Black Hundreds, an umbrella name for pogrom enthusiasts, ultramonarchists, and mystics of hate. A blacklist, or worse. Still, he spoke of yet another revolution that would free humanity from historical conditions. A Bolshevik revolution that would end history. He spoke of the rights that Jews would be granted. He told me that I was needed and that he could protect me. That was when I understood that a civil war was coming. A dark and obscure thing had been shaken in the Russian soul: some ill-defined suffering with virulent roots which would seek to put an end not only to history but also to itself. I tried to tell Alexander, but he didn't listen. Or he couldn't listen. We argued politics through the night, but it was pointless. He accused me, like the Provisional Government, of wavering. He believed in something new, an announcement of some type of paradise at hand for workers, farmers, and soldiers. I didn't know what I believed. But it was clear that I had to leave Petrograd.

A few days later, in early July, I left by train for Vitebsk. I spent some time with my family and walked the streets of the city, reacquainting myself with the babbling of the rivers, the fragrance of the shops, and, of course, the people, the beggars, soldiers, and rabbis who, like me, were wanderers. Even now, across an entire ocean, I can see them all. They are like ghosts that I brought with me to Chicago. It was on one of those walks that I met Benjaminas' mother, Alinochka. I stopped by a winter circus that had suddenly materialized. She was standing near a ticket booth watching two little acrobats perform. The acrobats wore white makeup and moved like little snow foxes. She held one hand to her mouth, amazed by the acrobats, and in the other she held two leather-bound books, one with a title in Russian and one with a title in Italian. I watched her for a few minutes and then, in a rare moment of courage, I introduced myself.

Of course, I don't remember what I said. How could I? Your mother's eyes, Benjaminas, they were like amber. I don't remember what she said either, but her voice, ah! Her voice was like that of a scholar's. This is one of those moments the old Russian writers call "struck with love," so I will say now that I was suddenly struck with a bolt of lightning out of an impossibly blue sky.

After I told my father about Alinochka, he suggested that I take an apprenticeship as a tailor. My father was originally from the city of Vilnius. In 1915, just before the German occupation of that city, a second or third cousin of his from there had moved to Vitebsk to open a tailor shop near the city center. He was an avid traveler and had business all throughout the Liteh. Due to the current political circumstances, my knowledge of languages could come in handy. I agreed to this and started immediately. Nearly six months later, in June of 1918, I married Alinochka. The wedding, which took place in a suburb of Vitebsk, was small and joyful.

In the intervening months, the new Bolshevik ruling party of Russia signed the Treaty of Brest-Litovsk with the Central Powers. Due to the peace treaty, new nation states were created including the Kingdom of Lithuania, the Ukrainian State, and the Belarusian People's Republic. There were others, of course, many actually, but they were mostly all German puppet states, which would serve as buffers.

Both the Germans and the Russians wanted to stall for time. Regardless of the treaty, the Germans were preparing for an eventual all-or-nothing clash with Russia. And the Bolshevik ruling party in Russia was biding its time so it could turn its attention to the escalating civil war and the confederation of the increasingly barbaric anti-Bolshevik forces known as the White

Army. Then, with the eventual defeat of the White Army, the ruling party could turn to world revolution, which it viewed as not only necessary, but inevitable. As a result, borders quickly changed hands and, in many circumstances, became overwhelmingly vague. It was increasingly difficult to make sense of the continent.

All of this, of course, was nothing new to us, the Jews of the Liteh, who, throughout the centuries, had seen other wars and other borders appear and disappear. We regarded national identity as largely fictitious and borders as transitory. We simply breathed and ate and slept and prayed outside the realm of borders. In fact, the old men, especially the devout old men wrapped in prayer shawls, spoke of the one-thousand-year-old swamps and forests of the Liteh as boundless landscapes that gave way not to nations but to the sky, which, for many, was another way of saying the very thoughts of YHWH. Do you understand, boys? Sovereignty had nothing to do with borders. Needless to say, we continued to use the old names and maybe we even convinced ourselves that we lived in a different era. In some ways, the Liteh was an immense time machine, like in one of those stories in *Weird Tales* that Benjaminas always reads. This, I believe, turned out to be our tragic mistake.

But at that time none of this mattered to me. What difference did the Bolsheviks or the White Army make? What difference was there between the Germans or the Russians? Everybody wanted the same thing. To fill their ranks with farmers and laborers and children. Even the Liteh was just a place between the others. None of it mattered. I knew I was naïve, but the troubles of Petrograd, war, and peace ceased to exist. When one is that young and that in love not even time and death exist. So, what did exist? Your mother, Benjaminas, she existed.

During the day, I worked as a tailor's apprentice. In the evenings, I walked the streets of Vitebsk with her and we talked and talked. Sometimes, if there was a little money, we went to a café or a small theater that had plays by Vsevolod Meyerhold.

Then, one day in mid-April 1920, an official of the ruling party in Moscow came to see me. I invited him into my modest house and we had tea. For nearly five minutes he didn't say anything and just sat at the table drinking tea. He then commented on the quality of the samovar on the stove. I told him it had been a wedding present. He asked about my wife and I told him she was pregnant and doing well. He nodded. When his tea was finished, he took out a leaflet. I immediately recognized it as one I had translated during the February Revolution. The corners were torn and the ink was smeared, like someone had rubbed ash on its cover.

In a quiet, but severe tone he asked me, "Is this leaflet your work?"

"It is," I replied.

"Is it reasonable to assume then that you were asked to translate this leaflet?"

"Yes, I was asked that," I said, "but I left that life behind."

I had no idea why the official was asking me all these questions, nor did I understand exactly what he wanted with me.

"Tell me, Saul Druer, do you know Alexander Sidorov?" the official asked me.

For a long while, I was silent.

The official looked me in the eye. "Please answer the question and I'll be sure to leave without troubling you any further."

"How should I know him? I heard that name once or twice in Petrograd, but I never met him," I said.

At that moment, I wondered exactly what this official wanted with Alexander Sidorov. I then imagined Alexander still protesting in the streets of Petrograd, his father's Turkish sword at his side. It was a ridiculous image—frozen in time by a permanent and overwhelming memory—but it was also an important image. It led me to understand that this man was not an official from the ruling party in Moscow. What's more, I suspected that he was with the White Army, or, at the very least, that the White Army had hired him. He was some sort of professional. Regardless, the civil war had found me. It existed.

I stood up and told the official that my wife would be home soon. He thanked me for the tea and stood up, too. He shook my hand and relaxed a little. The look in his eyes changed and for a moment they even seemed pleasant. Although, of course, how could they be? He was an imposter. Before leaving, he told me a joke about a Ukrainian woman who gives birth to a spider or a spider who gives birth to a Ukrainian woman. Something like that. I don't entirely remember the joke, but I do remember that it somehow seemed like a threat.

That night, Alinochka and I argued about what should be done. She was afraid and wanted to leave immediately for Paris, where she had two cousins who would help us start a new life. She said that I could not erase the events of Petrograd, no matter how hard I tried. She said that we had been living these past few years in a dream. But I wanted to stay in Vitebsk. Business was fair and I felt safe in my hometown, where I knew the people on the streets and where the ruling Bolshevik party had considerable support. Like I said, we argued, and nothing was settled. But nearly three days later, in the morning, a letter decided it for us. The letter was hand-delivered by a polite and spotless Red Army soldier. It was sealed by the Bolshevik ruling party and addressed from Alexander Sidorov.

I sat for a long while at the table before opening the letter. I must have drunk four or five cups of tea. I was sure that my fate was sealed in its contents. I closed my eyes and thought of nothing and everything, all at once, just as my own grandfather had taught me. I envisioned myself wandering through a dark labyrinth. My hands grasped for the walls, which were solid and unbroken. In some form or another, I had been wandering this way for thousands of years. And yet, suddenly, I was also very aware of the entirety of the labyrinth, each corridor and tunnel and secret passageway. I had never seen the center and I was certain I never would, but I was also certain that it was bathed in luminous moonlight. How badly I wanted to find the center! To lie in that moonlight and let it blanket my skin and let whatever needed to happen to me happen. But I was lost in that labyrinth and there was nothing I could really do about it.

When I finally opened my eyes, I was able to give myself over to fate. In the first two pages or so, Alexander wrote about his health and good fortune and explained in detail about his recent move to Moscow, following Yudenich's failed siege in Petrograd, in which he had played a vital role. He wrote that he was in charge of new operations in the Don, but that he was not at liberty to say more. He also wrote for some length about Moscow: an extraordinary city brimming with new artists and workers, a city that would be the center of the world in ten years, a city on the brink of history's end. Afterward, the tone of the letter changed, and he became more personal. I don't have the letter with me. It was too dangerous to keep it. But I remember some of his exact words: *I often think of our last argument just before you left for Vitebsk. If only there were a way for me to show you. If only there were a way to reconcile that day, I would invite you here, to Moscow, but I know in my heart you would not come. In any matter, dear friend, I believe your life is currently in danger.*

Following this, Alexander briefly stated that the man who had visited me had been with the White Army's intelligence section. Then he gave me detailed instructions for emigration to the United States. For evident reasons, he couldn't condone emigration to the United States, but he also understood that many Liteh Jews were going there. In his letter, I could sense a certain triumph, but also regret, and, if I'm not mistaken, a sad resignation in the certainty that our paths were diverging. For a long while, I stared and thought about those words: *dear friend.*

As a child in Vitebsk and as a student in Petrograd, I never had friends. Friendship was what other people experienced. For most of my life, I held the belief that I was surrounded by a thick mist. But here was a friend. One that understood me. At the end of the letter he wrote: *It's impossible to know where we will end up, but one day I think we will see each other again. I will find you, or, with any luck, you will find me. I have a certain confidence in this.* I reread Alexander's letter nearly ten times and committed it to memory before destroying it in the fireplace. Two days later, another polite and spotless Red Army soldier hand-delivered a thick envelope. There was no letter in it. Instead, it was full of money orders, traveling papers, and visas for Alinochka and me. Through Alexander's friendship, I felt as if everything was connected in ways that were both microscopic and vast.

After three days of preparation, we left Vitebsk for Brest on a supply train. The train stopped in Minsk and Red Army soldiers boarded. They were clean-shaven and young, yet most looked tired beyond their years. From there, we traveled south by night into the Ukrainian territories that were claimed by both the Bolsheviks and the forces of the Ukrainian People's Republic, who were in alliance with the Polish Army. In the outskirts of a small town, I was surprised to see a small unit of Ukrainian soldiers board our train. When I asked a Russian soldier about the Ukrainians, he explained to me that the Poles and Russians were both turning the Ukrainians against each other.

"The greatest hell," he said to me, "is when you're forced to kill your own brother." At some point we slept, but I don't remember when or for how long. The miles were ceaseless and full of flat plains and plateaus for as far as the eye could see. Sometimes on the western horizon, we could see strange outcroppings, possibly natural borders or the ruins of villages, which, later, in my dreams, took on the shape of human faces. In the sky, gray rain clouds formed in the east and then dispersed and then formed again.

At one point, the train stopped in the middle of a wheat field. A unit of soldiers got off the train and started marching east. I asked Alinochka to stay on the train and I got off with one of the captains to get a better look. It took a moment, but then I saw where the soldiers were headed. Hundreds of corpses lay on a road in the near distance. I couldn't tell if the corpses were those of the enemies or ours. I guess it didn't matter. Farther east, the entire wheat field was burning. Thick smoke rose from the field and cut its way eastward in the sky. The captain barked orders and passed around binoculars. I don't remember for how long we watched the flames, but by the time the soldiers returned half the landscape was shriveled and black, a volcanic wasteland more than a wheat field. The captain told me to board the train. Inside, my beautiful Alinochka was sleeping and holding the small mound of her belly. That mound was you, Benjaminas.

Telling you all of this now, I realize that you were there for everything. How strange! At that moment, I felt deeply thankful for Alinochka and for life. I had never felt that before and I thought of fatherhood and the corpses and in some small perceptible way I wonder if this was the moment I truly understood that I could die. The sensation felt like I was passing through a wall. Finally, the train left and we headed west toward the Carpathian Mountains, leaving the burning field and civil war behind.

At the western Ukrainian border, we transferred to a passenger train headed for Budapest. From there we transferred to another passenger train for La Spezia, Italy. Although I was worried about the border crossings, all of our visas and papers were in working order. Alexander had thought of everything. After the Ukrainian border crossing, the trip was rather routine and Alinochka and I were grateful for the safety and increased comfort. By the first week in May, we arrived in La Spezia, a coastal port city that also served as a naval base. Many streets and buildings were still devastated by the previous war, but the city was also full of construction crews. New public buildings and monuments were being built everywhere. We couldn't believe it. The city was restless and teeming with people. We lived quietly and happily in a small hotel room for five months. During the day, we walked the streets of La Spezia and talked and talked. In the evenings, we read Italian newspapers and novels. Then, one morning in mid-October 1920, we boarded a ship headed for New York City.

Saul unfolded his hands and stared at the candle. "It took nearly nine days to cross the rest of the Mediterranean and the Atlantic Ocean," he said, "and each day was like a nightmare. As it turned out, we had third-class tickets. We spent most of our days and nights crowded together in small, luggage-filled rooms. Like rats. We slept and ate like rats, too. When we washed, we were forced to use salt water, which caused sores and infections. It was horrible. Anyway, these are details." He touched the cards on the table and smiled. "All that's important is that we survived."

Saul looked at his son.

"Maybe we should stop there," he said, "it's late. And Maxwell does not want to hear every detail about the Atlantic crossing. Of course, he is tired."

"I'm not tired," said Maxwell. He picked up a stray card, a queen of spades, and imagined the Atlantic Ocean as his father had once described it—as a vast and horrific prophecy, a graveyard, a giant violet in full bloom.

"The rest of the story is something I only told your mother, Benjaminas. I have never told anyone else. It's like a memory locked away. I want you boys to understand that," he said.

"You should continue, tateh."

"But—"

"If you stop now, tateh, you will never tell it."

"Okay, I will tell."

★ ★ ★

On the fourth day at sea, a man was murdered, said Saul. The rumor of the murder was like a whisper, maybe two or three people in our section of the ship had heard about it. Soon, though, the rumor took shape and quickly spread through the entire ship. The details were few, but clear. An Italian man in first class had been stabbed multiple times and left to bleed to death just outside his cabin door. At first, I didn't think too much about the murder. These things happen all the time, especially on a ship full of thousands of people. But on the morning of the fifth day at sea, a handful of Italian sailors came to our section of the ship.

The sailors were mostly quiet, but one was armed with a pistol and he demanded in Italian that we move away from our luggage. He was the one in command. Some of the passengers—those that understood Italian—moved away and stood off to the side, even if there was not much room. Alinochka and I translated for those who didn't understand.

Then the sailors started grabbing our luggage at random. Since most of the trunks and suitcases were locked, they had to wait for the owners to unlock them. The sailors then spilled the entire contents of the trunks and suitcases on the ship floor. They searched everything in great detail: clothes, papers, books, cigarette cartons, etc. But they didn't find anything important. For the most part, the sailors looked annoyed or bored since they had probably been searching luggage all night and all morning, but the sailor in command stood straight as an iron rod and watched the entire process closely. After some time, he disappeared. The sailors stopped searching. They passed around cigarettes and looked at us like we were rats.

When the commanding sailor returned, he motioned for the male passengers to line up. We did. He then examined each of us closely—our shoes, our shirts, our hands, our faces. You have to understand we were shabby and covered in dirt. More than a few of us, including me, had stopped bathing regularly due to the harsh salt water. I imagine we smelled horrible and I was under the impression that the sailors thought that this was our normal condition, that we were, in fact, rats. It was embarrassing and shameful. But what choice did we have? When the commanding sailor came to me, he motioned to two sailors. They grabbed me roughly. I protested in Italian and told them that I hadn't done anything, but one of the sailors slammed his fist into my temple and everything went momentarily black.

I remember that Alinochka screamed. I took a few deep breaths and opened my eyes, but I couldn't see much, just a stack of luggage and a few wretched passengers. Everything was blurry. I turned my head slowly, toward the direction of Alinochka, but I couldn't see her, either. She continued to scream, at first in Yiddish, and then in Italian. Your mother, Benjaminas, had such a fierce voice! I really couldn't believe that this was happening. I wondered briefly if the civil war had somehow followed me to this ship. Maybe, Alinochka had been right, I thought miserably, and I couldn't escape Petrograd. Not even in the middle of the Atlantic Ocean. But, as it turned out, that was not the case. The civil war had been a collective and widespread horror. But, for the most part, it was behind us. What was about to happen was more like the nightmare of a madman.

I was taken to a cell near the first-class luggage hold. The cell was narrow and gray. It looked new, if somewhat unfinished. There were two cots, a metal chair, and a single dull light bulb, which hung from a thin wire in the ceiling. Two guards stayed to watch over the cell. They smoked and talked about their hometowns and relatives. Their voices echoed through the cell terribly. There were two other men in the cell, both sitting on a cot and speaking to each other in whispers. They nodded at me. I sat in the chair and felt my temple. A razor-sharp pain spread through my head and I felt a sticky residue, which I realized was blood. Still, I knew I would be okay. I was breathing fine and my vision had returned to normal. Some time passed. Three other men were brought in, which made the total six men. One man, pale and thin, paced the cell back and forth. A few of the other men talked in Polish and Russian, exchanging rumors about possible thefts and the murder of the first-class Italian passenger. The legality of the cell where we were being held also came up, but no real conclusions could be made about this. I listened and remained silent. It wasn't long before I realized that we all shared at least two major traits: we were all third-class passengers and Jews.

When the commanding sailor returned, he held a sheet of paper, which I thought might be orders or a list. He said something to the guards and they laughed. Then he opened the cell and one of the guards spoke slowly in Italian:

"Who goes first?"

I translated this into Polish and Russian. One of the men who had been sitting on the cot stood up confidently and said to us in Yiddish, "All of this is a mistake." He then walked out of the cell.

The guards never brought him back. Every so often the commanding sailor took out another man until it was just the pale, thin man and me in the cell. A few times, he looked at me, shrugged his narrow shoulders, and in Russian said, "I don't know." Once, he looked me in the eyes and said, "Back home, I was a teacher. Maybe a Rav one day." I could tell from his accent that—like me—he was from the Liteh, most likely Pinsk or one of the surrounding villages. He was maybe twenty. He could've been a distant cousin, I thought.

We waited. I can't be certain just how much time passed. Three or five hours. I thought of Alinochka. I worried that she might suddenly go into labor and that I would not be able to be at her side. Sometime later, the commanding sailor retuned and motioned to me. I'm not sure what I felt just then. Maybe nothing, since there was little I could really do. Or maybe a quiet sort of terror. Both probably. I was escorted out of the cell by two guards and led down passageway after passageway, sometimes turning so often I thought that we were doubling back toward the cell. The interior of the ship was immense. I couldn't help but imagine that I was being led through a labyrinth.

Eventually, we arrived at a large, sparsely furnished cabin. At the far end a small porthole looked out into the ocean. A few empty bookshelves lined the walls and in the center of the room was a long oak table. Behind the table was a black leather chair. Sitting in the chair was the captain. The guards took their positions, one at my left side, one at my right side. They saluted the captain.

The captain wore a spotless white uniform and had a thin, groomed mustache. His skin was smooth and he had a slender, built frame. He must have been in his mid-forties. He wore a small leather scabbard, which I assumed was fit with a knife.

"Would you rather we speak in Russian or Italian?" the captain asked me.

"Russian," I responded. Although I was confident in my Italian, I thought it might be best to speak in my native tongue in order to avoid any misunderstandings.

"Okay, good. Well, first, let me introduce myself. I am Captain Argenti of the SS *Beatrice*. Your name is Saul Druer, correct?"

I nodded.

The captain folded his arms and sighed. "Well, this has been a very long day, so let's get to the point, Mr. Druer. As captain, I normally wouldn't be as involved in something like this, but I am sure you are aware that a man was recently murdered. He was stabbed fifteen times and left to die. An Italian man. A friend of mine actually. We are all quite upset."

"I'm sorry for your loss," I said softly.

He took out a gold timepiece from his uniform pocket and checked it quickly. He then put it on the oak table. Half of his right pointer finger was missing. It ended just above the knuckle. "Is my Russian okay?" he asked.

"It's good. I understand," I replied.

"Do you mind if we switch to Italian? I have been speaking Russian all day and my throat is parched. It's an unforgiving language."

"That's fine," I said in Italian.

"We are looking for the murderer, of course. Do you understand?"

"I do," I said, "but this has nothing to do with me." I wanted to get this over with as soon as possible.

The captain stared at me for a long, long time. I remained silent. The simple fact of the matter was that I hadn't murdered anyone.

He flashed a grin and ran a finger along the gold timepiece. "Of course, of course," he said, "I don't think you murdered anyone. But we do have procedures here. Technicalities, you understand. I served on this very ship during the war and was in charge of its conversion to a passenger ship. The SS *Beatrice* is a wonderful ship. We want to avoid bad luck, especially regarding a murder." He picked up the gold timepiece and checked it again. Slowly, he said, "An unsolved murder would affect the ship's integrity, you understand. All this," the captain said and lifted his gaze as if to encompass the entire ship and the entire problem of the murder, "all this has to be handled at sea. The sea is the proper place for this sort of thing."

The captain motioned to the guard standing at my left. The guard took out a small notepad and began writing. The captain continued, "So, just to be certain, Mr. Druer, I have a few questions. Let's begin. Where were you yesterday morning?"

"I was in the third-class steerage with my wife all morning. She's pregnant and nearly due."

"Ah! A soon-to-be father. If she goes into labor shortly, you should know we have a doctor on the SS *Beatrice* for this sort of thing. A good doctor. Normally, he is reserved for the first-class passengers, but we'll make an exception, of course." The captain glanced at the guard to my left, who was busy writing. The guard nodded and wrote something down on a new sheet of paper.

"So, you see," I explained, "there would be no reason for me to leave my wife's side. Let alone to murder somebody I have never even met." The man in the cell had been right. All of this was some horrible mistake.

"Of course, of course, just a few more questions, Mr. Druer, and then if everything checks out you can return to your lovely wife."

The captain picked up the gold timepiece and stared at it for a moment. He then put it back on the table and covered it with his hand. "Did you get a good look at the men in the cell with you? Do you know any of those men?"

I shook my head. "I don't know any of those men. This morning was the first time I had seen any of them."

"Are you sure?" asked the captain, and made a rough noise with his throat.

"Yes, I'm sure."

"Of course, of course," said the captain. He looked at the guards and said something in Italian, but I didn't understand. He spoke a dialect that sounded like Italian, but could've been anything. The guard with the notepad said something in return and both the guards and the captain chuckled.

"Okay, Mr. Druer," the captain continued, and leaned forward in his chair, "I'll let you in on something here. You'll be let free. All the men I spoke to before you were let free. I thought that maybe one of them or even you might have something to do with the murder. Not directly, mind you, but as an accomplice. Maybe, even indirectly, you understand?"

I was silent. I did not understand the captain's point.

"In any case, I believe you're innocent. I believe the other four are innocent, as well. I thought that maybe…" And here he trailed off somewhat. "Anyway, it seems as if I was wrong. Too bad, eh?"

There was something monstrous in the way the captain said *too bad*.

I looked out the porthole. The ocean wobbled, and beyond I could glimpse the light of the setting sun.

"I don't like traveling west," he said. "There are always problems westward. Too many refugees like you, Mr. Druer. Not all of them are bad, of course, but they cause problems nonetheless. Now, eastward, that's the way to travel. On our return trip, the ship will be full of goods and rich Americans. Everything will be quiet and smooth. The sea is kinder somehow when we travel east, toward Rome." He glanced at his gold timepiece and then put it back into his uniform pocket. He then took out a thin knife from his scabbard and handed it to the guard standing at my right. The guard saluted and left. The other guard remained. "Have you ever been to Jerusalem, Mr. Druer?"

I shook my head.

"Sometimes, I think about how the Roman soldiers under Pompey came to that forsaken part of the world. I wonder what they thought. It was definitely a very different place than the grandeur of Rome. Of course, they conquered the land in no time at all. But still the Jews gave the Romans trouble. Revolt after revolt. For centuries. My father used to tell me how some Jews even became pirates near the seas of Phoenicia and Egypt. Maybe, you've read about this?"

I nodded and stared out the porthole. The light was now bloodred, or maybe I am imagining that color right now. Regardless, the sun was still setting.

"And I imagine," the captain continued, "that you've never been to the Dead Sea then? Well, you should go one day. It's really an astonishing place. Due to its high salinity, the water is so buoyant you can't sink. Even if you tried. Actually, it's quite relaxing to just lie on its waters and float. That's not all. The minerals and salts in the Dead Sea have healing properties. With my own eyes, I have seen it cure migraines, arthritis, and cancer. Of course, it took true Romans to notice this. On the advice of his Roman superiors, the Judean king Herod the Great even set up a health resort there for himself. So, you can understand why the Romans, who lived, breathed, and died by the mercy of Neptune, took a particular interest in the Dead Sea. They truly understood the power of the seas. Ah! Well, I'm speaking in circles. So, the Jewish rebels. Well, the Romans had an interesting way of dealing with the Jewish rebels. Do you want to hear about it?"

I didn't say anything.

"Of course, you do. Well, the Romans knew the Dead Sea could heal, but also that it could be used as a form of punishment. In any given Roman unit, there was at least one artist who was prone to painting. The Romans, as you know, were extraordinary artists. Well, there are many similarities between the brush and the knife. The Romans understood this well. They brought captured rebels to the banks of the Dead Sea and tied their limbs together, like you would a sacrificial lamb or a pig, and then the artist made hundreds of deep cuts into their flesh. Right into the face and lips and limbs and torso and the genitals. Then they threw the rebels into the Dead Sea.

"I can tell you from personal experience that even just one small sliver is painful in the Dead Sea. The salt enters the flesh and the pain is almost unbearable. But hundreds of deep cuts. That sort of pain is inconceivable. Most rebels tried to drown themselves, but the prospect of that was difficult, since the Dead Sea kept them afloat. It's a time-consuming way to die, which is the point, of course, but eventually the rebels died. They bled to death in the sea. If they were lucky, they lost consciousness first. The truly lucky suffered a heart attack and died immediately. Once, I'm told, nearly two hundred rebels were punished in concert this way. Can you imagine the horror of that? So, you understand, the Dead Sea is both an Eden and a particular type of hell. You really should visit one day. It's your ancestral waters after all."

The captain then stood up, blocking the view of the porthole. "But you're going west," he continued, "toward this New Rome. So many of you are going west. Do you know what they do to Jews in the United States, Mr. Druer?"

I was silent for a long, long time.

The captain motioned toward the guard, who placed his hand on my shoulder.

"Let's go."

Once again, I was led through the ship and down passageway after passageway. At one point, we walked through a large dining room, which was decorated in various shades of gray marble. Dazzling stripes of gold lined the walls and reminded me of the bright rays of a warm sun. Well-dressed first-class passengers were smiling and eating roasted chicken and potatoes. It smelled wonderful. I hadn't eaten anything all day. In some ways, the short walk through the dining room was worse than being held in the ship's cell. The guard, who winked at me, was well aware of that fact. I was then led to the deck of the ship. Thousands of stars were in the sky and a cool breeze blew over the deck. Everything was eerily quiet. At that point, the guard handed me off to a commanding sailor and left.

I was led to a rubber lifeboat. The lifeboat hung over the edge of the ship, ready to be dropped into the ocean. I wasn't exactly sure what was happening, so I kept quiet and gave the commanding sailor a hard stare. He handed me an official-looking note. It said: *It's not the Dead Sea, but it'll do. Captain Argenti.*

The cool air suddenly felt frigid. I wondered if the captain had lied to me and if he had brought the other prisoners here. I thought the worst. Was the captain quietly executing us like Jewish rebels, one by one? Had their lacerated and raw bodies been dumped into the ocean? It seemed impossible. The commanding sailor then told me to get into the lifeboat. I refused. He wore an indifferent expression, which, I think, is more menacing than an angry expression. Someone who is indifferent will do anything. He took out a pistol from his belt buckle. He released the safety, aimed the muzzle at my chest, and shrugged.

There was nothing I could do, I realized. Maybe, the captain's note had been an empty threat. I hadn't been tied up. I didn't see any other sailors, let alone one with a knife. In desperation, I thought that I could somehow survive at sea in the lifeboat, that another ship might come by and that this possibility far outweighed the possibility of surviving a gunshot wound to the chest. I took a deep breath and got in the lifeboat.

From above, I heard a mechanical crank, and the lifeboat slowly descended along the hull of the ship. My poor, poor Alinochka, I thought sadly. What would they tell her? What would she tell our child? Near the surface of the ocean, however, the lifeboat suddenly stopped. To my left, just under the foaming waters, four tremendous propellers were spinning.

Then I saw the teacher. A fine mist, created by the propellers, spread through the air and obscured his body, but I immediately knew it was him. He was hung up naked by ropes—his legs and feet tied together behind his back—and suspended two meters above the propellers. Long, deep cuts covered his entire body. Some of the cuts were in the shape of letters or indecipherable symbols. His once pale skin was a horrific shade of pink, the color of a freshly caught and sliced salmon. Thin layers of salt encrusted his wounds. A considerable amount of blood was dripping from these wounds into the churning ocean, leaving a thin trail of crimson behind the ship as it moved through the water. The sight of that trail of blood in the ocean still haunts me.

I couldn't tell if the teacher was alive or dead. This is what the captain meant by his note. This was his punishment. He was a madman. I vomited over the side of the lifeboat until my stomach clenched. Then I started yelling. The oppressive sound of the propellers drowned out my voice, but I was sure I could get someone's attention. Before long, the commanding sailor popped his head over the ship's railing and pointed his pistol at me. He then adjusted the pistol and fired a warning shot into the ocean.

The teacher looked at me. His face, like his body, was covered in hemorrhaging cuts, though these were crisscrossed in strange and horrible patterns. A bloody rag was stuffed into his mouth and tied tightly behind his head with a thick rope. He was alive, but barely. I could tell that it must have taken substantial effort to keep his eyes open. I imagined that the pain he was suffering was horrifying, nightmarish. I have never felt as much sorrow in my life as when he looked at me just then. I tried to say something in Yiddish, but nothing came out. He turned away and closed his eyes.

I remained in the lifeboat, unable to help the teacher. Whether he had murdered the Italian or not didn't matter to me. Nobody deserved this. I sat down and felt true helplessness and despair, like an abandoned child. I tried to close my eyes and think of the labyrinth, the familiar darkness and the cool, hard touch of the walls, but I couldn't. There was nothing about this or fate that made any sense. Time passed, but it was difficult to tell how much. A few rock-like clouds floated in the sky to the south. The moon was out, but its light was thin and vaporous. The stars flickered violently, yet how could that be? They were just stars. Once or twice, the teacher spasmed and I thought that he might somehow fall into the ocean. At one point, he looked at me again, his eyes clear and wide, but it was as if he were looking right through me. As if I were a ghost.

More time passed. The teacher inched toward death. It was miserable. I couldn't watch anymore, but there was nothing I could do to escape the image of the dying man. I stared into the ocean, transfixed by its waves and cold, moving surface. The sea has a hallucinatory power. Just beneath its surface I saw Vitebsk.

I saw its cathedral and monastery and synagogues. I saw its three rivers, which were steel blue tunnels boring down into the ocean floor. I saw clearly the people of Vitebsk, old rabbis wandering aimlessly, peasants carrying scythes, vengeful soldiers marching toward some distant, fiery catastrophe. And then I saw Alexander Sidorov. I saw his face. I saw his Turkish sword, the fin of a restless shark circling the dark waters.

I imagine all of this must have lasted a few minutes, but I have no way to tell. At some point, I fell asleep and dreamed that I was drowning. I was overcome with the vague and yet extremely relentless sensation of having entered the sea, of being swallowed up in its cold, fierce, and starless waters.

When I woke, the lifeboat was full of water and the sun was rising from the eastern edges of the Atlantic Ocean. The teacher was slumped over. His eyes were open. At first, I thought that he was staring into the rising sun, but then I realized that he was dead. Shortly after, the lifeboat ascended. On the deck, a quiet and boyish sailor nodded at me and I walked away free.

That afternoon there was a small funeral for the Italian man who had been murdered. For some uncanny reason, I attended. Sailors wrapped his body in an Italian flag and then they put him on a bier. A few family members gave eulogies and there were prayers. He was then lowered into the ocean. There was no ceremony for the teacher. For all anyone knew or cared, he had disappeared. That must have been the sixth day at sea.

The next morning, you were born, Benjaminas. Given everything that your poor mother had been through, there were a few serious complications. But a good doctor came to see her and, after a long, nerve-wracking day, everything was fine. The captain had sent the doctor, as promised. Your birth filled me with such joy, but it was also preceded by a nightmare. It's difficult even today for me to explain what all this meant to your mother and me. But maybe now you can understand this nightmare a little more. Without you, Benjaminas, without even the idea of you nestled in your mother's belly, I would have died with the teacher. If not a physical death, then an inner death, a metaphysical death as they used to say in Petrograd, which in many ways is worse. Meaning and purpose would have slipped away from life. Does this make sense? Without you, I really would have become a living ghost. But maybe this is too much. Maybe, I am embarrassing you now?

"No, tateh," said Benjamin. He took the cards from the table and started stacking them one by one. Then he turned to his father, sadly, and asked, "Why didn't you tell anyone about the teacher?"

Saul looked at his son for a moment.

"It's simple," he said, "or maybe it seemed simple then. I was afraid for your life and your mother's life. The captain, I believed, was a madman. In a very real way. I never doubted that he would do something horrible if I told anyone on the ship. At the funeral for the Italian man, during one of the prayers, I caught a glimpse of the captain standing on the deck. I'm deeply ashamed to say it, but I even thought about killing him. In the end, I'm not that type of man. You should never be that type of man, as you boys both know. For years, I dreamed that the captain was a Roman dybbuk. I dreamed that the spirit of a long-dead and suffering Roman soldier had been drawn to some sort of severe melancholy or psychosis in the Italian captain, and that it was controlling him. But, I don't know, those were just dreams."

Saul stared at the candle, as if he was trying to transfer those dreams to its flames. "And now, it's very late," he said, "we should be sleeping."

"One more thing, tateh," said Benjamin, "what happened to Alexander Sidorov?"

At this, he smiled. "I don't know. Sometimes, I imagine that one day a polite and spotless Red Army soldier will deliver a letter here from Alexander. It's a foolish thought, I know."

Saul stood up. "Now, we really should be sleeping," he said, "I've been talking through the night like someone possessed with sod ha'ibbur."

"Okay, tateh," said Benjamin.

"Maxwell," said Saul, "you may stay here for as long as you need."

After Maxwell washed up, Saul asked him if he needed help bringing the cot down from the roof. Maxwell told him that he would like to sleep on the rooftop for one more night. Saul nodded and smiled at the boy. It was very late. The kitchen was dark. Still, faint moonlight entered through the window. There were shadows everywhere in the kitchen, but somehow they were pleasant shadows, the shadows cast by flawless geometric figures.

They went to the rooftop and when they reached the door Maxwell opened it with a key that Benjamin had given him. A few pigeons rested on the ledge, cooing softly. A cool breeze blew over the roof. From somewhere in the distance, the rattle of a train could be heard. Maxwell hesitated a moment and then said, "If it's okay, I have a question, too."

"Of course," said Saul.

"Where is Benjamin's mother, Alinochka?"

The father regarded the boy.

"She became very ill and passed away when he was just five," the father said. "After all these years, she was the only other person who knew about how we came to this country. She really knew the story. All the dark and joyous aspects of it. In fact, even though I experienced all those things on the ship, she understood them much better than I ever could. Memories should pass through a mother. If she were here, I think, she would have told you our story much better than I ever could."

They walked in silence to the storage shed and stopped there.

"And your mother?" asked Saul, somewhat reluctantly.

"My mother," Maxwell began, but he couldn't finish.

"I understand," said Saul, "it's the same with us."

In the mornings, after rye bread and coffee, Maxwell and Benjamin returned to the market to search for Maxwell's father, but there was still no sign of him. They went to the police station, but the police were disinterested. One sluggish, pock-marked officer told the boys that everybody's old man went missing at some point and then half-heartedly asked Maxwell a few questions and filled out a yellow form. Another officer just shrugged and told Maxwell that unless he was greatly mistaken he would never see his father again.

Sometimes, as they searched, Maxwell felt feverish. He thought it was the overwhelming sense of aimlessness that made his body burn, but later he understood that the sensation was anger at his father for deserting him. Afterward, more often than not, they left the market and took El trains to neighborhoods that were vaguely reminiscent of foreign countries. At seven or eight, just before dusk, they'd take the streetcar back.

On no few occasions, they ended their days on the rooftop, where they sat with their feet dangling over the ledge, sharing a half-smoked cigarette, fiddling with a cheap radio kit. Sometimes, with the air of failed detectives, they recounted the events of the day and the search for Maxwell's father. Other times Benjamin talked nonstop about the people who lived in his neighborhood, which he had nicknamed the Isle of Pale (after the now defunct Pale of Settlement in the also now defunct Russian Empire). He told Maxwell about the rabbi who ran a counterfeit synagogue, the young woman from a shtetl outside Kiev who had once walked from Kiev to Istanbul and who now never left her apartment building but could still be found every winter night, like a sleepwalker, on the rooftop across the street bundled in a black cloak playing a violin, the alderman who once walked the streets with the infamous anarchists Emma Goldman and Ben Reitman, the Orthodox grocer whose favorite thing to say in English was *moderation in all things, including moderation*, in short, about all those Jews for whom, according to Benjamin's father, a paradox was *everything*.

Once, as even further illustration, Benjamin told Maxwell a joke that his father had told him. A poor man from Kaunas beseeched God every week for charity. Every week God listened to the man's tales of woe and doled out gifts that, little by little, improved the man's condition. One day, God, who was really quite busy during those troubled years, appeared and said to him, "Listen, you know I will continue to help you every week. You don't have to convince me anymore. A little less cringing, a little less moaning, and we would both be happier."

To which, matter-of-factly, the poor man said, "My good YHWH, I don't teach you how to be a god, so please don't teach me how to be a human."

Maxwell enjoyed listening to Benjamin's stories and, speaking truthfully, one might call him Maxwell's first friend. Each day, it became a little harder for him leave the city and Maxwell spent more and more time with Benjamin, whether searching for his father in the huge market and its surrounding neighborhoods or smoking and talking on the rooftop overlooking the Isle of Pale.

Chance or fate or the old mad pirate's Caribbean devil had it that Benjamin too was the first and only person Maxwell ever told about *A Model Earth*. One August day, while Maxwell was looking through Benjamin's back issues of *Amazing Stories* and *Weird Tales* in the rooftop shed, he discovered the opening chapter of his mother's novel *Lost City* in the June 1929, Vol. 13, No. 1 issue of *Weird Tales*. At first, since he hadn't known anything about the excerpt, which was titled "The Dominicana," he was taken by surprise, and since Benjamin was working that day at the delicatessen, he had no one with whom to share his surprise. Instead, he read the excerpt of his mother's novel three times. Each time he wept.

Later, when Benjamin returned, he told him:

"My mother wrote this."

Benjamin took the issue and read the name of the author. "Adana Moreau is your mother?" he said with astonishment. Then, after a long pause, he added, "What a huge goddamn coincidence."

To which Maxwell replied that there were no such things as coincidences and that rare things like this happened in the universe all the time.

"What rare things?" said Benjamin, even more perplexed.

As dusk fell and they shared a cigarette, they tried to decide which rare things could be mistaken for coincidences or vice versa and were unable to agree. Later that night, Benjamin told Maxwell that the only thing to do at that point was for him to read *Lost City*. Maxwell agreed that this was the best solution and he lent Benjamin the copy he had brought with him from New Orleans.

The next morning, at the kitchen table, Benjamin told Maxwell that he hadn't slept all night (or maybe he had slept a little and dreamed that he hadn't, he couldn't remember). He said it really didn't matter if coincidences existed or not because *Lost City* was a great science fiction story. He stressed the word *great*. Maxwell said he didn't know the difference between a great science fiction story or just a good one or even a terrible one. Benjamin said the difference lay in possibility, in the possibility of the story and the possibility of the language in which the story was told. Immediately he began to cite examples. He talked about Mary Shelley and H. P. Lovecraft, he talked about Yevgeny Zamyatin and E. E. "Doc" Smith, he raved about Aldous Huxley. He said he had read all those authors and that Adana Moreau was their equal or maybe, in some ways, she was even better. Then, naturally, he asked Maxwell if his mother had written anything else.

"Yes," he said tentatively, "she wrote a sequel called *A Model Earth*, but she destroyed it in a fire just before she died."

"Did you read it?" asked Benjamin.

"I did."

"Can you tell me about it?" he asked with some hesitation. For a few seconds Maxwell said nothing and only studied his face. Then he nodded.

As they wandered the market that day, which was plunged in frenetic late-summer activity, Maxwell told Benjamin the plot of *A Model Earth* from start to finish. What little he couldn't remember he made up. When he was finished, Benjamin started pacing the already overcrowded sidewalk in excitement.

"Is it good?" asked Maxwell over the din of the market.

Benjamin stopped dead in his tracks, looked Maxwell in the eyes, where he was certain there were still a few traces of *A Model Earth* to be told, and said, "You know the answer to that already, Joe. It's better than good and you need to write it all down again. You have to finish the story."

Maxwell thought about it for a moment and then shook his head.

"You have to understand. It's still possible to get it all down. It has to exist again. Others need to read it."

Just then, Maxwell saw his mother sitting at the kitchen table with a typewriter, her long coffee-colored hair forming the swirl of an Arabic numeral on her back as she bent her head down, her gaze fixed on the manuscript, typing to a rhythmic beat that matched his own heart, a small heart beating in the chaos of her final days.

"I can't," he said.

For several nights, Maxwell had terrible dreams in which time was reversed and his father was *his* son, and his grandfather was his grandson, and great-grandfather was his great-grandson, and so forth, through the entire line of his African pirate dynasty, until the end was the beginning.

Sometimes, to calm himself after he woke, he drew geometry problems from memory on a small notebook until he could fall back asleep. Other times, he woke shaking and was overcome by the irresistible urge to go outside and walk.

After another week with no leads, Saul pointed the boys to an article in the *Daily Illustrated Times* that he thought could help. The article was about a mother, who, in 1919, had gone to Paris in search of her son. He had joined the Allied troops in 1914, but disappeared shortly thereafter. The woman didn't find her son. However, years later, while living in an apartment near the Maison de Victor Hugo in Paris, a soldier-turned-grocer who resembled her son, who had nearly the same high forehead and burning cobalt blue eyes, brought her a bag of vegetables. He had fought in the Austro-Hungarian ranks and had lost his mother during a British tank assault. In some ways, the woman he saw resembled his deceased mother. She had the same dark hazel hair and nearly the same laugh, high-pitched and tender, a laugh that could be heard through the wheat fields of his small village as a child. Upon seeing the soldier, she laughed and called him *son* in French. Upon hearing the woman's laugh, the soldier called her *mother* in Hungarian, and entered the apartment, which suddenly felt as familiar to him as the fiery green waters of the Danube.

"But how can this help us, tateh?" said Benjamin when his father was finished. "The people in this story are delusional."

"It has nothing to do with delusion, Benjaminas," said his father, "it has to do with forgetting, and then remembering."

"Like an amnesiac? Still, this does not help us, tateh," said Benjamin.

"Yes, it does," his father said. "After I read the article, I went to the offices of the *Daily Illustrated Times* and convinced the reporter, a man who is clearly interested in missing people, to help us look for Maxwell's father."

"How did you convince him?" asked Maxwell.

"I told him your father is a pirate," he said with a smile.

A few days later, they met the reporter, a skinny man with red hair and a long jawline like a Moai stone statue, in a busy diner on South Canal. To start, the reporter, who was somewhat skeptical throughout the interview, asked Maxwell when he had arrived to Chicago. He replied that it had been on July 5th or July 6th or maybe even July 7th. He didn't know for certain because he had been trapped in a boxcar.

"A bullman?" asked the reporter.

Maxwell nodded.

"What a piece of shit," said the reporter, and Saul and Benjamin nodded solemnly in agreement.

"That's what the other bullman who let me out said, too."

The reporter (who chose not to write any of this down) laughed. Then he took out a pack of cigarettes and offered one to Maxwell, who nodded as a way of saying thank you, and stuck it behind his ear for later. After this the reporter suddenly turned more serious and began to write down the information Maxwell gave him: date and place of birth, names of parents and where they had met, description and profession of his missing father, names of any surviving family members or friends who had known his father, why and how he had come to Chicago, address of where he was staying (which would not be published, the reporter reminded him, and which Saul then offered freely), etc. When he was finished with his questions, the reporter told Maxwell that he would see what he could do help to him find his father, but he couldn't make any promises. Then they shook hands and the reporter left the diner, in a hurry.

Afterward, Saul, who had been saving for some time for just such an event, took the boys to the Century of Progress World's Fair, which, according to a young, eager attendant at the front gates, was a *brief city sprung out of the prairie and flung into the dust of the not-too-distant future.* They visited the Maya Temple, the Crystal Maze, and the House of Tomorrow. The fair center was more carnivalesque, with Ripley's Believe It or Not, The Temple of Mystery (where, to the boys' astonishment, a magician named Carter the Great sawed a woman in half, then hung himself), replicas of foreign villages, and the Streets of Paris, where young men loitered, gangster types with missing teeth straight out of a crime novel. Farther north there were public spaces cloistered along the shores of a large blue lagoon, above which, at some two hundred feet, ran the suspended cables and rocket cars of the Sky Ride. The aquarium and the museum were there, too. In front of the Hall of Science there was a fountain with moving robots, where they stood for some time in the sweltering heat, drinking cold milkshakes and immersed in a sweeping debate about whether robots would one day become human-like, if, like Frankenstein's monster, they would reminisce and feel hunger and suffer or, at the very least, take on the dim sensations of suffering.

The Hall of Science featured a stratosphere gondola, a deep-sea submersible, and a chemistry exhibit, in which a scientist calmly explained that the secrets of the atom would one day reveal themselves to contain the power to destroy the world.

At some point, they wandered into a large black dome, where an astronomer from Harvard University, a small woman with tight black curls and a red Pashmina shawl wrapped tightly around her shoulders, introduced herself and then talked about the proliferation of instants that followed the birth of the universe some billions of years earlier from a primeval atom, the Cosmic Egg, and led inevitably or accidentally (scientists still had no idea) to them being in that room listening to her. Then she flipped a switch and the black dome was flooded with galaxies and nebulas. She explained that the Earth spun around once every twenty-four hours, the moon orbited the Earth every twenty-seven days, the Earth orbited the sun in one terrestrial year, and the sun orbited the center of the Milky Way galaxy once every 230 million years, which was a *galactic year* and which meant that the last time the sun was in its current position, the dinosaurs ruled the Earth. In turn, the Milky Way, according to Edwin Hubble, was hurtling through space and time in an expanding universe bursting with billions of still other galaxies.

"With repetition," she said and spread her arms, encompassing the darkness, the dust, and the burning stars, "even the extraordinary becomes ordinary."

Later, before dusk, they rode the Sky Ride. From the vantage point of their rocket car, the city, like all American cities, was endless. To the east was a vast lake that had once been a glacier, a sea, thought Maxwell in awe, that was not a sea.

Afterward, they ordered hamburgers, French fries, and Coca-Colas in a restaurant overlooking the blue lagoon. They watched the Arcturus ceremony, a light and water show. When the food arrived, they talked about all the things they had seen that day and shared the French fries from the center of the table, like a family.

On August 27th, an article with the headline "Son of the Last Pirate of the New World" appeared on page six of the *Daily Illustrated Times*. In the article, the reporter, in a rather tabloid-like fashion, first described his meeting with a half Negro, half Dominican boy who had arrived to Chicago from New Orleans to look for his father, the *Last Pirate of the New World*. Then, switching tones, the article gave a highly detailed history of pirating in the Americas, starting with the Spanish Empire in the late 1500s and the French pirates and privateers who plundered Spanish and Portuguese treasure ships and colonial ports, including Brazilian ports on the Atlantic Ocean exporting gold and Spanish Caribbean ports in the seas of the Antilles trading in African slaves. Then, moving through the centuries, the article observed the lives of the pirate and privateer brothers Jean and Pierre Lafitte, who by 1811 had, along with freemen and escaped slaves, established a self-styled and independent black market kingdom called Barataria—named, of course, after the fictional territory governed by Sancho Panza in *Don Quixote*—on a bay near New Orleans. Then, in a somewhat surprising turn, the article implicated US Navy and Marine officers in purchasing black market arms and alcohol from Barataria descendants, then still living near New Orleans, during the occupation of the Dominican Republic (1916–1924). Those same descendants, the article continued, who truly could be considered the last pirates in a lineage spanning some four hundred years, also supplied crime organizations and speakeasies throughout the South with alcohol. All these events, combined with the northward migration patterns of Southern Negroes since the start of the Great Depression, meant that there could conceivably be pirates and the children of pirates living in the city. The long and terrible arms of the French and Spanish Empires, the reporter concluded, reached even into the heart of modern-day Chicago.

Lastly, almost as an afterthought, the article contained a telephone number for the journalist and an illustration of the *Last Pirate of the New World* (as described by his son) in case anybody reading knew his whereabouts.

In September, at the explicit urging of his father, Benjamin returned to the school at the neighborhood synagogue, even though he was convinced that, like the Martian heat-ray in *War of the Worlds*, it would only end up liquefying his mind. Since the synagogue and the neighborhood public school wouldn't accept Maxwell, he spent most of his days alone in the kitchen reading a book on astronomy.

Occasionally, he was happy in that apartment. Other times, he leaned against the kitchen window and closed his eyes, determined to conjure up his home on Melpomene Avenue, or rather, his home on Melpomene Avenue in a parallel universe, one that wasn't empty and diminished, one where there was a bed, a black typewriter, and a kitchen table around which at that moment sat the old mad pirate, his father, and his mother.

Some days, especially when the weather was pleasant, he took long walks through the neighborhood, walks that invariably ended with three or four of the older neighborhood boys following him for a few blocks, sometimes silently, crisscrossing the street when he crisscrossed the street, and other times calling out to Maxwell in words that made no sense to him, maybe in Yiddish or Russian, in any case, words that sounded like the constant dripping of a rusted steel faucet and that struck him, finally, as threatening.

Still, one late September morning he decided to walk to the *Daily Illustrated Times* building. A young, busy secretary in dark glasses pointed out the reporter who had written the article about him. The reporter was sitting at a desk in the center of a very long, narrow room, where others sat typing.

There was a brief pause before the reporter finished typing and looked up. The reporter asked Maxwell how he was doing and Maxwell asked if he'd heard any news about his father.

"I did have one call," he said, finally, "an old, senile Mexican woman who told me about how her husband, a Mayan from Bacalar, had been killed by pirates hired by Yucatecos."

"So, nothing," said Maxwell.

"Nothing," said the reporter, "I'm sorry, son. But I'll keep my ear to the ground. He's bound to turn up."

Maxwell suspected that the reporter's words were true. And yet, later that night, as he sat alone on the ledge of the rooftop, smoking a cigarette and watching the flecks of stars just above the vaporous lights of the city, he couldn't help but think that they were not the entire truth.

Maxwell never told Saul or Benjamin about the older neighborhood boys who followed him, but, as it turned out, he didn't have to. Around this time, on a cool, windy October day, as Maxwell was leaning against the kitchen window, he saw two of the boys and two men approach Saul on the sidewalk. Both older boys wore skullcaps. They looked tired and thin and twitchy. One of the men wore a faded gray button-down coat and leaned on a baseball bat like a cane. Maxwell immediately recognized the taller one as the man Benjamin had said was his rabbi.

"It's too dangerous for him here," said the rabbi in English.

"What is too dangerous?" said Saul. Then he asked whether the rabbi wasn't ashamed, whether he had lost his mind, whether he didn't understand that by showing up with others and a baseball bat that they were, as far as he could see, the ones instigating the danger.

"We only need to talk to the boy," said the rabbi, spreading his arms in supplication, "nothing more."

For a few seconds, Saul searched his face. "Tell me, Rabbi," he said, "did you not escape Kiev within an inch of your life? Did you learn so well from the bloodthirsty Cossacks and Russian priests who came for you and your family when you were a boy?"

The others looked at Saul as if they were seeing him for the first time.

"I don't think you should speak to the rabbi like that," said the man with the baseball bat and then he pointed it in Saul's face.

The rabbi held a hand up. "Not like this."

Before leaving, the rabbi said something else to Saul, the thin words of which got lost in the wind.

So, it wasn't much longer before Maxwell made up his mind to return to New Orleans. This was something else he never told Saul or Benjamin, even if, in some ineffable way, they already suspected it.

On October 19th, they celebrated Benjamin's thirteenth birthday. Since the brief encounter with the rabbi and his thugs, Saul thought it best if they had his son's Bar Mitzvah at home. That morning he asked the neighborhood butcher for credit and, in the evening, they ate rye bread, borscht, and large strips of steaming brisket, followed by Mandelbrot cookies, an extravagant meal for each one of them during those hard times.

Afterward, they played poker and Saul told a story about a trip to Minsk and Nevel he had taken with his father after his own Bar Mitzvah. He then told the boys a joke that his father had told him on that very same trip, a Russian joke about how the Devil, who for centuries had been planning the end of the world, falls in love with a beautiful girl in Moscow and cancels his plans and how they get married and start a family and then grow old together, although the Devil, who, of course, doesn't grow old so much as fleshly and forgetful, one day blurts out to his wife that he's been the Devil all along. But the Devil's wife, who is still beautiful after all those years and is still mortal, just laughs and says, "I knew that from the first moment I met you, stupid. How else do you think the world is still spinning?"

After Saul had gone to sleep, the boys went up to the rooftop. They sat on the ledge and shared a cigarette, talking nonstop, and laughing and laughing as if the world truly had been lost and then saved by a hair.

The following morning, Maxwell woke early, before dawn. Benjamin was asleep, a single white sheet wrapped loosely around his body. For a second, Maxwell thought about waking him to say goodbye, but quickly decided against it. Instead, he placed his copy of *Lost City* at the foot of Benjamin's bed.

In the kitchen, Saul was sitting at the table, sipping coffee. When he saw Maxwell, he wasn't surprised. At first, he wanted to tell the boy that he didn't have to go, that he could stay for as long as he needed, that he could find him a school or a job, that he would confront the rabbi and his thugs again and again if needed, that everything would change, but Maxwell just smiled and shook his head, as if to say, but what exactly would change? Of course, neither of them knew. Saul handed Maxwell a wrapped brisket sandwich, three dollars, and a large envelope.

"Benjamin wanted you to have this," he explained as Maxwell took the envelope.

Outside, it was cold, as cold as anything Maxwell had ever known, and the street was like a long frozen passageway at the end of which a giant reddish eyeball was slowly blinking to life. At the Illinois Central Station, Maxwell bought a one-way ticket to New Orleans. Since he had a little time, he sat on a platform bench, watching the nameless crowds. A woman dressed in black mourning clothes ran down the platform, holding a paper lantern. A cheerful-looking soldier with one arm hugged a little girl. Porters stood talking near a newspaper stand. Every few minutes, a train left the station with a low, thundering bellow and Maxwell imagined that they were headed to other universes.

At some point, he ate the brisket sandwich. Then he remembered the envelope. Inside were seven sheets of folded notebook paper, each, except the first, covered back to front with black ink. The first page was the title page and on it was written *A Model Earth*. Underneath was the following note: *It's only a few pages, but I'll find you and send the rest when it's finished.*

Maxwell closed his eyes and thought of nothing and everything, all at once, just as Saul had taught him, as if he were walking through a dark labyrinth, the center of which was bathed in moonlight, or, like his missing father, sailing through an endless dark blue sea toward something unknown. Then he opened his eyes and began to read.

THE DESERT AND THE STORM

October 2005

Puedo ayudarte? she said after opening the Quality Suites motel door to Room 307. Then, after a short silence, during which she gazed past Saul, Javier, and Ms. Zora toward the highway in the distance now lit up by the near-equatorial orange sun, Javier said, Señora Ortiz?

For a moment, Victoria Ortiz just stood there in the threshold of the Quality Suites motel door to Room 307, scratching her forehead above her gray eyebrows, and then she nodded in recognition of Javier's voice and said, oye! El Periodista, so, you came here checking in on him too, eh?

Sitting on a couch watching a TV show about glaciers was an old man with salted black hair. When he saw them, he stood up without saying anything. Then he moved toward Ms. Zora, smiled, and gave her a hug. He was tall, as tall as anyone Saul had ever known, and he had the gait, self-possession, and calm gaze of someone who spent a great deal of time outdoors. Briefly, Saul imagined him hiking through a Martian landscape with its iridescent stones and polar ice caps, its deadly crater walls and wandering rovers. Despite everything, thought Saul, he's still alive, and we're here.

In Spanish, Victoria explained to Maxwell that Javier was the journalist who had been looking for him before the Storm. Then Saul introduced himself as Benjamin Drower's grandson and handed Maxwell the box containing the manuscript to *A Model Earth*.

Maxwell sat back down on the couch and opened the box. He read the title and the name under the title. He thumbed through the nine hundred and twenty-four pages of the manuscript. He smiled at Saul with a mixture of slight, almost imperceptible, joy and bewilderment. Then he placed both hands on the manuscript and said, so, he really finished it?

I don't understand, said Saul. What do you mean *he finished it*?

Thank you for bringing this to me. It feels like an impossible thing to hold in my hands right now, said Maxwell after a long pause, the type of pause, thought Saul, that announced he was trying to remember something from his distant past. Something otherworldly and pleasant like the slow unfolding of a long-lost triptych.

But the truth of the matter, he continued, is that the last time I saw your grandfather, Saul, was in Chicago in 1933. I only knew him for a short while, maybe only a few months, but we still became very good friends. I don't know how much you or Ms. Zora here know, but my mother did finish *A Model Earth*, which was a sequel to *Lost City*. Sadly, before her death, she destroyed it. But before then, quite by accident, I read it all and a few years later, after I met your grandfather in Chicago, I told him the entire story of *A Model Earth*. In fact, he was the only other person I ever told in my life. We were so young then, what the hell did we know, but he insisted that it should be written down again, which was something I thought I would never be able to do. So he decided he would instead. And all these years later, he said after a short pause, I can't believe it's here.

I had no idea, said Saul, taken by surprise. My grandfather never told me about *A Model Earth*, and, like you, I only found it by accident. He died this past December. At some point before then, I don't know when, he tracked you down to the Universidad de Chile and then asked me to send a package to you, but, at that time, I had no idea that there was a manuscript inside. In fact, it was his last request before he died, but, by the time I sent it, you had already left Santiago and the package was returned.

I understand, said Maxwell, and I'm very sorry to hear about your loss, Saul. Then he fell silent and gazed at the TV, but showed no signs of watching it. Saul had seen that faraway look in his grandfather's eyes many times. On the TV a massive Himalayan glacier was rapidly receding into a valley covered in rocks and gray pools of water. The Anthropocene, said a woman's voice. The word *Anthropocene* to Saul sounded like the passage of a fitful breeze through an empty wasteland.

How did you two meet? Saul asked finally.

Maxwell smiled and then told them about his childhood, a time in his life he hadn't thought about for many years, but which, since his return to New Orleans, had consumed his thoughts. He told them about the Isle of Orleans, as his mother had called it, and about his mother's literary adventures, about her fierce magnetic attraction to science fiction, about her close friendships with Ms. Zora's grandmother, the prolific librarian Afraa Laguerre, and a young publisher named David Ellison who stopped publishing, but who still left a tremendous rip in the fabric of Southern literature, as if literature were truly nothing more than cloth concealing a burning reality. He told them about his mother's death in August 1930, about how, shortly after, his father left New Orleans to look for work, and about his few years spent with the old mad pirate and his failed journey to Chicago to meet up with his father, who, by then, had already vanished. His disappearance was still overwhelming to him after all these years, even if he had finally learned to accept it. It had been a naïve, reckless journey, but it had brought him and *A Model Earth* to Benjamin Drower, a journey, he understood more fully now, marked by light or waves or whatever it was that linked his past to his future across the bayous and the windswept fields of Kansas and the lakes and lonely train tracks also linking New Orleans to Chicago.

Afterward, they left the motel room and sat in the busy courtyard. Maxwell carried the heavy manuscript with both hands. An early-evening breeze passed through the courtyard, suffusing everything with the scrambled scent of barbecue meat and laundry detergent. By then the sun had already set. For some time they discussed Benjamin Drower's life, or rather, in something like his own words, the narrative path he had followed in life, a path, thought Saul with some solace, that had converged (however briefly, however accidentally) with each of their own.

At some point, the conversation veered toward the more recent past and the Storm, a territory through which they moved with the caution of a desplazado crossing an unknown border.

You were a hard man to find, said Javier to Maxwell. If you don't mind me asking, what happened after you retired and left Santiago? What happened during the Storm?

The story Maxwell Moreau told them, at length, was as follows: During the second week of December in 2002 he gave his last lecture at the Universidad de Chile, where he had been teaching since 1995, a lecture about what some theoretical physicists called the Big Freeze, the accelerating expansion, thinning, and ultimate death of the universe, after which, he explained to his vaguely terrified students, there would be no stars and no light. With a great big smile, he then released them for the semester. When he could he liked to end all his courses in this manner because there was something useful in impermanence, asymmetry, and possibility, even if he didn't always know what, something sinuous, elegant, and eel-like, something of an Amazonian river that wound through and gave life to dark, muddy lands, yet, in due course, still emptied out into its own death at sea.

After the class, he turned in his office keys and walked the streets of Barrio Brasil. He ate outside at a small quiet restaurant in a plaza, talking to the waiters and waitresses there who were his friends and who occasionally sat down with him between dinner rushes and then again after the restaurant had closed to drink chicha fermented from apples and tell jokes until 1:00 a.m. or 2:00 a.m., when everybody went home for the night.

In late January, Maxwell attended a ceremony at the university to celebrate the recent presidential decree giving Chile's support to the Atacama Large Millimeter/submillimeter Array (ALMA). During the ceremony, he sat in the back of the auditorium and read a strange little Bolivian novel about a mysterious crime on a spaceship with no planet of origin, a novel that fit nicely into the pocket of his gray slacks for just this sort of occasion.

Afterward, he ate dinner with the chair of the physics department, a cultural attaché from Germany, a vice-president of an information technologies business, and an assistant to the secretary of the interior of Chile in a lavish restaurant in Las Condes, on a brightly lit street flanked by glass and steel skyscrapers and tall boutique apartment buildings, some of which looked like abandoned Pinochet-era offices. The place, thought Maxwell, couldn't have made him feel more awful, but the presence of the chair, who had long stood by his work and who had the long blooming laugh of someone raised, like him, in a working-class neighborhood, made him feel at ease.

All in all, the conversation that night proceeded in three stages: First they talked about the approximate cost of ALMA, $552 million US, an enormous cost for an enormous endeavor. Then the chair told a story about a journey he had taken to the White Desert in Egypt in 1966, during which, half-starved, broke, and lost among the dunes, he had stumbled upon a Bedouin camp. At first, the Bedouins didn't trust him, but eventually, after exhausting his very limited Arabic, they understood that he was a student, a *Chilean stargazer who had stupidly forgotten to look where he was going,* and they invited him to travel with them on the condition that he bury the silver cross he wore on a silver chain. He wasn't a religious man, the chair explained, and a little later in life he would understand that he was an atheist, but he had still worn that cross, given to him by his grandmother, for nearly his entire life. But he ultimately agreed to bury it.

For two months, he traveled and worked with the Bedouins in the White Desert. It was one of the happiest times in his life and, on his last night, they presented him with a small parting gift, a khanjar dagger with a short pistol grip shaped hilt and a short, curved blade like the letter *J* resembling a hook, a dagger, he only understood years later, that was an emblem of sorts depicting humankind's fleeting, intricate, and often squandered relationship with the desert.

After his story, the chair took out a long black box from under the table and handed it to Maxwell. Inside was the khanjar dagger. Without your tireless efforts in the Atacama Desert, he said, ALMA would never have happened at all. Maxwell thanked the chair and the others clapped. Of course, they wanted Maxwell to give a speech, but all he could do was say thank you, but no, no, and smile and soon enough the coffee and brazo de reina arrived and the conversation turned to other, more personal matters. In other words, as they drank coffee and ate dessert, they talked about themselves, about their dreams both fulfilled and unfulfilled, about their family vacations, the long hours spent in pointless meetings, the long hours spent alone but happy, or as close to alone and happy as they could possibly be in this new hyper-connected century. Out of all of them Maxwell said the least and after some time he stood up, thanked everyone for a pleasant evening, and left.

In February, with the help of two of his former students, he sold most of his belongings and donated his books to a local library. Some days later, he packed a large hiking backpack and left Santiago in a rented gray pickup truck, following the coast north along Route 5 with views of rock-strewn mountains, wild sand beaches, and a flat blue ocean.

The following afternoon, Maxwell arrived in Calama. He'd last seen Victoria Ortiz a few months earlier when she was in Santiago visiting her granddaughter. But this was the first time he was seeing her home, which was near the Cathedral San Juan Bautista, topped by a shining copper-plated spire, and which looked like a little citadel.

Victoria greeted Maxwell warmly and they sat on the couch and drank strong, bitter coffee in large mugs while they talked about Maxwell's retirement, which, he confessed, didn't feel at all like a retirement. What does it feel like then? asked Victoria. He thought about it for a moment, but didn't have a good answer. Then they talked about how bright and hot it was in Calama during the day and how at night the cold obliterated every memory of the warmth. When she laughed, her brow creased and a few strands of hair fell from her bun and then rested along her cheek, like, imagined Maxwell, the Spanish shepherdess in *Don Quixote*.

Afterward, they walked to a supermarket to purchase a few items for dinner. As they walked along Calle Ramírez she took his hand into hers.

★ ★ ★

A few days later, in the morning, they drove in Victoria's white pickup truck from Calama to the expansive plateau at the bottom of the Cerro Chajnantor. At some point, while looking in the glove box for Victoria's map of the Atacama Desert, Maxwell found a human mandible. The mandible was partially toothless, stained russet, and fractured along one side. He had no idea if it was either thousands of years old or thirty. He held the mandible in his hands unsteadily, Hamlet-like, as if it were able to contort the air around it with fear, astonishment, or horror. It's not my son, said Victoria, but its somebody's son.

They arrived around midday and set up camp next to the test instruments that Maxwell and his graduate students had installed some five years earlier. Then they went for a short hike around the plateau, not more than five or six kilometers total. When they reached the eastern edge, they gazed across the volcanic peaks, and the scattered mountain villages of Argentina beyond. They kissed for a long time and then Maxwell told Victoria about the chair's adventures in the White Desert. He took out the khanjar dagger and handed it to Victoria. She turned it over in her hands skillfully. Do you think the chair's story is bullshit? she asked him with a wry smile. It hadn't occurred to him. I don't know, he said, maybe it doesn't matter either way.

Later, after dinner, Maxwell set up his portable telescope and they spent the next few hours reading the translucent night sky, which was aflame with stars. Through the telescope's eyepiece, they could see swirling snake-shaped nebulas, the blue, orange, and brown cloud bands of Jupiter, the rings of Saturn, the constellations of Scorpio and the Southern Cross, the globular cluster Omega Centauri, and even the timorous outlines of the Large and Small Magellanic Clouds some two hundred thousand light-years away, all of it right at the tip of their noses, giving Maxwell the familiar impression that there was no border between space and the Earth, and that one inevitably dispersed into the other and then fragmented into beauty.

You once told me that a theoretical physicist could re-create the entire universe on paper without ever leaving his office, said Victoria, as she pressed her eye against the telescope. So, why help with this ALMA project, what else do you expect to find out here in the middle of the desert?

For a few seconds, Maxwell was lost in thought. Then he said, unusual claims like evidence for parallel universes require a very high burden of proof. The ALMA telescope or one like it could potentially detect gravity from one universe leaking into ours. Or a NASA satellite might detect other universes nestled within the black holes that formed some three hundred million years after the Big Bang or even signs of a collision between our universe and another. In other words, a telescope like ALMA could one day give us evidence of a multiplicity beyond our imagination.

But what surprised him most and what he didn't say to Victoria was that all he could think of when he had first gazed into the Atacama Desert's translucent night sky was the fiery constellation of his mother's slender face framed by her long, coffee-colored hair and all the lives that she had lived in those other universes just beyond his reach.

On March 20th, the same day the United States invaded Iraq, Maxwell boarded a flight from Santiago to Panama City, where he had a short layover before boarding another flight to New Orleans. On the final leg of his trip, he sat next to a one-armed businessman from Colombia. They talked for a while, as the man flipped through the pages of a news magazine, and Maxwell learned that the man had lost his arm fighting FARC rebels. According to the businessman everything was about to change. The norteamericanos are at war, he said, and a new era was about to begin. But then again, the norteamericanos are always at war. They are at war in my country even as we speak. So, maybe, nothing ever changes, he said, laughing slowly, with his eyes and teeth shining in the dark cabin, and scratching his prosthetic arm as if it were a sleeping cat or still an arm. Right, said Maxwell, and he turned away and stared out the window at the purple clouds that looked like the arched cloister of a cathedral. They love war, the one-armed businessman said some minutes later just as Maxwell was drifting toward sleep. It's their national pastime, he said, baseball, free enterprise, and war.

Despite the considerable humidity, the first year in New Orleans was peaceful, uneventful. With his savings, he bought a modest two-story cottage on South Telemachus Street, a relatively quiet street lined with old elms, swaying palms, massive elephant ears, and the occasional banana tree. In the mornings, he sat in the kitchen and worked on a long essay about the multiverse titled "The Outer Limits," which was to be published in September 2004 in an anthology inspired by the work of the late Hugh Everett III and titled *A Brief History of the Future*.

Afterward, he went for long walks. These walks inevitably took him to the waterway Bayou St. John which routed itself through a neighborhood of the same name. The waterway had been in use since pre-Columbian times and it pervaded the entire neighborhood with a freshwater scent and the awareness of something primeval always moving nearby. Other times, he took the Canal Streetcar to the Carondelet stop and wandered the old stone quadrangular streets of the French Quarter, which, at first glance, seemed very different from those of his childhood. Long gone were the frenetic courtyards of Sicilian tenement buildings, the huge black Spanish jars, and the melancholic sounds of the accordion—but on second glance the streets of the French Quarter didn't feel very different at all. It was as if the teeming, operatic city of his childhood was an invisible city inside yet another invisible city, and so on, back through the decades and even centuries, a great big invisible belly heaving slowly under the near-tropical heavens, as the Argentine writer Julio Cortázar might say.

Occasionally, his next-door neighbor Antoine, a chef who came knocking on his door one June night to introduce himself, stopped by to help cook. Antoine spent a good deal of time in Maxwell's kitchen radiantly musing over food, ecology, Darwin, and mass extinction, which, according to him, was inevitable for the human species. Maxwell, in turn, talked to Antoine about the multiverse or the events that had precipitated his return to New Orleans or his happy, sometimes accidental, travels through Europe, Asia, and South America. At some point, Antoine started calling him Traveler.

Afterward, if it was cool enough, Maxwell sat alone in a black wicker chair on his front porch listening to the faint, boiling blasts of trumpets and trombones coming from a nearby elementary school or to the drumming rain that often seemed like it would never end, reading or thinking about a few unsolved problems in physics, or so he claimed in emails written to colleagues, but in truth he wasn't thinking anything at all.

What did Maxwell read that first year in New Orleans? He read *The Data*, which was, as one might expect, a book about how the basis of the physical universe was data made of bits of interconnected information that would dissolve little by little until there was nothing left. He read *Mars*, an apocryphal dark comedy written entirely in dialogue in which Mars converses with the Earth every seventeen years. He read *The Fifth*, a crime novel about a detective on the brink of solving the case of a serial killer living in the 5th dimension, a novel which inexplicably ends mid-sentence, just moments before the case is fully solved, like the writer too had suddenly disappeared into the 5th dimension. He read *Our Messenger*, a tragic biography of Peter L. Jensen, who invented the loudspeaker only to later regret his invention when fascists started using it with great success, wondering, while he read, if the Internet would one day face the same fate. That book inevitably led to *The Samurai and the Statue*, a historical novel of sorts following the life of a poor old sculptor living in Rome from the summer of 1924 to the winter of 1925 as he attempts in vain to sculpt a Cubist bronze sculpture of Hasekura Tsunenaga, a 17th century samurai who headed a diplomatic mission to the Vatican, passing through New Spain and various port-of-calls in Europe. What Maxwell enjoyed most about *The Samurai and the Statue* was that the writer made little attempt to accurately represent either the life of the Roman sculptor or the life of the 17th century samurai (even if the writer hadn't painted a careless or ordinary picture of either), but rather did want to present a theory of their relationship and the relationship each had with the Old World. He also read *The Census Taker*, a prescient novel about American apartheid in 2050. Then *Uruk*, about an android in the third millennium named Gilgamesh. In a thin but immeasurably elegant collection of poems by the Cuban poet Norberto Codina, he found the following: *el ser humano es infinito*. Of course, numerous books followed. When he finished a book, he exchanged it for another at one of the cramped used bookstores that could be found in the French Quarter or in one of the surrounding neighborhoods.

It was around this time, as he wandered the city in search of other bookstores, that he happened upon the New Orleans Rare Book Center and Ms. Zora. While he was looking through a rather impressive bookcase, she approached him and asked if he needed any help. She wore a black wool shawl wrapped tightly around her thin shoulders, an unusual sight in New Orleans, where there was only water and sun. Her hair was long, way past her shoulders, and black. At first, as if unstuck in time, he recognized her immediately as Afraa Laguerre, but on second thought realized that this was impossible. He didn't say anything, what could he even say to her just then without sounding like a rambling old man, but later, when she rang up his purchase, a biography on Nezahualcoyotl, the 15th century poet and ruler of Texcoco, he saw the photographs on the wall behind the front counter and was struck for a second time by the stunning image of Afraa Laguerre.

Or rather, images. In one small black and white photo, in which she was about the same age as when he had known her, she stood in a stylish courtyard with an unknown writer (at least to him), but what Maxwell really saw was a woman with a fearless smile and gaze like Audrey Hepburn or Dorothy Van Engle, which is to say a strong-willed, intelligent gaze, the gaze of someone who had committed her life to unanswerable questions, to the abyss.

Afraa Laguerre, he said slowly and in something like a whisper. That's right, she said, my grandmother and the founder of this place. My mother was a writer, said Maxwell. What was her name? she asked. Adana Moreau, he said. Well then, said Ms. Zora with a great big vatic smile, we have a lot to talk about.

It wasn't too long after that Maxwell and Ms. Zora went searching for his mother's tomb. He remembered, vaguely, like in a waking dream, that it was in St. Louis Cemetery No. 2, but he wasn't sure exactly where. As they searched the damp aisles of the cemetery, Maxwell talked about a trip his family and Afraa had taken to an island off the Gulf Coast shortly after the publication of *Lost City* in 1929. He had been nine then. The island, from what he remembered, was long and thin, so that you could turn your head one way to see the sunrise, which was faint at first, then strong and dense, and then later turn your head the other way to see the sunset, which, inevitably, tinted the sand and trees a soft red. During one of those sunsets, they went for a walk along a western stretch of beach. While Maxwell and his father hunted for seashells and crabs and strange rocks, Afraa and his mother talked for a long time about books, about books found by ineluctable chance on old but tidy shelves, and books that devoured readers, not the other way around, like a fanged beast.

A little later, he helped Afraa build a campfire on the beach. His parents went up to the water's edge, gazing out to sea. They stood inches apart, like Aztec stone statues, obsidian and immortal, or rather that's how he saw them then, and maybe even now. At some point, he heard his mother laugh. Then his father said te amo, te amo, te amo, three times, like a pirate's charm, and they kissed.

A few years after that, said Maxwell, they were both gone from me. They entered something like a labyrinth of time and never left.

Maxwell and Ms. Zora walked in silence until they reached a brick tomb near the western edge of the cemetery. His mother's name had faded, but was still, if obliquely, legible. It's still here, said Maxwell and he smiled. Before they left, Ms. Zora laid a small bouquet of blue roses in front of Adana Moreau's tomb.

In April, a few days after Maxwell's eighty-fourth birthday, while thumbing through an illustrated 19th century book about trees in the Amazon, he found an old postcard with a black and white photograph of an immense cypress tree. He suddenly realized that during all this time he hadn't written Victoria Ortiz. He discussed it with Ms. Zora while she reshelved a few books. What a waste of time, she said. I don't know how I could've forgotten, he said.

That night, on the back of the old postcard, he wrote a letter to Victoria in which he told her about his house on South Telemachus Street, about the sky in New Orleans (shades of Cézanne, Kahlo), about the sounds of drums and guitars that he sometimes heard coming from a neighboring house that was home to a group of Brazilian musicians, about the streetcars at dusk, their lights already on, heading home.

Three weeks later, he received a postcard from Victoria with a photograph of the incandescent night skyline of Santiago, where she was staying with her granddaughter for a few weeks. In the postcard, she told Maxwell about the rumors that Pinochet's health was failing, about how in interviews he still clung, like a toxic lichen, to the falsehood that he had done the country good, about her treks into the desert, which continued without pause, and about her involvement in the planning of something called the Museum of Memory. Other postcards followed.

The following year, in late July, while visiting Santiago for the month, Victoria's granddaughter bought her a laptop and taught her how to use email. Shortly after, Maxwell and Victoria's communications became more frequent and, soon enough, at hyper speed, all pretext finally dissolved. Every few days now, they wrote each other long emails which were, more or less, faithful simulacrums of the conversations they once had in person and which were, in a word, about the need for companionship, especially at their ripe old age, joked Victoria in an email written on August 22nd, because the truth was that they both still felt very young and almost infinite, like Sisyphus, Maxwell happily responded the following day, who cheated Death again and again to be with his wife.

On Wednesday, August 24th, Maxwell woke early, took a cold shower, made a cup of Cuban coffee, and turned on the computer. He wrote an email to Victoria. Then he spent a few hours on the Internet searching for odd bits of news, names in theoretical physics that no one remembered anymore, forgotten theories. At some point, he read about a tropical storm some two hundred and thirty miles east of Miami, wondering vaguely if he knew anybody in that city. Some hours later, the tropical storm was given a name.

Later that afternoon, he stood on his balcony and gazed east, toward where he imagined the storm to be, and he didn't see anything. The sky was gray and pinkish and slumbering, like the backdrop of a Finnish painting. The day grew hotter and hotter.

That Saturday evening, his next-door neighbor Antoine stopped by to see if Maxwell was evacuating like the others before the Storm or if, like him, he would ride it out. He thought about his prospects in Houston or Atlanta or Memphis and decided to stay.

On Sunday morning, he filled his bathtub with water. Then he put plastic jugs of water in the freezer. Later, Maxwell went with Antoine to the hardware store to purchase supplies and plywood to cover his windows. On the highway, a few traffic helicopters passed overhead. When they reached the Home Depot, it looked to Maxwell like an enormous, frantic launching operation for a spacecraft.

Later that evening, after Antoine had boarded up his restaurant with a few employees, he came over to Maxwell's house with a bottle of good whiskey, two large crabs, and andouille sausage, of a spicy variety, he told Maxwell, direct from a butcher friend of his in the West Bank.

Tonight, he said, I'll do all the cooking.

As he cooked, Antoine talked excitedly about the storms of his childhood, about how the green parrots would vanish from the city beforehand, about the sound of rain on tin roofs, about lightning like vast rings of Bengal fire, the streets like shallow Venetian rivers, the green scales and white, knife-like teeth of a Nile crocodile head on the fireplace mantle of his family's shotgun house, the deep sweaty pores of his sister's forehead as she slept fast and hard next to him in bed, oblivious to the wind and the rain and the air charged with a fleeting electric value that prickled his skin, and memory.

After dinner, as the rain started to fall and as the wind picked up wastrel speed, Antoine said, let me tell you something, Traveler. Sure, said Maxwell. For the first time in a long time, I feel good and I can't explain why.

For a few seconds, the wind howled, and both were silent. Then: does that make any sense, Traveler?

Yes, said Maxwell, I think it does.

I feel alive, said Antoine.

Around 5:30 a.m., Maxwell woke from a dream. In the dream, he was talking with a crocodile. The crocodile was mudstruck, delirious. His breath like vaporous clouds. What happens when galaxies devour each other? the crocodile asked.

After Maxwell woke, the first thing he noticed was that the plywood covering his bedroom window had blown off and that the window had shattered, letting in hot blasts of wind and rain. The house shuddered, breathed in and then out. The roof thundered with water, like an army of Tartar horsemen had suddenly gathered there. Across the street, through a sheet of lashing rain, a palm tree was lurching forward at a grotesque forty-five-degree angle. He watched as a long length of old white fence tore from the earth and went spinning, like a scarf, into the darkness. Two plastic chairs galloped, then lifted off the ground. He heard car windows popping. At some point, all the buildings on the street went dark and then there were only vague shapes, as if the street had been drawn with charcoal. Maxwell ran downstairs to the first-floor bathroom. He sat on the edge of the porcelain tub, still filled with water, thinking that, at any moment, he would be sucked out of the house, skyward, and simply disappear into the all-devouring sound and fury.

Later, after the Storm had passed just east of the city and after a few hours of much-needed sleep, Maxwell went for a walk. The light drizzle of warm rain that had veiled the city that late morning had cleared, and the day was incredibly peaceful, as is often the case after storms, a cloudless day, pale yellow, the vault of a smoke-blue sky like a bell jar suspended over the city.

As he walked, first along Canal Street and then along North Cortez Street, he took deep breaths and the sharp, pleasant smell of a thousand busted-open oak trees hummed through the warren of his sinuses. Power lines sagged sad and low, and debris littered the street. The roofs and siding of some houses had been peeled back, like giant butterfly wings, but most of the houses looked more or less intact, including his own. Occasionally, he saw someone else wandering the neighborhood, like him, a sleepwalker, and they stopped to chat about how they had survived the Storm.

So, as the worst of it appeared to be over, he thought of other things as he walked. He thought about the Atacama Desert, about the eleven dimensions of M-theory, about the film *The Exterminating Angel* by Luis Buñuel, a psychological horror film he had first seen in 1981, fifteen years after its release, six years after Franco's death, in a small theater in Madrid.

But, at some point, he felt water coursing over his ankles, then his shins, and he headed directly back to South Telemachus Street. He knocked on Antoine's door, but no one answered.

Maxwell's house was airless and stifling hot, like a tomb, so he gathered his supplies and took them to the balcony. He turned on his battery-powered radio and twisted the dial, but there was no signal, just static, like the hollow roar of the ocean. Then he tried calling Ms. Zora, but the signal was busy. Likewise, the Internet was down. The water on South Telemachus Street rose and rose. At some point, he rechecked his camping gear and food supplies. He made pasta on his camping stove, but by the time it was ready he wasn't hungry.

The following morning, Maxwell woke to Antoine's voice. Traveler, you still here? he heard, distantly, as if through a pinhole. He was drenched in sweat and his sleeping bag was bunched up under him. It was dawn or just past dawn now, he couldn't tell. Still, the sun was flaring. South Telemachus Street was a long, dark river, maybe seven feet deep. The water smelled like putrid fruit. The air around his house was hot, apoplectic. He stood up slowly.

There you are, Traveler, said Antoine, you had me worried for a minute. Listen, he said, the levees breached, the water's still rising, it's toxic, you have to stay up there.

Antoine was standing on the bow of a fifteen-foot Sea Ray. He wore a faded Hawaiian shirt and a bright orange life vest. Between his bare feet was a .22 rifle. In the Sea Ray with Antoine were seven other people: an elderly woman with two young kids, one holding a little shaking dog on her lap, an elderly man wrapped in a mint-green bedsheet, a middle-aged couple, and an adolescent girl wearing a Batman backpack who was contemplating Maxwell with a faraway look. In fact, all of Antoine's passengers sat lost in thought. In turn, Maxwell stood on his balcony gazing at the strangers' faces, which were like something out of a Goya painting, lucid, if dazed, survivors of a grotesque thing. They did not seem like strangers to him at all.

You good, Traveler? said Antoine. Maxwell thought for a few seconds. Yes, I'm good, he said slowly, like he was a time traveler recently arrived in a city about which nothing was known for sure. Nobody's coming, said Antoine, no Army, no Navy, no other boats except a few others in the neighborhood like mine, no buses, no nada. In other words, Traveler, Homeland ain't secure and we're on our own, so after I check on some addresses I'm coming back for you.

Antoine took the helm of his boat, started the engine, and turned on the CD player. Maxwell watched as the Sea Ray headed toward Canal Street, the tender, liquescent sounds of Bob Marley's "Waiting in Vain" drifting over the flooded ruins of New Orleans.

★ ★ ★

That morning, after Maxwell cooked oatmeal, he grabbed a flashlight and went halfway down his stairs into his dark and flooded house. At some point in the night, the front door had busted open and a large section of wall had collapsed. Bobbing hypnotically on the stagnant water were gasoline cans, a mattress (not his), a shower curtain, a teakettle, wooden dining room chairs (his), a package of chips, Ziploc containers, and a painting of a cactus he had purchased at a secondhand art store. Over the surface of the water floated clouds of fine ochre dust. Ah, yes, he said to himself slowly, the paramāṇu. Through the dust, dragonflies swarmed like little helicopters. He followed them with the beam of his flashlight for a while.

Later, Maxwell was finally able to find a working radio station, WWL-AM. He listened as others trapped in the city called in to give advice or plead for help. One man explained rather calmly that when the water came he had escaped to his attic and busted through the roof with an ax. Another caller couldn't speak or rather her words were unintelligible behind deep sobs. Yet another woman called to tell the broadcaster that she was stuck in an elm tree. Where are you? the broadcaster asked. The woman shouted an address on North Roman Street, corner of Egania. Where the hell is everybody? she asked. Send somebody! Please. There are fucking rats in the tree. Please don't let me die. Stay with us, the broadcaster said, hold tight to that tree. Stay with us, he said again when there was no response. I'm not going to make it, said the woman, finally, her voice trailing off into a thin, static-like haze, I'm tired, I'm so tired. Some seconds later, the phone call ended and Maxwell switched off the radio.

Still, for a long while after—even weeks later—he thought about that woman in the elm tree, about unreality, about dying or rather a type of isolation that, at least initially, resembled dying, about a sky-gray amphitheater like an enormous medieval crypt.

Antoine returned in his Sea Ray just after dusk. Without the glare from streetlights or houses, the ink-black sky was now fiery and all-consumed with stars and constellations.

I've never seen so many stars in my life, Traveler, said Antoine with a deep sigh.

Maxwell, who was out on his balcony, squinted and looked to the star Beta Aquarii, a rare yellow supergiant some six hundred light-years away, yet, that night, visible to the naked eye. Maxwell pointed and said, look.

What am I looking at? said Antoine.

Beta Aquarii, said Maxwell, in the constellation of Aquarius.

The water-bearer? said Antoine.

That's the one, said Maxwell, the flood-bearer, the avatar of the apocalypse.

Well, Traveler, at least the apocalypse is pretty, said Antoine and they both laughed and laughed.

Just before dawn, Maxwell settled himself in the back of the boat and Antoine explained that they were headed to the embankment of Bayou St. John on Moss Street, where people were gathering to be taken out of the city. On South Telemachus Street, Antoine navigated the Sea Ray with mathematical, pirate-like precision between submerged cars, mammoth elm tree branches, and floating debris, all the while singing along to the lyrics of Israel Vibration's "Ambush" playing on the CD player: *I'm just a buffalo soldier/survival is my game.*

In the distance, on another street (or rather, another tributary) Maxwell made out the silhouette of the Lindy Boggs Hospital, like the silhouette of a half-submerged castle. He saw nearly vertical electrical poles that looked like the masts of 18th century sunken ships. He saw two boys, no more than twelve or thirteen, paddling in a white, floating refrigerator with its top pulled off. When the boys waved at them as they passed in the Sea Ray, he thought vaguely of a postapocalyptic Mark Twain novel never written or written and never found. On Canal Street, he saw a corpse facedown in the water, bloated, unrecognizable, and trapped in the branches of a fallen tree among newspaper advertisements for secondhand sales, black plastic garbage bags, and tubes of toothpaste. He thought about looking away, but he didn't look away. He felt obligated to something or someone, maybe the victim. Maybe they had known each other or had passed each other more than once on Canal Street. He saw a dawning pink sky that led to nowhere, but through which, at great heights, soared helicopters like carrion fowl.

On South Cortez Street, near the embankment, they passed a one-story shotgun house with the word HELP spray-painted in red on a bedsheet hung from the roof. On the roof, there was a middle-aged woman wearing a blue head scarf, a toddler grasping the legs of the woman, a skinny, shirtless teenage boy, and an elderly woman holding the head of a bald, female mannequin like it was a floating device.

City's on fire, said Antoine.

Then he steered the Sea Ray toward the roof and called up to the family. With Antoine's help, the family climbed down into the boat, one after the other, first the toddler, then the elderly woman, then the middle-aged woman followed by the teenage boy, after which there was a brief and immobile silence, like they'd all just been struck by lightning, whether a beautiful or incredibly terrible bolt of white lightning, Maxwell couldn't tell. A silence that was nevertheless broken when Antoine said that he could get them out of the city. For a moment, the family looked at each other, still wordless, before finally saying, thank you, my God, thank you, their tones ranging from relief to humor to sorrow. Then the elderly woman looked directly into Maxwell's eyes, slipped the bald female mannequin head silently into the water, and started to weep.

As Antoine steered the Sea Ray away from the roof, Maxwell watched the mannequin head bobbing senselessly in the water, like she was, in turn, watching the boat leave, craning her neck, rising above the flat toxic water on tiptoe, unblinking in her synthetic gaze, until the boat disappeared from view.

When they arrived at the embankment, Antoine turned off the engine and then raised it out of the water. He got out of the Sea Ray and stood, shin deep, in the rippling water by the stern. He then led his five passengers onto the thin strip of dry land where there was a crowd of fifty or so people sitting in lawn chairs or standing in a long line behind a camouflage-toned Army Blackhawk helicopter. They stood cautiously on the embankment and looked out over the city, at the water endlessly stretching in every direction, at the boats coming in one by one, at the people wading through the water carrying garbage bags full of possessions, at the slender plume of black smoke rising from a nearby burning building, at the empty skyscrapers in the distance. There was a small crowd gathered around a radio tuned to WWL-AM and the family joined them.

At some point, Antoine handed Maxwell two bottles of ice water and an Army MRE lunch. Maxwell smiled and said, thank you. Antoine nodded silently and then waded through the shin-deep water back to his Sea Ray. Before climbing aboard, he turned around and looked at Maxwell. His forehead, his neck, his arms shone in the fierce calcitic daylight, touched by a burning, joyful madness. He smiled and called out to Maxwell. See you in a parallel universe, Traveler, he said.

Some hours later, Maxwell boarded the deafening Army Blackhawk helicopter with four others. Once they were above the city, he saw that the floodwaters reflected the light of the blue sky and the white clouds, so it seemed as if the city was floating in midair, like a cityship.

★ ★ ★

A few days later I arrived here, said Maxwell and he glanced at the highway beyond the parking lot of the Quality Suites motel, and added with a smile, when I emailed Victoria to tell her what happened, she came right away.

After Maxwell wrote down his contact information for Saul, they all said goodbye and walked to Romário's Cadillac, and when Saul looked back Maxwell was already immersed in the manuscript. They drove east, back the way they had come, and the road seemed to take on an extra-temporal quality, like they were traveling backward in time. We're already meeting ourselves coming the other way, he thought as the Cadillac sped on and on and on.

They arrived in New Orleans around 10:00 p.m. and Javier parked the car in front of Ms. Zora's bookstore. She thanked them for keeping Saul's grandfather's word to deliver the manuscript to Maxwell. I can tell you boys that it means the world to him, she said. And Saul suddenly saw the Hebrew letters for *world*, letters which resembled wisps of smoke. It was the same word he remembered just then that his parents had once taught him how to write on a blank page as white as the sands of an ancient desert in the Torah. עוֹלָם, he had written, during those last days together in Tel Aviv.

Ms. Zora suddenly seemed very tired, but this too only lasted a moment, and she hugged Javier and Saul and thanked them again. Before saying goodbye, they asked her what she was going to do now. Ms. Zora shrugged her shoulders and said, you never know. Then she sprang up the porch steps with her son. Come back anytime, she said before closing the door behind her.

As Saul and Javier walked to the French Quarter, they shared a cigarette, both lost in thought. When they reached the cathedral, they sat facing it on the steps leading into Jackson Square.

After a short silence, Saul said, I still don't understand why he never told me about *A Model Earth*.

I was wondering the same thing, pana, said Javier, maybe he finished writing it down again before you arrived to Chicago, or maybe he was unsure if he would ever be able to finish. Or he could've finished it during that brief resurgence the dying often feel hours or days before their death. But no matter how much we think we know, we end up knowing so little of our parents and even less of our grandparents, most lives are forgotten as soon as they've occurred. After a few years, a few decades, a century, most lives are unknown, he said in a tone of sadness that surprised Saul, after which they both fell silent again.

And yet, said Javier some seconds later, in spite of all that, your grandfather spent his life recording other people's stories. I don't think *A Model Earth* would have been any different to him. He wanted to ensure that Adana Moreau's story wouldn't be lost again to time.

I remember one night when I called him from Quito, continued Javier, and we somehow got to talking about how Quito had been the final Incan city and Atahualpa, the final sovereign emperor of the Incan Empire just before the Spanish conquest. I don't remember his or my exact words, but I do remember that I told him that far too much of the history of the Incas had been forgotten, concealed, and erased. It was all a great loss. But he told me that I was only half-right. He said that the history of the Incas and those they conquered, the Cañaris and Quitus-Caras, for example, should be perceptible everywhere I went in Quito—in the labyrinthine streets, in the endless markets, in the garbage bins, in the dirt, in the music, in the eyes, in the florid multiplicity of languages and DNA, a DNA, he reminded me, that I too shared. Incan history *breathed*, and I breathed too because of it. At some point, he said that maybe in a way we were both right, that "history casts itself across our existence *like a shadow of another world*."

Last night, said Saul, you told me there was little or no point in thinking about Earths in parallel universes because it denies our existence on this one or even erases it completely, as if by thinking of those other, inaccessible Earths we would only be transformed into fictions. And in some ways, I think you're right, this branch of reality, this Earth, is the only one we experience and know. But, continued Saul, it's only by thinking of all those other Earths, of all my other branches of reality—the realities I've abandoned or inextricably erased, like Sol Marías, or the realities I've pursued aimlessly or half-heartedly, or even the vast majority of realities in which I have little control of anything at all—that I can make any decisions in this one. I think, he said slowly, that the fundamental elegant variability of the multiverse, as Maxwell Moreau might say, finally forces me to now make choices I would otherwise never consider or even imagine. Does that make any sense? he asked and fell silent.

Yes, pana, I think it does, said Javier.

In other words, said Saul, I've decided that I'm going to stay here for a while and see what I can do to help Victoria and Maxwell, and others, too. Yeah? said Javier, now smiling, and he looked at Saul, his gaze lucent. He took out a cigarette but didn't light it. I was waiting for you to say something, pana, he said and they both laughed.

On the walk back to the car, Javier received a text message from the photojournalist that said they should meet him at Café Brazil. By the time they arrived a large crowd had gathered, a musty and disheveled crowd mottled with dirt and dust and gray fibers of drywall and yellow stains of sweat, a crowd composed, thought Saul, of those who were returning home and those who had never left.

They found the photojournalist at the bar and together ordered a round of whiskey. Occasionally, the electricity flickered on or off and the room went dark. When this happened, people cheered or groaned. Javier and Saul listened as the photojournalist talked about a woman he interviewed some days earlier but hadn't photographed. She had lost her child in the Storm. As she told her story, she wept into her palms.

Her face was the same face he saw no matter where he was on the planet, whether in Santa Fe, the steppes of Mongolia, the Euphrates River, or New Orleans, it was the same exact face, the same sorrowful, thinking face as etched by the German artist Käthe Kollwitz in dark chalk on brown Ingres paper, a dark-hatched face turned down toward the dirt, to the earth, to the abyss beyond the edges of the paper, in other words, the face of a mother, the face of slow love and slow grief.

Javier asked why he hadn't photographed the woman. Roberto didn't know.

Some minutes later, a short, wiry man walked onstage with a small jazz band and introduced himself as John Boutte. He looked at the audience for a long while. The audience, in turn, looked at him. Here we are, the audience seemed to say, we can see you and you can see us, and that's all we need right now. Now, I want you all to do me a favor, said the singer, I want everybody to scream as loud as you can. The singer's voice was soft and fiery, a slow blue flame. Whatever else you want to do tonight, said the singer, just scream. And so, the crowd screamed, AHHHHHHHHHH! Now, get up and do it again, said the singer. The crowd scrambled, laughed, and took deep, vast breaths and screamed, AHHHHHHHHHHHHHHHHHH-HHHH!, an enormous roar gaining speed, like the winds of the Storm that had brought each one of them there, and for three or four seconds the Isle of Orleans seemed to rise from the depths. Now, said the singer, get up and do it again.

The following morning, Saul called Maxwell and they made plans to meet later that afternoon at his house on South Telemachus Street. Javier and Saul drove to a hardware store in Metairie and picked up supplies that Saul could use to start clearing and gutting Maxwell's ruined house. While they waited in the long checkout line, Saul watched a few dozen other customers, whose movements at that early hour were slow and haggard, but defiant, like each customer had just escaped from a madhouse and were now, together, heading somewhere slightly less mad.

After they had unloaded the supplies in front of Maxwell's house, they sat on the hood of the Cadillac and shared a cigarette. Before I forget, said Saul, I have something for you. He reached into his pocket and took out a key chain. He unfastened a small orange key and gave it to Javier. What's this? asked Javier. It's a copy of the key to the self-storage unit with my grandfather's things, said Saul, now smiling a little like it was finally *his* turn to play a trick. There are nine boxes in there packed with just over fifty years of cassettes of all of his interviews. He called them all his Vox Humana, the human voice, so that's how I labeled them.

Damn, pana, said Javier, are you sure? Yes, said Saul, take them, I have no idea what to do with them, but you will. Javier took the key and said, thank you. Some seconds later, Javier's cell phone rang. He picked it up and smiled when he heard Maya's waterfall-like voice on the other end. I'll see you soon, pana, he said in a low voice, somewhat apologetically, holding the cell phone between his ear and right shoulder. Then he hugged Saul and got into the car. Yes, mija, he said, I'll be home tonight, but very late. What did I see without you? Well, I saw a white cathedral and a river and an egret. It was standing on the tin roof of a stilted house that had been knocked over by wind. Yes, mija, just like Baba Yaga's house. Recuerdas Baba Yaga? he said and smiled. As Saul listened, it occurred to him that Javier's story was part of a familiar game Javier and Maya had been playing for a while now, a game that, due to his long absences as a foreign correspondent, served to fill in the innumerable gaps of a memory not shared but rather invented, like connect the dots or Mad Libs, a game that conjured images of fierce adventures, vulnerable distant lands, and a childhood discovered or redis-covered in the constant liquid movement of telling.

Javier started the car, nodded at Saul, and drove away. For a few seconds Saul stood there in the empty street and thought of Maya, with a little red hat and a fall coat, walking around and around Palmer Square Park with her father. He thought of Marina in her light blue scrubs and lab coat standing outside the glass doors of a hospital, gazing up at the glimmering sky-scrapers of her new home. And finally, he thought of all three of them eating and laughing together at the kitchen table, the light of a clear, hard-edged moon filtering through the win-dow, a young winter moon with the sharp curve of a khanjar dagger. It was no longer an orphan's moon, if it ever was one, but he had no idea what it was now. Maybe, it was a rupture in the sky where the moon should've been. Or maybe an airless, nameless moon from another world. Maybe not.

EPILOGUE

March 1933–April 1933

The pirate finished a letter to his son. He then folded it three times, in equal parts, and put it in a large manila envelope with a star map of the northern constellations. He had purchased the star map some days earlier from a Jewish refugee at a stall in the Maxwell Street Market. After paying the man, the pirate explained it was a present for his son and that his birthday was in a few days.

"How old?" asked the refugee.

"Thirteen," the pirate said, smiling with an air of pride.

"That's good," he said, "good, good."

He put the envelope on the cheap wooden wardrobe, where he wouldn't forget it, and walked to the bathroom, where he washed himself in cold water. There were no mirrors in the bathroom, but it didn't matter. The pirate, who was slowly becoming something else, another version of himself, a version he would not have known how to justify as a younger man, doubted he would recognize himself in any mirror. Afterward, he lay on the iron bed, half-asleep, listening to oblique rain fall outside his alley window and gazing at the faded painting above the desk where he had written the letter, a painting of a man and woman on horseback and a white prairie schooner being pulled by two pairs of oxen. They were already on their way, he thought, dragging their animals and property and rifles over the parched earth, and, later, fields of ice and snow, heading west, writing letters to their family about a vast prairie-length fear of death and boredom, letters that were really poems that took the shape of nautilus shells, poems with closed interior chambers spinning, spinning, and written in hard Cyrillic. The sky in that faded pastoral painting was starless and the color of smoking cobalt. What strange land were they wandering? he thought. Why was it even theirs to wander in the first place? What the hell did they know that he didn't?

The following morning, he woke early and went to a nearby diner for breakfast. He ordered oatmeal, eggs, and bacon. Afterward, he deposited the manila envelope in a mailbox. At some point, it started raining and he returned to the Jonava, walked up the stairwell to the third floor, and knocked on the door of Room 31. From behind the door, he heard a voice, thin and riled, as if ailing.

"Yeah, coming," said the voice.

"It's Titus," said the pirate.

"Yeah, okay."

The man who opened the door smiled at the sight of him. He was bald with deep lines running across his head like the tributaries of the Mississippi River. He wore a gray button-down shirt and black slacks with a hole near his left kneecap. His name was Reese. He invited the pirate into the room, which looked like an exact copy of his own room, except Reese had a painting of a white prairie schooner being pulled by two pairs of oxen along a mountain path instead of a prairie. Also, there were no signs of the man and woman on horseback. A window, exactly like his—dirty, small, and open—looked out over the same alley below. The scent of flowers, gasoline, and wet asphalt drifted into the room.

"So, two months?" asked the pirate.

"Yeah," said Reese, "two trips a week, tops, but fast. Michigan ratified a few days ago. Others will follow. Then everything will change."

"Okay," said the pirate.

The bald man nodded. He went to his desk, where he took out and then unfurled a large, crisp map of Lake Michigan. The lake was blue-green and the deep ochre lands surrounding it were veined with the black-ink names of towns and cities that seemed to the pirate somehow foreign.

"I've been dreaming of this map every night for weeks," the bald man said and smiled thinly, like a solitary huntsman.

The pirate checked out of the Jonava and told the hotel clerk that he would be back in a few days, but he didn't seem to listen or care one way or the other. The pirate had a leather backpack he had picked up in Fort Worth and he came out of the hotel and set it on the edge of the curb. He was there for a long time before Reese pulled up next to the hotel in a black Ford.

They drove along residential streets and then backstreets, some unlit, to a lakeshore warehouse on the edge of the city. Reese parked the car and they walked to a dark blue sailboat docked on a pier extending from the warehouse. There, two other men were waiting for them with a large thermos of hot coffee and flashlights.

"Let's go," said one of the men, but the pirate was unsure which one had said it. They both had flat black hair and flat, full faces, like brothers or like business partners who through the years had started to resemble each other.

"Hey," said the pirate, climbing aboard. His dusty boots left prints across the bow and he could see the water beading coldly there and running in tiny rivulets into the lake. Then they were moving. In front of him, the vast lake lay smoking in winter's last cold mist.

Some hours later, they docked at an old 19th century timber yard just south of South Haven, Michigan. Then the two men vanished and some minutes later reappeared, each driving a truck with its lights off. The pirate got into the cab of one truck, and Reese into the other. They drove on back roads, past little houses with no lights and rows of trees and fields still lingering in frost, one truck following the other. While they drove, the man talked to the pirate about his wife, an avid moviegoer, and how when he was home in Detroit they made it a point to go to at least one movie a week. Afterward, without fail, his wife would talk not about the movie they had just seen, but about the types of movies she really wanted to see, in other words, movies that didn't yet exist, a war movie, for example, about a fierce French soldier who tricks both her allies and enemies by dressing as a man, like Joan of Arc, or a comedy about a roulette player, a priest, who night after night only manages to break even, or an adventure movie about the colonization of Mars. As the brother or business partner talked, the pirate watched the dark road just beyond the sprayed yellow headlights of the truck, thinking with some melancholy that Adana would've been good friends with the man's wife.

Just after dawn, they arrived at a large warehouse outside Detroit. A stout man with sharp eyes and gray hair who was responsible for organizing distribution teams handed the pirate a shipping permit and informed him that the shipment would have to be taken to Venezuela. Then he started to laugh, and it took the pirate a moment to understand that he was laughing about the permit—stamped by a bribed Canadian customs officer—not at him. An hour later they were done loading the barrels of whiskey and they left in the two trucks. This time, on the way back, the pirate drove the truck and the business partner slept.

When they arrived at the timber yard, they waited until night-fall to load the sailboat. Once they were out on the lake, they sat on the deck, ate sandwiches, and drank cold coffee from their thermoses. One of the business partners steered the sailboat west, against the cold fitful wind. The pirate thought of the Taíno ability to navigate three or four hundred miles by sea using only the direction of the wind, the shape of the clouds, the color of the sky, and their knowledge of the stars. He thought of the let-ter and star map of the northern constellations he had sent his son and smiled to himself. At some point, Reese told him that it would take longer heading back and it was his turn to sleep, so the pirate went to the mid-cabin, lay across the hard, long bench, and closed his eyes.

Some minutes or hours later, he couldn't tell, he awoke to the sounds of shouting and footsteps on the deck above. He then knew immediately, like waking suddenly from an icy dream, that it was dawn and that they had been stopped near the shores of Chicago by a patrol boat. The first thing that struck the pirate when the prohibition agent and policeman appeared in the mid-cabin was that they were both wearing wool coats like his. For a few seconds, they were silent, as if contemplating whether to arrest him or beat him to a bloody pulp and forget about him. Then the policeman pulled out a pistol and told him to head to-ward the deck. The agent stayed in the mid-cabin to search for the barrels of whiskey, which, presumably, he would later sell, and then split the profits with the policeman.

On deck, behind him, the pirate heard the policeman sniff in the stark cold like a hound sniffing for blood. He told the pirate to keep his hands where he could see them. The pirate nodded and raised his arms. The policeman walked him to the bow of the sailboat. In the distance, the pirate could just make out the sad, gray purlieus of the city. Then he heard Reese's braying, terrified voice. He was shouting something at the policeman or maybe something at him, something he couldn't quite make out, something incomprehensible that, at least obliquely, sounded like a warning.

The Last Pirate of the New World heard but did not feel the shots as they passed through something vital in him. He felt only himself falling, twisting in the air, and the shock of cold water as he broke through the surface of the lake and began to sink, faceup, into its depths. He thrashed and kicked and struggled to draw breath, but no breath came. A tide of warmth then flooded him, and, as he sank farther and farther, his thoughts dissolved into the dark water. Within seconds the sensation was that of having no thoughts at all and that he too was dissolving, disappearing, like a river that stops being a river once it reaches the sea, his final breath now escaping from his nostrils and mouth in a bright foam of tiny bubbles which expanded and split or collided into yet others, each single sphere translucent and aflame with the light of the dawning sun, each single one rising away from him and toward a distant and vast surface.

★ ★ ★ ★ ★

ACKNOWLEDGMENTS

A novel is a family, a city, sometimes an entire world.

First and foremost, I would like to begin by thanking Mom and Dad for their sacrifice, endless love, and support. To my sisters, Melanie and Nicole; to Aunt Carolyn; Mary Josten; and my grandfathers, Don Napo and Vic Drower, whose extraordinary stories breathed life into my own.

A thousand and one thank-yous to my inimitable agent, Chris Clemans, for his passion, unwavering support, and brilliant, astronomical guidance. I am deeply indebted to the whole crew at Hanover Square Press/HarperCollins, including Emer Flounders and my editor, John Glynn, whose grace, vision, and incandescent belief in this book are a life force all its own.

Thank you to Gabriel Levinson, hermano-in-arms; there's no one else with whom I'd rather wander this mad Library of Babel. Thank you to Mahmoud Saeed, whose friendship and conversations about writing, the writing life, and history mean the world to me. To Edward Peacock, whose wisdom and belief in the human species continue to inspire me.

Thank you to my dear friend Ingrid Rojas Contreras, whose letters and shared writing through the years were like a compass. To Sarah Bruni, hermana-in-arms, whose incredible kindness, talent, and love of literature are a guiding light. To Isabelle Minville, for whom there are no creative limitations. To John Burke, dear friend, critic, ingenious thinker. To Melanie Pappadis Faranello, who, at every stage, offered priceless advice and pushed me forward. To Kathy Daneman, for her brilliant guidance and support. To Sarah Dodson, William De Souza Lobo, Heather Momyer, Heather Dewar, Bradford Rhines, Antonio Jiménez Morato, Aroldo Andrés Nery, Jimena Codina González, Jesus Ruiz, Katy Simpson Smith, Maurice Carlos Ruffin, Kali Fajardo-Anstine, Gerardo Cárdenas, Stacy Parker Le Melle, Laura Sims, and Idra Novey.

I am beyond grateful for my luminous, rebellious Chicago fam. I don't know what I'd do without you and your encouragement. Chris Sullivan, Eric Roberts, Chris Heinl, Joe Aliotta, Ted Clyde, Kush Mangat, and all the countless others with whom I shared the best of all possible worlds growing up. To Davis Chin, Thomas Mundt, Cam Honsa, and Karolina Zarychta Honsa. To Ramsin Canon, Waleeta Canon, Kenzo Shibata, Marvin Benjamin, Michelle Kaffko Ebner, and Carrie Smith.

Thank you to all my former students at El Cuarto Año High School and Antonia Pantoja High School; your fight means everything. Thank you to my teaching colleagues and the Chicago Teachers Union. A writer's life is vastly improved when lived in solidarity with others.

I am indebted to the Illinois Arts Council and the City of Chicago Department of Cultural Affairs and Special Events for their institutional support.

Without my wife, Alicia Josten Zapata, my editor-in-chief, my one true island, this novel would have not been possible.